TALES OF THE WILD WEST

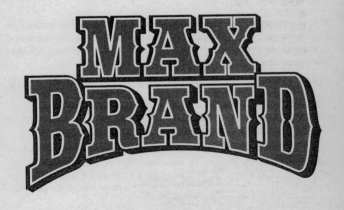

LEISURE BOOKS   NEW YORK CITY

To Jon Tuska, who made it all happen

A LEISURE BOOK®

September 2000

Published by special arragement with Golden West Literary Agency.

Dorchester Publishing Co., Inc.
276 Fifth Avenue
New York, NY 10001

ISBN 0-8439-4769-1

The name "Leisure Books" and the stylized "L" with design are trademarks of Dorchester Publishing Co., Inc.

Printed in the United States of America.

TALES OF THE WILD WEST

TABLE OF CONTENTS

Foreword

On paper, over a span of twenty-five years, Frederick Faust produced more than four hundred Western tales. In book format, beginning in 1919 with THE UNTAMED, and including titles now scheduled for publication through 2001, his Westerns total some two-hundred and twelve volumes in many hundreds of editions around the world. These books have been printed by a variety of publishers under seven names—as Evan Evans, David Manning, George Owen Baxter, John Frederick, Peter Henry Morland, Frank Austin and, most often, as Max Brand. This current volume presents seven stories that have never been included in any previous Faust collection.

It has often been stated that Faust, living for many years of his life in Europe, knew nothing of the real West and that his many tales in this genre were based strictly on legend and myth. This is only partially true. Faust's West, his geographically mysterious "mountain desert country," is largely a reflection of his passion for Classical mythology. It is a never-never land populated by his "good bad-men," stalwart women, great horses, and greater villains, and ruled by sheer strength—the strength of both spirit and body. However, when his critics claim that Faust knew nothing of the true West, they are in serious error.

Frederick Schiller Faust (of German and Irish descent, born in Seattle) grew to manhood in the American West. Orphaned at an early age, he handled wagon teams, worked a haypress, broke wild mustangs, and labored from dawn to dusk as a ranch hand in California's San Joaquin Valley. Each night, around a flickering campfire, he would listen to veteran cowpunchers and mountain men, thrilling to their numerous "tales of the Wild West." Young Faust absorbed their colorful way of talking, their profanity, and their slang, filing away these impressions for his own Western "yarns" (as he liked to call them).

That his mountain desert country was "unreal" and that Faust lacked the knowledge and ability to describe the true Western landscape are other persistent falsehoods. A glance at a typical page of a Max Brand novel such as LUCKY LARRIBEE (Dodd, Mead, 1957) proves just the opposite:

> The valley fell away in great steps down the central canyon, where the waters were mostly hidden by the precipitous walls. Far down the ravine they saw the glint of the current rounding turns. On their side, the mountains rolled slowly up to great peaks, the heads and shoulders of which were blanketed with snow. Beyond, they could look across a withering expanse of desert, and in the valley itself there appeared the ledges and cliffs of many colors, according to the nature of the strata through which the water had chiseled its way.

Although this description could probably apply to many Western locales, any Californian will recognize the eponymous Sierra Nevada mountains of Faust's youth, coursing with river and stream, rich valley on one side, the great Mojave Desert on the other.

Additionally, beyond his early background and personal

knowledge, Faust maintained a massive card file of Western facts to use as basic research. Here was detailed information on horses, clothing, guns, wagons, weather, cattle, American Indian tribal customs, farm equipment, terrain, and so on.

Faust knew the West in all aspects, and, if he chose to write of it mainly on a mythic scale, this was his deliberate choice, a choice that set him apart from the bulk of Western fictioneers and lent individual distinction to his work.

Here, then, are seven fresh examples of his storytelling genius, a further celebration of Frederick Faust's West. Saddle up for a ride through Max Brand country.

It's a trip you'll always remember.

William F. Nolan
West Hills, California
1996

The Laughter of
Slim Malone

*There are no heroes in "The Laughter of Slim Malone,"
an early Faust Western that appeared in* All-Story Weekly
*in the issue dated June 14, 1919. Malone is a smooth-
talking stagecoach bandit who robs for personal gain, who
hides from the law, and who has no desire whatever to "go
straight." If he has to shoot up a posse to maintain his
outlaw freedom, he has no qualms about doing so. When
Faust began writing for editor Frank Blackwell at Street &
Smith's* Western Story Magazine *in 1920, he was, by magazine policy, no longer able to offer his readers an all-
crooked protagonist. Therefore, this earlier tale is definitely
not characteristic of a typical Max Brand Western. In the
mid-1930s, after he'd left Blackwell, he was again free to
create darker characters—as he did in "Lake Tyndal," also
in this collection. Here, then, is a portrait of a man who
lives by his wits and his guns and who, literally, laughs at
the law.*

14

Time has little to do with reputation in the Far West, and accordingly the name of Slim Malone grew old in the region of Appleton, and yet the owner of the name was still young. Appleton was somewhat of a misnomer, for the region had never known anything save imported apples or any other sort of fruit since the time of its birth into the history of whiskey and revolvers. But a misguided pioneer in the old days had raised a few scrubby trees and had named the town forever. The dreams of the early agriculturists had died long ago, but the name remained to pique the curiosity of travelers and furnish jokes for inhabitants.

The town lay at the conjunction of three gorges in the heart of the Rockies, and the little plain where it nestled was crowded with orchards that bore everything but apples. The six original trees that had given the town its name now stood in the back yard of Sandy Orton's saloon—old trees with knotted and mossy limbs that suggested a venerable age due to the hard climate rather than to the passage of years. They were pointed out to casual travelers with great pride, and they were the established toast of Sandy's place. But Sandy's was frequented by a loud-voiced and spendthrift crowd not usual to agricultural towns.

In the old days, when Appleton was a name rather than a fact, the hilarity had been as absent as the men, but after gold was discovered in the three gorges that led from the settlement into the heart of the mountains the little town became a rendezvous of a thousand adventurers. The stages to and from the railroad thirty miles away were crowded with men eager to face the hardships of the climate and the great adventure of the gold fields.

It was then that Slim Malone appeared. It was said that he had first come upon the scene as the owner of the Red River strike that was finally owned by Barney Gleason. It was further rumored that Gleason had beaten Slim Malone out of the claim by a very shady deal at cards. Gleason refused to discuss the matter, and Slim Malone was rarely within vocal range, so the matter had never been sifted.

Gleason was rarely more vocal than a grunt, and, when Slim Malone appeared, people generally had other things to think about than questions concerning his past.

A certain percentage of lawlessness is taken for granted in a mining town. People are too busy with their own concerns to pay attention to their neighbors, but when three stages in succession, passing from Appleton to Concord, the nearest railroad station, were robbed by a rider on a white horse, the community awoke and waxed wroth. The loss was too much in common to be passed over.

The first effort was an impromptu organization of half a dozen angered miners who rode into the Weston Hills. They found fresh hoof prints after an hour of riding and went on greatly encouraged, with the pistols loosened in their holsters. After some hours of hard travel they came upon a white horse in the midst of a hollow and then spread into a circle and approached cautiously. But not cautiously enough. While they were still far from the white horse, the bandit opened fire upon them from the shelter of a circle of rocks. They rode into town the next day with three of their number badly hurt and the other three marked for life. That started the war.

As the months passed, posse after posse left Appleton and started to scour the Weston Hills for the marauder. The luckiest of the expeditions came back, telling tales of a sudden fusillade from an unexpected covert and then a swift white horse, scouring into the distance. The majority came back with no tales at all save of silent mountains and the grim cactus of the desert.

In the meantime the stages from Appleton to Concord were held up with a monotonous regularity by the rider on the fleet white horse, and the mining town grew more and more irate. Men cursed the name of Slim Malone. An adventurous singer in one of Appleton's dancehalls invented a song, featuring the marauder, and it was taken up by the matrons of the town as a sort of scarecrow ballad to hush their children.

Then the new mayor came to Appleton. He owned three

claims on Askwarthy Gulch, and he ran on the double platform of no license for the Appleton saloons and the end of Slim Malone. The women used their influence because of the first. His name was Orval Kendricks, but that didn't count. What mattered was his red hair and the statements of his platform. Slim Malone celebrated the new reign by holding up two stages within the first five days.

But the new mayor lived up to the color of his hair and proved worthy of his platform. He held a meeting of every able-bodied citizen in town three days after his inauguration, and in his speech, the men noted with relief, he forgot to mention the saloons, and he concentrated his attention on Slim Malone. He stated that the good name and the prosperity of Appleton depended upon the capture of this marauder at once. Divorced from the mayor's rather resounding rhetoric, the populace of Appleton realized the truth of his remarks and applauded him to the echo. His silences were as much appreciated as his words.

After a carefully prepared peroration he built up to his climax by the proposal that the community import Lefty Cornwall, at a salary of five hundred dollars a month and a five thousand dollar bonus, to act as sheriff until the apprehension of Slim Malone. Then the crowd applauded again to the echo. In their midst were men who had lost more than five thousand at a blow, owing to the strenuous activity of this Slim Malone. They were equal to any measures for his suppression, even if it meant the importation of Lefty Cornwall.

The fame of Lefty had begun in Texas where he mortally wounded one Mexican and crippled two others in a saloon fight. Since then it had increased and spread until he was a household word even farther north than Appleton. He came from that sun-burned southland, where a man's prowess was gauged by his speed and dexterity with his "irons," and even on that northern plateau of Appleton men knew that to cross Lefty Cornwall was death or murderous mutilation.

At first, there were some dissenters. Men stated freely

Max Brand

that Lefty would never dream of coming as far north as Appleton for a paltry five thousand dollars. There were even a few dissenters who claimed that, should he come, he would never be able to cope with Slim Malone, but these were laughed and hooted down by a radical minority who came from the southland and knew the fame of Lefty Cornwall in detail. The mayor accounted for the others by stating that he had already communicated with Lefty and had received his assent by letter. This announcement dissolved the meeting in cheers.

Appleton decreed the day of the arrival of the new sheriff a festival occasion. The farmers from the adjoining tableland drove into town; the miners from the three valleys rode down. When the stage arrived from Concord, the incipient sheriff dismounted in the midst of a huge crowd and cheers that shook the signboard of Sandy Orton's saloon.

Now the mayor of Appleton in his platform had declared deathless war against the saloons, but since his election he had been strangely silent upon the liquor question. He was as canny as his red hair suggested, and he had a truly Scottish insight into the crucial moments of life. He perceived the arrival of Lefty Cornwall to be such a moment, and he perceived at the same moment the correct way of meeting that crisis.

It was with surprise no less than pleasure that the throng heard the lusty voice of their chief official, inviting them to Sandy Orton's saloon, and where they were in doubt, his beckoning arm put them right. They filled the saloon from bar to door, and those who could not enter thronged at the entrances with gaping mouths.

The mayor was equal to the occasion. He mounted the bar much as a plainsman mounts a horse, and, standing in full view of his fellow citizens, he invited Lefty Cornwall to join him in his prominent position. Nowise loath, Lefty swung onto the bar in the most approved fashion and stood, locked arm in arm, with the dignified official of Appleton. In the meantime the bartenders, thrilled equally with surprise and pleasure, passed out the drinks to the crowded room. It was apparently a moment big in portent to Appleton, and not a heart there but pulsed big with pride in their mayor.

"Fellow citizens," began the mayor, raising a large, freckled hand for silence.

A hush fell upon the assemblage.

"Boys," continued the mayor, after a proper silence reigned, "I haven't got much to say."

"Here's to you!" yelled a voice. "I hate a guy that's noisy."

The mayor frowned and waved a commanding hand for silence. "I spotted you, Pete Bartlett," he called. "If you like silence, you must hate yourself."

The crowd roared with approving laughter.

"Boys," began Orval Kendricks again, when the laughter had subsided, "this here is a solemn occasion. I feel called upon to summon the manhood of this here town to listen to my words, and I reckon that most of the manhood of the town is within hearin'."

A chorus of assent followed.

"It don't need any Daniel Webster to tell you men that this here town is hard hit," continued Mayor Kendricks. "It don't need no Henry Clay to tell you that these diggin's are about to bust up unless we have the right sort of strong-arm man in town. We've been sufferin' patiently from the aggressions of a red-handed desperado who I don't need to mention, because his name just naturally burns my tongue."

"Slim Malone!" cried a dozen voices. "We're followin' you, chief!"

The mayor thrust his hand into his breast and extended the other arm in imitation of a popular woodcut of Patrick Henry. The crowd acknowledged the eloquence of the attitude with a common gaping.

"There may be some of you guys," cried the mayor, rising to the emotion of the moment, "there may be some of you guys who don't know the man I mean, but I reckon that a tolerable pile of Appleton's best citizens spend a large part of their time cursing Slim Malone."

Max Brand

"We ain't through damning him yet," yelled a voice, and the crowd voiced their assent, half in growls and half in laughter.

"He has tricked our posses as an honest man would be ashamed to do," continued the mayor, warming to his oration, "he has shot our citizens, and he has swiped our gold! I'm askin' you, man to man, can a self-respectin' community stand for this? It can't! What's the answer that Appleton makes to this desperado?" He paused and frowned the audience into a state of suspense. "There's only *one* answer to this gunfighter, and that answer stands at my right hand," bellowed the mayor, when he judged that the silence had sunk into his hearers sufficiently. "The name of the answer is Lefty Cornwall!"

The following burst of applause brought a momentary blush into even Lefty's cheeks. At the reiterated demands for a speech, he hitched at his revolver in its skeleton holster, removed his sombrero, and mopped his forehead with a ponderous hand. When it became evident that the hero was about to break into utterance, the crowd fell silent.

"Fellows," began the gunfighter, "makin' speeches ain't much in my line."

"Makin' dead men is more your game," broke in the wit of the assemblage.

A universal hiss attested that the crowd was anxious to hear the Texas gunman out.

"But if you are goin' to do me the honor of makin' me sheriff of this here county and this here city of Appleton," he continued, letting his eye rove down Appleton's one street, "I'm here to state that law and order is goin' to be maintained here at all costs. Right here I got to state that the only costs I'm referrin' to is the price of the powder and lead for this here cannon of mine."

The crowd broke in upon the speech with noisy appreciation and many cries of: "That's the stuff, old boy!"

"I been hearin' a tolerable pile about one Slim Malone," went on the new sheriff.

"So have we," broke in the irrepressible wit of the assemblage, only to be choked into silence by more serious-minded neighbors.

"Sure," agreed the sheriff. "I reckon you've heard a lot too much about him. But I'm here to state that all this talk about Slim Malone has got to stop . . . and has got to stop sudden. I'm here to stop it."

He hitched the holster a little forward again as he spoke, and a deep silence fell upon the crowd.

"Fellow citizens," he continued, spitting liberally over the side of the bar, "whatever gun play is carried on around here in the future is to be done strictly by me, and all you men can consider yourselves under warning to leave your shootin' irons at home, unless you want to use them to dig premature graves."

This advice was received with an ironical chuckle of appreciation from the crowd.

"As for Slim Malone," he went on, "I'm goin' out into the Weston Hills to get him, single-handed. I don't want no posse. I'll get him single-handed or bust, you can lay to that. If I come back to this town without Slim Malone, alive or dead, you can say that Malone has the Indian sign on me."

Having finished all that he had to say, Lefty felt about in his mind to find a graceful manner of closing his speech, when the mayor came to his assistance. He recognized that nervous clearing of the throat and wandering of the eyes out of his own first political experiences. Now he raised his glass of colored alcohol and water, which in Appleton rejoiced in the name of bourbon.

"Boys," he shouted, "there ain't no better way of showin' our appreciation of our new sheriff than by turnin' bottoms up. Let's go!"

Every hand in the barroom flashed into the air, and after a loud whoop there was a brief gurgling sound that warmed the heart of Sandy Orton. It should have been the signal for a day's carousal, and the good citizens of Appleton were nowise averse. They desired to hear the voice of their new sheriff in friendly converse. They desired to see him in that

most amiable of all poses, his foot on the rail and his hand
on the bar. They wanted to look him over and size him up
just as a boy wishes to fondle his first gun. But the sheriff
objected. He was sorry to spoil the fun. He said that they
could go ahead and have their little time, but that they must
leave him out. He had business to perform that didn't admit
of drinking.

There might have been adverse criticism of this Spartan
strenuousness, but at this point a diversion occurred in the
shape of four wild riders who broke into Appleton and
brought the word that Slim Malone had been out again.
This time he had held up a mule train on its way to carry
provisions up Bender Cañon to Earl Parrish's claim. With
his usual fine restraint Slim had taken no lives, but he had
winged two of the drivers badly and had helped himself
from the provisions without unnecessary waste. He had
even lingered to give first aid to the two drivers whose
courage had overcome their sense of proportion.

If anything had been needed to spur on the new official
of Appleton, it came in the form of the message Slim Malone had left with the wounded men before he rode away.

"Tell the new sheriff," he called, as he sat easily in the
saddle, "that I've heard of him, and that I'll organize a little
party for him as soon as possible, so that we can get better
acquainted. Tell him that the one thing he lacks to make
him a good fighting man is a sense of humor."

Lefty Cornwall heard this message in silence while he
spat with vicious precision into a distant spittoon. Afterward, and still in silence, he retired and worked an hour
cleaning his already shining revolver and patting and oiling
the holster. He performed these grave functions in the house
of the mayor, and that dignitary announced later that he
had wound up by practicing the draw and point, walking
and sitting down, and at every angle. The mayor was impressed past speech.

When Lefty issued forth at last, he found a score of hard
riders, standing by their horses in the street.

"And what might all this here gang be for?" inquired Lefty mildly.

"We're the posse, waitin' to be sworn in," announced one of the men.

"Swearin' in takes a terrible lot of time," said Lefty, "and, besides, I don't know how it's done. I don't want no posse, as I said before. I wouldn't know how to handle it. Anyway, twenty men on horseback make enough noise to scare away a whole gang of bandits. You might as well start lookin' for trouble with a brass band, because you'd sure find the trouble."

He hitched at his belt in his customary manner when at a loss for words, and his right hand dropped gracefully upon the handle of his gun and drooped thereon somewhat sinisterly.

"This here Malone," went on the sheriff, "may be a tolerable badman in his way, but I ain't no shorn lamb myself. I'm goin' out to get him, and I'm goin' to get him by myself. I reckon that's final."

They accepted his announcement with cheers and set about offering all the information in their power. It was generally believed that the bandit lived somewhere at the far end of Eagle Head Cañon, about fifteen miles from town. His dwelling had never been spotted, but he was most frequently seen riding to and from this place. Thrice posses had raked the cañon as with a fine-toothed comb, but they had never come upon a trace of his habitation; but the cañon was thick with caves and heaped with giant boulders that offered innumerable places of concealment, and the legend was strong that Slim Malone lived in that place.

The next thing was to find a proper mount. This proved a more difficult task. The sheriff knew horses from nose to hoof, and he was hard to please. At last he selected a tall roan with a wicked eye and flat shoulders that promised speed. These preparations made, he swung to the saddle, waved his hand to the crowd, and galloped out of town.

There was not much bluff about Lefty Cornwall, as the curious-minded had frequently discovered in the past, but, as he swung into the narrow throat of Eagle Head Cañon, he began to realize that he might have gone too far this time. While he was in the town, it had been easy enough to make ringing speeches. Now that the evening began to come down by lazy, cool degrees a certain diffidence grew in him.

He had fought many men during his brief life, but he had never come across a reputation as strange or as fascinating as this of Slim Malone's. If the challenge that the bandit had sent him was irritating, it also roused in his mind a certain degree of respect and, as he rode up the cañon, winding slowly among the boulders, a hundred doubts infested his mind.

If he had been back upon the level reaches of the Texan desert, which he knew, these uncertainties would probably have never entered his head, but here every half mile of his journey was passed under the eye of a thousand coverts from which a man could have picked him off with the safety of a hunter firing from a blind at partridges. Moreover, a curious loneliness akin to homesickness came in him, located, as far as he could discover, chiefly in the pit of the stomach.

The mountains were blue now and purple along the upper reaches, and, as the sun left off, the moon took up her reign over the chill blue spaces. It was very solemn, almost funereal to the thought of Lefty Cornwall. And the silence was punctuated with the melancholy howling of a far-off coyote.

It was complete night before he reached the upper end of Eagle Head Cañon, and he was weary from the stumbling gait of his horse over the rocks. Moreover, the mountain night air was cold—very cold to Lefty. He wanted desperately to turn back, but he had not the heart to face the inquiries that would meet him in town and the covert smiles that would welcome the hero, returning empty-handed, the man who needed no posse.

Lefty was a very brave man, but like almost all of the physically courageous he dreaded derision more than actual pain. Yet, in spite of this, he finally decided that it was better to go back to town and face the smiles than to remain through the cold night in these dread silences. He wished heartily that he had taken one other man with him, if it were only for the companionship. As it was, he felt it was no use to hunt further, and he started back down the cañon. He had not gone far when his horse stumbled and commenced to limp.

Lefty got off with a curse and felt of the forehoofs. The difficulty proved to be a sharp, three-cornered rock that had been picked up under the shoe of the left forefoot. He was bending over to pry this loose between his fingers when he caught the glint of a light. In his excitement he sprang upright and stared. At once the light disappeared. Lefty began to feel ghostly. His senses had never played him such tricks before.

He leaned over and commenced work on the stone again, but, as he did so, his eye caught the same glint of light. There was no possible mistake about it this time. He remained bent over and stared at it until he was certain that he saw a yellow spot of light, a long, thin ray that pointed out to him like a finger through the shadows. This time he took the bearings of the light carefully, and, when he stood up, he was able to locate it again. Lefty's heart beat high. He threw the reins over his horse's head and commenced to stalk the light carefully. Sometimes, as he slipped and stumbled over the rocks, he lost sight of it altogether, only to have it reappear when he had almost given up hope of finding it again. And so he came upon the cave.

The light shone through a little chink between two tall boulders, and, as Lefty pressed his eye to the aperture, holding his breath as he did so, he saw a long dugout, perhaps a dozen paces from end to end and some five paces wide. Behind a partition at one end he heard the stamping of a horse, and, as Lefty gazed, a magnificent head rose behind the partition and looked fairly at him. His heart stopped as that great-eyed gaze turned on him, the ears pricking and the wisp of hay motionless in the mouth. But after a moment the horse dropped his head again and went on crunching his fodder, stamping now and then and snorting as he ate.

At first he saw no other occupant of the place, but by moving his eye to one side of the aperture he managed to get a glimpse of the bandit himself. There was no question about his identity. From the descriptions that he had heard while in Appleton, he knew him at once, the expressionless gray eyes and the thin, refined face with an almost Greek modeling about its lower part.

He was tilted back in a heavy chair, smoking a pipe and reading, and Lefty saw that he sat facing a blanket at the far end of the room. Evidently this was the entrance. So far as Lefty could see, the bandit was unarmed, his two long guns lying on the table half a dozen paces away.

Very softly he crept along the side of the boulder and finally came to a passage, as he had expected. It was just wide enough for a man to press through, and from the chisel marks at its sides it had evidently been artificially widened from time to time. At the end of the narrow passage hung the blanket.

If Lefty had proceeded cautiously up to this point, his caution now became almost animal-like. Behind that blanket he had no idea what was happening. Perhaps the bandit had heard a noise long before and was now crouched against the wall in another part of the place, ready to open fire at the first stir of the blanket. Perhaps he had stolen out of the cave by another entrance and was now hunting the hunter. This thought sent a chill down Lefty's back, and he turned his head quickly. Then he resumed his slow progress. At the very edge of the blanket he paused for a long and deathly minute, but Lefty was not a woman . . . to fail at the last moment.

He swung the blanket aside and crouched in the entrance with his gun leveled. The little round sight framed the face of Slim Malone, who still sat reading quietly and puffing at a black-bowled pipe.

"Hands up," said Lefty softly.

Even then, with his bead on his man, he did not feel entirely sure of himself. It seemed that this could not be true. Opportunity had favored him too much. There must still be some turn of the game.

The expressionless gray eyes raised calmly from the book. It seemed to Lefty that a yellow glint came into them for a moment, like the light that comes into an animal's eyes when it is angered, but the next moment it was gone, and he could not be sure that it had come there at all. The rest of the face was perfectly calm. Malone lowered the book slowly and then raised his hands above his head.

"Ah, Sheriff," he said quietly, "I see that you have honored my invitation."

"Right-o," said Lefty, "I'm here, all right."

He felt strangely relieved after hearing his quarry speak. He stepped through the entrance and straightened up, still with the revolver leveled. It was beyond his fondest hopes that he should be able to bring the desperado alive to Appleton, and the thought of his complete success warmed his heart. Also the immediate prospect of that five-thousand-dollar bonus.

"In order to remove any strain you may be under," went on Slim Malone, "I'll assure you that I am quite unarmed. My guns are both lying on the table there. In order that you may make sure, I shall stand up, with my hands over my head, and turn around slowly. You can examine me to your own satisfaction."

He did as he had said, and Lefty's practiced eyes saw that there was not the suspicion of a lump under the clothes.

"Now," said Slim Malone, as he faced his captor again, and his smile was strangely winning, "I hope that I may lower my arms, and we can commence our little party."

"Your end of this here party is all over, my beauty," said Lefty grimly, "except that the boys at Appleton may give you a little impromptu reception when we hit town. They seem to be rather strong on celebrations."

"So I understand," smiled Slim Malone. "I have no doubt they will be glad to see me."

"Ain't no doubt in the world," grinned Lefty, warming to the perfect calm of this man. "Between you and me, pal, I'm sorry to have to turn this little trick, but. . . ."

Malone waved a careless and reassuring hand. "Business is business, my dear fellow," he said.

"That bein' the case," said Lefty, "I'll have to ask you to turn around and put your hands behind your back while I put these here bracelets on. I don't want to discourage you any, but, while I'm doin' it, this here gun will be in my hand and pointin' at your back."

"Naturally," nodded Malone; "quite right, of course. But before we start on our little jaunt back to town, won't you have a drink with me? I have some really rare old stuff here, quite different from the firewater they put labels on in Appleton."

Lefty grinned appreciatively. "It's a good move, pal," he said, shaking his head with admiration, "and I know that you're hard put to it, or you wouldn't try such an old dodge on me. It's a good move, but down in Texas the booze stunt is so old that they've almost forgotten it . . . but not quite!"

"Ah," said Malone, with a little sigh of regret, "then I suppose we shall have to ride out in the night without a nip. Gets mighty chilly here before morning, you know."

This fact had gradually dawned on Lefty during his ride up the valley, and, as he looked forward to the journey back, he shivered with unpleasant anticipation. In Texas a summer night was one thing, in these mountains it was quite another.

"I suppose the booze is the real thing?" he inquired casually.

"There are little bubbles under the glass," said Slim Malone with subtle emotion.

Lefty Cornwall sighed deeply. The taste of the Appleton bar whiskey still burned his mouth. After all, this fellow was a man. He might be a criminal, but Lefty's own past was not free from shady episodes. Furthermore, he was about to make five thousand dollars on presenting him to the good people of Appleton.

"If you're sure you want a drink before we start, go ahead," said Lefty.

"The bottle and a glass are over there in that little dugout on the wall," pointed Malone.

In the little open hutch on the wall the sheriff perceived a tall bottle that shimmered pleasantly in the torch light. "Go ahead," said the sheriff, "I reckon you know I'm watchin' all the time."

"Surely," said Malone pleasantly. "I know you're on the job all the time."

He walked over to the hutch and picked up the bottle and the glass. He paused with the bottle tucked away under his arm. "Queer thing," pondered Malone, "the same pack that held this bottle of whisky held this also."

Lefty tightened his grip on the gun as Malone reached deeper into the hutch, but he straightened again and appeared carrying a large concert banjo.

"That feller had taste," he continued, crossing the room and laying the banjo down carelessly on the chair. "Just run your eyes over that banjo."

"Some banjo, all right," said the sheriff, "but hurry up with your drink, Malone. We've got to be on our way."

Malone uncorked the bottle and held it under his nose while he inhaled a whiff. "The old aroma, all right," he pronounced with the air of a connoisseur, "must be a vintage as far back as the 'Eighties. You won't join me?"

Now the heart of the sheriff was a human heart, but his will was adamant. "Not me, Malone," he answered. "I've been in the game too long. Can't drink on this sort of a job."

"Guess you're right," murmured Malone, letting the amber stream trickle slowly into the glass, "but it's too bad." He raised the glass to his lips and swallowed half of the contents slowly. "The stuff is so oily," he mused, "that you don't need a chaser. Just sort of oils its own way down, you know."

The sheriff moistened his lips.

"It certainly is a shame that you can't taste it," continued Malone, as he drained the glass.

The sheriff hitched his belt with his customary gesture. "It looks like the real thing," he said judicially.

"It is," pronounced Malone with decision, "and after the sort of poison they serve you around here. . . ."

The sheriff shuddered with sympathy. "I reckon," he said hesitatingly, "that you might pour me just a drop."

It seemed to him that, as he spoke, the yellow glint came into the eyes of Malone again, but a moment later it was gone, and he decided that the change had been merely a shadow from the wavering torch light. He took the glass Malone extended to him under the cover of the pointed gun and raised it slowly to his lips.

"Just stand a bit farther back while I drink, pal," he said.

Malone obeyed, and the sheriff tilted the glass. It was, as Malone had said, the real old aroma, and the sheriff drew a deep breath.

Now, there is a saying about liquor that the drink that does the harm is "just one more," and certain it is that one whiskey calls for another as surely as a question calls for an answer.

"I reckon it isn't quite as old as you say," said the sheriff, feeling his way from word to word cautiously. "I reckon it ain't more than fifteen years old at the outside."

Malone paused, with the bottle suspended over the glass to consider.

"I thought that myself when I first drank," he nodded, "but that was before I got used to it. All bourbon is a little sharp, you know."

The sheriff was inclined to agree. He also felt sure that one more drink would quite banish from his memory the taste of that one drink in Appleton. Moreover, the danger, if there was any, was slight, for Malone was taking drink for drink with him, and larger drinks at that. It was a sort of subtle challenge to the manhood of the sheriff, and he was as proud of his capacity for whiskey as of his speed with a gun.

It was perhaps half an hour later that the sheriff indicated the banjo with a careless wave of the pistol.

"Play any?" he inquired, "or do you keep it around as sort of an ornament?"

"Both," smiled Malone. "It makes the place more home-like, you know, and then I sing once in a while, but not often. Folks around here aren't particularly partial to my voice."

"I'm a pretty good judge," stated the sheriff, "blaze away, and I'll see you ain't interrupted. Been a long time since I had the pleasure of hearing any decent singin'."

He was, as he said, a fairly good judge, and he was delighted with the rich baritone that rang through the cave. After a time, as the whiskey and the music melted into his mood, he began to call for old favorites, darky ballads, and last of all for the sentimental ditties that have always charmed the heart of the rough men of the West: "Annie Laurie," "Old Black Joe," "Ben Bolt," "Silver Threads Among the Gold."

As he sang, the bandit commenced, naturally, to walk back and forth through the cave, and the sheriff sat back in the chair and with half-closed eyes waved the revolver back and forth in time. He failed to note that, as Malone walked up and down each time, he made a longer trip, until at last he was pacing and turning close to the table on which lay the revolvers side by side. He did not note it, or, if he did, his mind was too thrilled with the tender airs and the tenderer liquor to register the fact clearly. It faded into the pleasant blur of his sensations.

> Oh, don't you remember sweet Alice, Ben Bolt,
> Sweet Alice with. . . .

The music stopped. Malone had stooped over the table with the speed of a bird picking up a grain of wheat, and with the same movement he whirled and fired. The gun spun from the hand of the sheriff, and he stood, staring into eyes that now, beyond all doubt, flared with an animal fire.

"Put your hands behind your back after you've thrown those bracelets to me," said Malone. "I naturally hate to break up this party, but I think you've had about enough whiskey to keep you warm on the ride back, Lefty, my boy."

There was an insane desire on the sheriff's part to leap upon Malone bare-handed, but he had seen too many fighting men in action before. He knew the meaning of those eyes and the steadiness of the revolver.

"It's your game, Slim," he said, with as little bitterness as possible, "but will you tell me why in the name of God you aren't on the stage? It isn't what you do, pal, it's the way you do it!"

Appleton awoke early the next morning. Someone shouted and then fired a pistol. The populace gathered at windows and doors, rubbing sleepy eyes that a moment later shone wide awake, and yawns turned into yells of laughter, for down the middle of Appleton's one street came the sheriff. He was sitting the roan horse, with his feet tied below the girth, and his hands cuffed behind his back. Even the weary roan seemed to feel in his drooping head the defeat of his rider. Upon the back of the sheriff was a large piece of cardboard, upon which was printed in large letters the following:

I'm sending this back with my signature in token of a pleasant evening in my home in Eagle Head Cañon. I'm sorry to announce that I've moved.

Slim Malone

The Champion

Writing at the peak of his powers, 1937 proved to be a prime year for Faust in terms of productivity, variety of subject matter, and markets. He remained a star of the first magnitude in the pulp field with stories that year in Ad-venture, Detective Fiction Weekly, Argosy, Black Mask, Double Detective, and Complete Western Book. He had mastered the leading slick-paper publications with fiction in Collier's, The Saturday Evening Post, American Caval-cade, Cosmopolitan, This Week, The American Magazine, Liberty, and Elk's Magazine. Faust also had a wide mix of books published in 1937, including his finest historical, THE GOLDEN KNIGHT (Greystone, 1937), a rollicking saga of Richard the Lionheart published under the George Challis byline. As Frederick Frost, he saw the release of two fast-paced novels of global espionage, SPY MEETS SPY (Macrae-Smith, 1937) and THE BAMBOO WHISTLE (Macrae-Smith, 1937). And, as Max Brand, a Manhattan crime novel was published, SIX GOLDEN ANGELS (Dodd, Mead, 1937), along with two Westerns, THE STREAK (Dodd, Mead, 1937) and TROUBLE TRAIL (Dodd, Mead,

Max Brand

1937). Although the bulk of his magazine fiction that year was printed under the Max Brand pseudonym, Faust did allow magazine publishers to use his real name on two stories of particular merit—"Johnny Come Lately" in The Saturday Evening Post *(3/6/37) and "Three in the Dark" in* The American Magazine *(11/37). As his biographer, Robert Easton, stated in MAX BRAND: THE BIG "WESTERNER" (University of Oklahoma Press, 1970): "At forty-four, [as a failed poet], he was becoming hungry for an identity he did not have and a recognition which, if deferred longer, might never come."*

"The Champion," which first appeared in All-American Fiction *(11/37), centers around a hay-baling crew of farm workers in California. It deals, on an heroic scale, with the author's painfully real experiences as a young man, working for food and shelter on farms and ranches in California's central valley region. Faust was later to realize that these long, agonizing hours of grueling labor had weakened his heart. (He suffered from a series of heart attacks, many of them severe, throughout the last three decades of his life.) This story is an intensely powerful, unique, fact-into-fiction account of what it was really like in the still wild California of Faust's youth.*

Nearly thirty years ago, when beer was only five cents a schooner in the saloons near the Stockton Slough, Jumbo Cafferty looked with apparent suspicion on the change he received after buying a round of drinks. Like a champion prize fighter, Jumbo usually did most of the buying because he was known through the length of the San Joaquin-Sacramento Valley as the greatest haypress feeder in the land. There was even room in his huge body for an odd sense of humor. He picked up a quarter, shook his head over it, and bent it double between his thumbs and forefingers. He did the same to a solid fifty-cent piece and threw them back on the bar. "Why d'you pass out counterfeit in here?" he roared. "Whyn't you have honest money?"

The bartender, abashed, picked up the fallen coins and

bit into the fifty-cent piece. Then his eyes screwed up in his head, for, instead of sinking into lead, he had almost broken his teeth on the hard metal. Jumbo's followers bellowed laughter as though at a signal.

Then someone by the door yelled: "Hi, Jumbo! Here comes your girl!"

The many beers had rolled a mist over Jumbo's brain, but the thought of the widow, like a sea wind, cleared his mind again, and he went to the door with great strides. He pushed the swing doors open and stepped out into heat and dazzle of the California sun. It was true that Mrs. Rosa Pinzone was coming up the street with her span of bright sorrels, drawing the rubber-tired buggy. The silver mountings of the harness flashed like jewels in Jumbo's eyes, but they were not half so brilliant as the thought of Rosa. If she inclined a little toward plumpness, she made up for it by plenty of bounce. She was a dark beauty with brown eyes full of conversation, and her skin was as golden as the dust of poppies.

A month before Jumbo had decided to marry her and settle down at last on her two hundred acres of unmortgaged land. For four successive Saturdays he had given up his evening beer and driven with her to dances in Ripon, in Lodi, and points in between. He had two-stepped and waltzed and schottisched with her until six in the morning and gone contentedly back to work with a feeling like that of money in the pocket. And for all that, behold her now, shining under the wide brim of a Merry Widow hat, and at her side his enemy, his rival, that handsome devil, Frenchie, who was almost as famous as Jumbo among the haypress fans of the state. It was he who handled the reins.

Now she saw Jumbo. She waved carelessly. She spoke with laughter to Frenchie, who, in turn, looked back over his shoulder and laughed loudly.

Jumbo's big hands doubled gradually into fists. "I don't make it out," he said.

A voice answered him. "Frenchie and the Moffett crew

broke the haypress record a couple of days ago. He fed in close to forty-eight tons."

The tidings pierced the soul of Jumbo Cafferty. And then a stupor came upon him and remained in spite of all the beers he drank. It was late that night before he muttered— "Yeah, women are like that!"—and roused from his coma. "Where's the boss? Where's McCann?" he asked.

Someone said: "He's over at Shanley's Place."

Cafferty went to Shanley's and found the owner of the haypress playing cards in the back room, dressed up for Sunday in a white shirt without a collar.

"Who taught Frenchie how to handle a fork? Who taught him how to build a feed and then feed it?" asked Cafferty.

"You did," said McCann.

"Who taught Frenchie everything he knows?" asked Cafferty.

"You did," said McCann. "And what of it?"

"I'll tell you what of it," answered Cafferty. "The dirty rat has gone and broke the record that him and me set three years ago. He's gone and broke it behind my back. To-morrow we'll take that record and. . . ."

"Not tomorrow," said McCann, checking a bet. "Not on Monday. The boys gotta get the Sunday beer out of them."

"We're in the Minnehan hay right now," said Cafferty, "and there ain't enough of it for two days' work. We're in the Minnehan hay, and it's the cleanest stack of wheat and barley that I ever seen."

"The boys'll be cooked," said McCann. "They'll be all weak in the knees. Anyway, it ain't a championship crew. Harry Lucas, he ain't no first-rate feeder. And that bale-roller, Sammy Pleasant, he's too young and soft."

"I'll make him big and strong!" exclaimed Cafferty. He thumped a fist against the great arch of his chest. "I'll make 'em all big and strong. I'll scare hell out of 'em. Go get the wagon. We're gonna pick up the crew and start home now."

"It ain't closing time for another hour," protested Mc-Cann.

"We're gonna start now."

"All right."

"Hey, you can't quit," said one of the players.

"Argue with this bohunk. Don't argue with me," answered McCann, and got up with a grin and his winnings.

He and Cafferty went the rounds of the Stockton saloons until they had picked up the entire crew. Old Steve, the derrick driver, came, weeping and promising to kill Jumbo when he could find a knife to cut the blackness out of his heart. Whelan, the power-driver, and Harry Lucas, the second feeder, were both in the same place, and they fought Jumbo savagely to save their last hour for more beer until he bumped their heads together and lugged them out, one under each arm. Chicago, the wire-puncher, was a drunken, senseless log, and so was Sammy Pleasant, the young bale-roller. Jumbo put them in the bottom of the wagon where their heads rattled against the iron-bound floorboards all the eleven miles over the dusty, rutted highway until they came to the Minnehan hay field. It was smoothed by silver moonshine, and the high-shouldered haystack and the derrick rising above the adjoining haypress was like a black gibbet among the stars.

"Monday is no good to try for a record," repeated McCann, when he pulled up the rig beside the cook wagon.

"Any day is good if I wanta make it good," shouted Cafferty in high anger. "Any day is a Jumbo day, if I wanta make it!"

Jumbo Cafferty sat up in the black of the morning, put a knuckle in each eye to get the sleep out, and swept the straw out of his hair. The rest were struggling their feet into socks, wet with dew, and grunting as they pulled on their shoes. A half moon dazzled them from the west, and only in the east the stars were bright above the gray-green mist of the dawn. Bessie McCann stood at the door of the cook wagon, beating on a tin pan and shouting: "Turn out! Turn out! Breakfast! *Break*fast!"

Jumbo stretched himself luxuriously, swaying a little

from side to side, and twisting until he had flexed every pound of the muscle that draped his big bones with elastic ropes and rubbery sheets of strength. Then he turned to the east and the pale beginning of what he intended to make the greatest day in his life. He went to the cook wagon and, from a full bucket, sloshed some cold water into a wash basin.

It was young Sammy Pleasant, the bale-roller, about whom he was worrying, for Sammy, he was sure, would prove the weak link in the chain. *He was too handsome to be strong*, thought Jumbo.

It was Sammy who said, as they sat at breakfast: "There's no use trying. This is Monday, isn't it? And we're all sick with stale beer. We have to put off that try for the record, Jumbo."

There was a deep-throated, sudden assent from all the rest.

Jumbo looked up from his mush and milk slowly. He saw the eyes of Mrs. McCann, frightened and curious, fixed upon him. Then he rose to his feet. Three other men sat on the same bench, but the backthrust of his great legs shoved it away shuddering inches.

"Whatta you mean?" thundered Jumbo. He paused, and a slight tingling of tinware on the stove followed his roar. "Lying down? Quitting? Yellow? I'm gonna break him wide open, so's the *rest* of the world can know what's inside him."

He sat down. He could feel the beat of his pulse in the great artery that ran up the left side of his throat. There was no clatter of spoons or forks. The crew waited, silently, for someone to answer, but there was only a faint sighing sound as Jimmy McCann blew out a long breath of cigarette smoke.

It was still a murky gray-green dawn twilight when the derrick pulleys began to screech and the first hay dumped on the feeding table. Cafferty weighed the forkful. It was from the sun-bleached top of the stack, but the dew that soaked it made ample compensation. They would be baling heavy hay from the start. Then he built the first feed swiftly, putting on the layers until they were stacked high. He looked over the battlefield with a calm eye. The men were all in place. Jumbo leaned around the edge of the press and looked down at Whelan.

"What you say, Dick?"

Whelan was knotting the bandanna that he would pull up over his nose and mouth when the dust cloud became too dense for clean breathing. "I'm gonna ride 'em all the way, Jumbo!"

"Al-l-l *right!*" Jumbo yelled, and jumped back as Whelan tripped the beater and let it fall. It came down gradually, the apron lifting at the same time to force the feed of hay into the press, but such a morsel as Jumbo had prepared no Little Giant press in the country could swallow unassisted. Cafferty first jammed down the pyramided top of the load so that it commenced to spill into the box. Then he pulled out the lower layer a bit, gave the whole mass of the feed an assisting thrust, and helped the apron to close with the push of his left hand. As the door clicked, the weighted, iron-bound beater descended with a rush that made the press shudder and set all the guy cables trembling. Jumbo heard the hay crunch in the bottom of the box and stepped back as the apron fell. He built the second feed, then a third, a fourth, a fifth, each a diminishing mouthful, so that the bale would come out of the box compact and square.

"Bale!" yelled Dick Whelan, as the last feed rammed home.

Jumbo, building the first feed of the next bale with instinctive hands, listened hungrily and heard the clank of the iron as Sammy Pleasant knocked away the locking bar. Then came an instant of silence. No, not utter silence, for Jumbo could hear the hiss of the steel needles as Chicago punched the wires through. He would have two of them through and be picking up the third before Sammy had the door wide and was at the tying with his gloved hands. Yet, so quick was Sammy that a moment later his impatient voice, with a thrill of triumph in it, was piping—"Wire! Wire! Wire!"—to prove that he had had to wait for the final strand. It was the old duel between roller and wire puncher.

And now Jumbo heard the bale bump on the dusty floor of the dog house beneath, and the soft slam of the door. He began to push down the top of the feed. He saw Sammy roll the bale onto the scales, weigh it, write the poundage on the redwood tag. As he slipped the tag under the central wire, Sammy shouted over his shoulder: "Two hundred forty, Jumbo!"

Two hundred and forty pounds? And out of the lightest part of the hay? Jumbo laughed with joy.

A dust cloud was rising. Out of that cloud Jumbo shouted encouragement to the crew while his heart swelled with love for them. Even Chicago, with his beautiful face, his crippled body, and the malicious devil inside him, seemed to Jumbo a glorious spirit.

They put out Jumbo's tally of twenty-five bales in under fifty minutes. Sammy Pleasant shouted the news, as Jumbo climbed from the feeders' table into the soft limbo of the stack and picked up the massive Jackson fork lightly with one hand.

"We're going to *kill* that record!" cried Sammy, shaking a fist above his head, laughing up at the giant on the stack.

But Jumbo felt the first cold touch of doubt, for the rolling of twenty-five bales had crimsoned the face of Sammy Pleasant, and, where the dust whitened his cheeks, the rolling sweat inscribed lines of an indecipherable writing.

"But he's proud! Book learning makes a man proud."

Sammy, in fact, had gone halfway through high school.

The sun was already hot, but Jumbo, who never had known fatigue, could sweat a gallon and feel no difference. However, what would happen to the rest when flesh began to melt away? Now his soul was pinched when he heard Sammy's voice calling out the lighter weights of Lucas's tally: "Two thirty-five, two twenty-five, two thirty-two. . . ."

Yet, after all, he could not expect Harry Lucas to jam

the press as he did and build the bales up like the solid grain of wood from top to bottom. Lucas was no Frenchie, swift-handed, dexterous, with the strength of a bull behind a cat's paw. Jumbo's heart softened, remembering Frenchie whom he had taken to his heart like a brother, confiding to him all the intricate little devices of the feeder's art. They had built the old record together and broken it over and over until it stood above forty-seven tons. He had given, always, a full share of the glory to Frenchie, but it was true that people looked up to him rather than to the foreigner for an explanation of the great runs the press had made in those days. So Frenchie had gone off by himself and now, with his natural strength and with his purloined craft, he had helped to put the high mark within eight pounds of forty-eight tons! The loss of Frenchie had been like the loss of a hand.

An audience began to gather before the middle of the morning for the news had spread through the district that the McCann press was trying for the record. Before the morning lunch period Sammy Pleasant shouted up at Jumbo: "Frenchie! Frenchie's here! He's got your gal!"

Jumbo saw the big fellow at once, in a blue silk shirt with a red necktie. His overalls fitted him as closely as a sailor's trousers around the narrow of the hips. He wore a hat of clean gray felt, pushed back from his face, and, as usual, he was smiling, for Frenchie seemed to find the world around him a little ridiculous. There was the widow, sitting beside him in her rubber-tired buggy, wearing her fluffy yellow dress with a red something at her throat, paying no more attention to Jumbo than to a man in a picture but adoring Frenchie with upward eyes. And yet, for the moment, Jumbo could forgive the two hundred acres and Rosa as well, he was so stirred by the sight of his old partner. Out of the hot days of struggle in the past he remembered only the singing voice of Frenchie, calling through the dust cloud: *"Courage! Le diablo est mort!"*

Jumbo delayed a first feed for a moment, as he danced on the platform and waved his great arms. "Oh, Frenchie!

Hi, Frenchie!" he shouted. "How y'are, boy?"

Frenchie turned at Jumbo's cry, lifted the hand that held a cigarette in a slight salute, and once more was laughing with Rosa.

Jumbo did not feel anger but only a sorrow for the old days when he had been to Frenchie a great and faultless god. He knew that no one ever had been to him what Frenchie was in the other years—a tower of strength, a wall to lean on.

A moment later Mrs. McCann came out with the mid-morning lunch of bread, butter, stewed plums, and a pail of steaming black coffee. Jumbo swung down from the table and went up to Frenchie. "Well, you come over to see how we can do it, eh? Wait! We're gonna stick that record where you'll never touch it."

Having spoken, he waited with a childish eagerness for a flash of the old warm friendship.

"You won't do it with Sammy Pleasant," Frenchie said. He pointed. "He's sick. He's going to crash on you in an hour or so."

"Don't kill yourself trying, Jumbo," said Rosa. "You're not young like Frenchie, you know."

Disappointment, in Jumbo, turned into anger that made him clench his fists, but since his boyhood he had walked in fear of what his big hands might do, so he swallowed his first wrath. Then he turned and regarded Sammy Pleasant. The big lad reclined with head and shoulders against the bottom of the bale stack, holding a cup of coffee that the shudder of his hand kept spilling.

Jumbo went toward his bale-roller and heard Frenchie's laughter behind him. He dropped to one knee beside Sammy Pleasant. "How you feel?"

"Fine."

Jumbo pushed his fingers into Sammy's hair and tilted back his head. Against the heel of his palm he felt the rapid blood in the temple, beating.

"I'm all right, Jumbo," said Sammy Pleasant. "Don't you

worry. I've got a lot left in me, and I'm going to pour it all in."

Jumbo stood up. "Stop piling them three high. Leave the tops till noon, and I'll throw 'em up."

From that point on, Sammy Pleasant rolled the top bales to the side and left them on the ground.

Jumbo looked down on the greatness of his own body and laughed. "The kid ain't like me. He's made big, but he ain't made same as me. God was taking His time when He made me."

He remembered what Rosa had said about youth and laughed again. He was thirty-five, but he never had thought about time. Time to Jumbo was a child unworthy of consideration. But then the thought of Rosa's smile and her two hundred acres stabbed him again. He saw that he could win both Rosa and the record by this day's work.

When twelve o'clock was announced by the banging of the tin pan at the cookhouse, the bale-roller's tally showed two hundred and twenty-one bales tied and weighed, at an average of two hundred and thirty-five pounds to the bale. That gave them within a few pounds of twenty-six tons for the eight hours of work, and Jumbo, as he went into the cookhouse, was jubilant.

It was a cheerful, noisy crew that sat around the table in the cookhouse until Sammy Pleasant, with half of his steak uneaten, got up from the bench and went out of the cookhouse, steadying himself with his hands against the wall. The other men stopped eating for a moment and looked at one another with empty, staring eyes, and nothing moved except the streams of sweat that ran down their faces, for in the cookhouse the heat of the stove was added to the hundred and ten degrees of that blistering day.

"He's big, but he's a bum," exploded Dick Whelan at last.

Jumbo got up and left the cookhouse, carrying Sammy's unfinished plate with him. His own stomach was clamoring for more food, but he turned his back on thoughts of himself and went down to where Sammy Pleasant lay under the wagon with his face in his hat, groaning a little with every breath he drew. Jumbo turned him on his back. The two hundred pounds of him were as loose as water.

"I'm fine. I wasn't hungry. I'm fine," said Sammy.

Jumbo fanned his face with his hat. "Take it easy. . . . I ain't gonna see you killed. Take it easy. . . . Let the record go. I wouldn't want anything to happen to you."

"I'm going to last it out," said Sammy. "Did you see Frenchie laughing? I'm going to last it out, all right."

"Not unless'n you eat," said Jumbo. "Leave your head rest on my knee, like that. . . ."

"I won't be a baby. I'm not sick."

"You just leave go all holts and take it easy," ordered Jumbo. "There's nobody can see us."

"I'm no man. I haven't got any guts," Sammy said, when the steak was finished, "like you got, Jumbo. There's nobody like you."

"I guess there *ain't* anybody like me, at that. I'll tell you what. I never was tired in my life. You lay there and rest while I go and throw up those bales."

He went off and spent the rest of the lunch hour completing the stacks, throwing the bales up lightly, not with the craft of a bale-roller but with sheer, clumsy excess of power. The whole audience from beneath the oak tree, except Frenchie, came out to watch him. Frenchie, of course, had gone back to spend the heat of the day lolling on the Pinzone porch.

Jim Coffey's boy touched his leg and said: "Jumbo, is it true? Are you the strongest man in the world?" And nobody laughed.

But just at the end of the lunch hour, as he hoisted the last third-rank bale into place, old Tom Walters came and confronted him. "You're going to make yourself sick, Jumbo Cafferty," he said. "The bigger you are, the more there is for the sun to fry. A man isn't meant to work straight through a day as hot as this. A man is meant to take an hour off for lunch. *God* means him to!"

Heat was raging through Cafferty's brain so that the trees

44

in the distance seemed to lift and fall on the waves of it. Those bales had turned to lead. Then he was back on the platform with the sun focused as with a burning glass on the back of his head and the dust cloud suspiring upward around the press. Straight up the dust lifted, for there was not a breath of wind, not a touch of mercy in that terrible afternoon.

Yet Sammy Pleasant was carrying on very well. He looked sicker than ever, but he was rolling and piling the bales steadily.

"How you making it?"

"That steak's working," yelled Sammy, white-faced but laughing.

Cafferty's heart opened. He and Rosa would have a son like Sammy, able to laugh, beautiful to behold, but harder in substance.

Then disaster struck suddenly, from an unexpected direction.

A Jackson fork is the gift of a genius to men who have to handle hay swiftly, in large masses, but it has four tines as sharp as needles, and the curve necessary to the steel prongs makes them clumsy and dangerous. Jumbo was on the twentieth bale after lunch when a voice screamed, and he saw the derrick was bringing in not only a forkload of hay but Harry Lucas, writhing on top of it. A tine had gone through the fleshy part of Harry's left forearm. Jumbo got him to the ground, and Bessie McCann bandaged the wound.

"There goes our record, and God help it," said Jimmy McCann.

"Jumbo, I'm sorry," said Harry Lucas, his long face twisting with pain. "I wanted to do it for you. We all wanta do it for you. But the fork just sort of flipped around and snagged me."

"Steve!" Jumbo shouted to the derrick driver. "Steve, you could handle a Jackson fork before you were more'n born, son. Listen, Harry," said Jumbo to Harry Lucas, "you

45

got hands enough to work the derrick horse. And we can go right on!"

"How can we go on?" asked Jimmy McCann. "With only one man to do the feeding . . . ? There ain't no man that can feed a press without being spelled for a whole half day!"

"Can't nobody do it?" said Jumbo. He laughed. "Take a look and see. *I* can! Harry, get out there to the derrick horse. Steve, let me see how good you are with that fork."

The spectators had crowded in around the press crew, and they began cheering when Lucas, with his bandaged arm, went out to take control of the derrick horse. Jumbo looked and saw that only Frenchie, sitting beside Rosa Pinzone under the shadow of a great striped umbrella over her buggy, was silent, smiling, with an inward, contemptuous knowledge. It was the only thing that could make Jumbo's heart sink.

He never had known fatigue before, but he knew it by the time he had pushed another ten tons through the jaws of that Little Giant press. A haypress feeder works like a sprinter, at full capacity all the time. Some track athletes can sprint almost an entire quarter mile, but no one, no matter what his powers, can sprint a half mile or a mile. That, in a sense, was what Jumbo was trying to do.

He called to Jimmy McCann. "Hey, Jimmy, fetch the flask over."

McCann brought the whiskey flask and handed it up.

"That stuff's no good on a day like this," he said. "It'll boil in you."

Jumbo said nothing, but, when the power horses were changed, he used the spare moment to pour a long draught down his throat. Afterward, he had false power for half an hour. Then the fatigue grew greater, in a sudden wave, and he felt choked. It was the dust that did it, he kept telling himself. No wind would come to slant the white smother away from the press. It boiled up, thick and heavy, thicker and whiter than fog, with the sun sparkling through its outer layers. One could feel it about the waist, like thin water.

When it reached the nose, it poured into the lungs like a liquid and set the men gasping. It often made of Sammy Pleasant, seen from the feeders' table above, a mere shadowy silhouette as he bobbed up and down, rolling his bale toward the stack. He was slow even in lifting the bales two high. Jumbo thought Sammy would faint.

The mid-afternoon lunch came at half past four, and Jumbo felt his knees give way under him. When he got to the lunch pails, the men stopped eating and looked at him. Young Sammy Pleasant pushed to his feet and came to him, wavering as though he were walking in a fierce wind.

"Jumbo," he said, "if it wasn't you, I'd say you were fagged out."

"Fagged?" shouted Jumbo. "I never was tired in my life."

Jimmy McCann brought matters back to a practical basis. He had the bale-roller's book in his hand as he said: "Boys, I want you to listen to something. We've bailed and piled thirty-eight tons of hay already. A haypress day is from dawn to sunset. Keep on at this rate, and you're gonna turn out fifty tons of hay and break every record that ever was on the books."

He had his answer not from the panting crew of the press but from the crowd of spectators. There were two hundred of them, now, shouting applause. Only Frenchie was silent and aloof, when it seemed to Jumbo that one word from his old partner would give him vital strength. But Rosa— bless her!—was clapping her hands vigorously. The very soul of Jumbo was comforted.

He munched a bit of bread, took a long swallow of whiskey, and began to pitch the bales, three high, to make the top row of the stack. But the lifting of every bale sent a wave of hot blood bursting against his brain. A mist formed across his eyes. Through it he could see Frenchie, standing somewhat apart. Then the brief lunch period ended, as he put up the last bale and turned back toward the press.

There came a time, about twenty bales later, when Jumbo began to forget the record and pray for the sun to go down. But it was plastered against one place in the sky, and there it remained hour after hour, burning its rays through the welter of dust.

Now a voice called softly to Jumbo and frightened him a little. For it placed him back in the old, happy days when to his own exhaustless strength was added the river of power that flowed in Frenchie. He saw it was not a ghost but Frenchie himself, who had climbed up to the platform and crouched in a corner, calling: "Jumbo, you can't do it. You'll kill yourself. You're dying on your feet now. Take a slip and fall and pretend you've knocked out your shoulder. Nobody'll know. . . . You're dying on your feet."

"Get off or I'll run the fork through you!" Jumbo yelled.

Frenchie disappeared, but his voice remained at Jumbo's ear saying: "*You're dying . . . you're dying . . . you're dying on your feet!*"

When Frenchie said something, it was apt to be true, but, of course, it was impossible that Jumbo should die like this. That wise God who had made him with such affectionate care would not throw away His handiwork in such a manner. This thought came to Jumbo rather dimly. All things were dim in the darkness of his eyes, the shadow from within that veiled everything. Through that impalpable curtain he saw Sammy Pleasant, all a-stagger with exhaustion, now piling the bales three high. He could not make the straight lift, but he laid the lower rows in two steps, giving each of the top bales two lifts. That was slow work, but the ground would be clean when the sun set and the work ended. Jumbo knew this work was done for his sake. It was just after this that he heard the voice of Frenchie suddenly rising: "Come on, Jumbo! *Le diablo est mort!* Ten bales more, Jumbo, and you smash the record to *hell.* . . ."

Cafferty knew that cheerful battle cry. He had learned its meaning in the gay old days. *The devil is dead.* The voice was a fountain of brightness that cleared his brain. Once more the pitchfork was light in his hands, building the feeds high and heavy, ramming them down the throat of the press. If only the descending sun had not been a streak of blood-red, staining his consciousness! If only a little time remained!

He heard Frenchie's ringing voice like quicksilver running through his blood, and flicking the others also, touching the whole crew, taking the stagger out of young Jimmy Pleasant with a word of praise.

"I gotta win," said Cafferty to his soul. "Even Frenchie wants me to. . . . Frenchie would be up here helping, if it wouldn't spoil the record. Frenchie . . . he's with me . . . and God wouldn't hold me back. Even Rosa is helping me now!"

For she had taken her stand near the dog house in spite of the dust that boiled out around her and whitened her dress; and from a pail of water she sprayed Sammy with her wet fingertips, continual little showers of cool drops.

"For me!" said Jumbo to his bursting heart, and envisioned the pleasant future, the two hundred acres, the well-matched mule team, the heavy wagons with red-painted, shining wheels, until his thoughts settled upon the bigness, the black beauty, of Rosa's kitchen range and remained there.

He discovered that for half of eternity he had been worrying about a certain sound, which was the noise his feet made as he lunged to thrust the feed down the throat of the press. Formerly, it had always been a steady, rhythmic beat, but now there was a stutter in it, and he found that he was staggering each time that he stepped forward. The hay grew heavy again. It seemed to have turned to sticks of molasses, heavy, clinging to the tines, and his legs had no sense in them whatever.

As he worked, he saw Sammy Pleasant falling from the second tier of bales as he tried to lift a third-row bale into place. He thought that was the end, but a moment later Sammy was pushing the bale into place. He saw the crowd that stood on the top of the bale stack, yelling itself hoarse every time a bale came out of the press. Hundreds of people had come for miles to see the end of that day.

The voice of Frenchie from beside the scales, where he

was adding up the tally of the bales, sang out to him: "Jumbo, one more bale and you win. Jumbo, Jumbo, *le diablo est mort!*"

"The devil is dead," said Jumbo. He laughed like a drunken, defiant Viking god. Then stilled.

Darkness like a hot, black night had gathered over Jumbo, but he found the hay through the instinctive swing and reach of the hay fork, built the feed by instinct, and helped the closing apron home. One red glint out of the west told him that the sun still watched him as the beater carried down the fifth feed and the bale was made.

After that, he felt himself falling. He heard the separate noises as his knees, his hips, his shoulder and elbows, and then his head struck the floor of the feeders' table.

He lived by fits and snatches, after that, for hours. First he was aware of Frenchie, kneeling by him and holding up a hand that stopped the cheering voices. Then they were lowering him from the table.

The next thing he knew was Jimmy McCann's voice saying: "My God, he's bleeding from the mouth . . . he's gonna die!" and then Frenchie, silencing McCann with a ripple of cursing.

"How's Sammy?" asked Cafferty.

"Sammy, he's all right."

"He's game, ain't he?"

"Maybe," said Frenchie.

"Send everybody away except you," said Jumbo. Frenchie sent them all away. "Make me stop trembling," said Jumbo. "It's like I was afraid. If they see me, they'll think I'm afraid."

Frenchie took his hand, and the trembling ceased. The doctor came. He spoke in a quiet, precise voice after he had listened with a stethoscope and taken his temperature. "Can you hear me, Jumbo?"

Something locked Jumbo's jaws, and he could not speak, but he heard Frenchie say: "He's gone again. It's like that. Comes and goes. Doctor, tell me what's gonna happen?"

Jumbo lost the doctor's words, but he heard the slow,

falling voice. When clear consciousness came back to him again, his body was so cold that he felt he was afloat on a black sea, with the waters about to lap over his mouth. Above him the Milky Way was a dust cloud, blowing through the sky, and the stars were drawing down closer and closer to the earth. Some of the stars were blotted out by Frenchie's shoulders.

"Frenchie, there's a lot to think about that I never thought."

"Ah, my old . . . !"

"Yeah, you never'll speak English very good," said Jumbo. He added: "But I like you the way you are. I like you fine."

"*Mon vieux!*" said Frenchie.

"What does that mean?" said Jumbo. "Don't be a fool like you was a woman or something."

But he knew by Frenchie's weeping voice that his life was feared for, and this made him want to laugh. Instead of laughing he fell asleep. When he wakened again, a cold wind was blowing breath into his body. The stars were dim in the east, and a gray light shone faintly on the dew that covered the head of Frenchie.

"Frenchie!" he said.

At the vigor in his voice, Frenchie leaned forward with a start. "*Tiens!*" he said. "The strength comes back to you! May all the doctors be. . . . Ah, hi, Jumbo, but I have been sitting here with some thoughts."

"Where is Rosa?" asked Jumbo.

"Tomorrow," said Frenchie. "I tell you tomorrow."

Jumbo lifted his head. "Now what are you talking about?"

"Listen, *mon vieux*," said Frenchie, bending over to peer into the eyes of his friend. "When Sammy dropped, Rosa comes to him, running, and takes his head in her lap . . . bah! . . . and calls him her darling!"

"Yeah?" said Jumbo, watching two hundred well-fenced acres fade from his vision.

". . . and her sweetheart," continued Frenchie, "and helps

him into her buggy . . . I spit upon it! . . . and takes his head on her shoulder and drives away. . . ."

"Yeah?" said Jumbo. "That kind of leaves the world to the two of us, don't it?" Jumbo held out his hand.

Frenchie took it in both of his. "My old . . . !" he said.

"You gotta learn English right," said Jumbo, disturbed. "I'm gonna take some time off and teach you."

He looked beyond Frenchie into the green east with a curious joy, for his eye seemed to travel across the horizon and through an opening gate of amber light. Then from the trees near the slough some crows got up and flew in single file across the brilliance, slowly laboring their wings up and down, as though they were drawing the day after them across the great world.

Master and Man

*"Master and Man" which appeared in the January 5, 1924
issue of* Western Story Magazine *is an extraordinary story
on several levels. In the pulp world of the 1920s there were
no black heroes. In fact, during this era of ethnic restric-
tions in popular literature, some pulp writers even wrote
about Negroes with the same disdain they held toward Mexicans and American Indians. Not so with Faust. "Master
and Man" represents a radical departure from any such
fashion of the period. The real hero of the story is a stalwart black man, Bobbie, who can not only outride, outfight,
and outshoot any white man in the mountain desert, but
whose unwavering moral code serves as a model for his
often cruel and dissolute white master. Here, in this truly
offbeat tale, Faust is far ahead of his time, demonstrating
a sensitivity and racial empathy that is revolutionary for
the period. "Master and Man" is also a story of redemp-
tion, replete with the action and drama demanded by pulp
readers—an unconventional high-water mark in the fictional career of Max Brand.*

I

"TOM AND BOBBIE"

In his bare feet he was six feet three and a half inches in height. He weighed two hundred and twenty pounds. He could carry that weight over a hundred yards in ten seconds, flat. He could jump over a bar as high as the top of his head. He could throw a sixteen-pound hammer fifty-five yards. And at Jefferson Thompson's place, in the old blacksmith shop, ten good men and true saw him lift a canvas sack filled with iron junk off the floor and onto a scales, and those scales registered twelve hundred pounds, the weight of a sizable horse.

His body was made not bulkily, but with smoothly sloping muscles, fitted one to another so deftly that his bared arm looked round and fat, almost like the arm of a woman. His limbs tapered to narrow, long hands and feet. He had the head of a Greek, with features chiseled with infinite care and strength—a long, high nose, a square, clipped chin, and big, confident, black eyes. His hair was like waving smoke, and his skin was as black as jet.

Such was Bobbie. Had he been white, he would have been one of the famous figures of the community, the very pride of western Texas. But, as it was, he was only the Farnsworth Negro, Bobbie. In fact, his great size, his singular skill in many ways, which enabled him to crush the rebellion out of a vicious mustang, or to throw a rope with either hand, or to work two revolvers at the same time at two different targets—all of these assets were lost sight of and forgotten in the damning phrase: "the Farnsworth Negro." The more formidable and exceptional he was, the more shameful it was considered that he should be treated like a slave. Apparently he freely accepted that treatment, which culminated on the famous occasion when his young master, Thomas Gainsborough Farnsworth, struck the big Negro squarely in the face with his fist and then beat him with his riding quirt in front of everybody in the town of Daggett. The occasion was an ugly one. Old Tom Farnsworth, who knew that his boy was wasting his time and squandering his money in a poker game in Daggett, reinforcing his waning spirits with bootleg whiskey from time to time, sent Bobbie in to give Thomas, Jr., a message that he must come home at once. Bobbie arrived just as the game was breaking up, and young Tom was sick and worried because his wallet, which had been fat, was now empty, and his future was mortgaged with certain I. O. U.s. So he flew into a passion and beat the Negro soundly with his fists and his quirt.

Bobbie was seen to endure this punishment without stirring so much as a muscle of his face, even when Tom, maddened by his own brutality, struck Bobbie squarely across the mouth with a lash of the quirt. There was neither complaint nor dodging on the part of Bobbie. The next day big Sam Chalmers and his brother, Jud, acting on the principle that a man who would endure such treatment at the hands of another must be a cur at heart, started to harry and worry Bobbie through the streets of the town of Daggett. Bobbie gave them the slip and went to the house of the sheriff.

"Sheriff Morgan," he said, "the Chalmers boys are bothering me some."

The sheriff looked with curious contempt at the huge body and the handsome face of the Negro, marked with great bars and wales by the beating of the day before.

"Can't you take care of yourself, Bobbie?" he asked. "Do I got to put you in a cage, by gum, to keep you from being spoiled?"

"Sheriff Morgan," said the big fellow, "I only want your permission to protect myself."

"Say, man," said the sheriff, whose heart was as big as his hand and as tough, "do you got to ask me for that?"

"I am a Negro," said Bobbie.

At this the sheriff dismissed Bobbie, but he remained thoughtful after his visitor had departed. Through a window he beheld Bobbie encounter the Chalmers stalwarts. Both of these men were proven fighters. They went at their quarry with a rush, and the sheriff scratched his chin as he watched them split upon Bobbie like water on a reef. They rushed at him again. Sam drew a gun, and Jud whipped out a knife, and then Bobbie struck once with either hand. That was the end of the battle. Sam was carried to the next house with a broken rib, and Jud was dragged to the same place with a shattered jawbone.

"The big feller don't know his strength," said the town of Daggett. But, thereafter, it grew more and more curious and more and more disgusted with Bobbie. If he were truly fearless, as it seemed to be proven, what could have kept him in the service of the Farnsworth family, enduring such insult and brutality as Tom had used toward him?

The explanation requires a backward look to a day when Bobbie was only ten years old. On that occasion his old grandfather, with a black skin growing gray and dusty with age, talked to him while they sat, fishing, under a willow tree. The source of the complaint was that little Bobbie was making serious objections to certain things that were required of him. Why, he had asked, should he have to polish the boots of his master? Why should young Tom be privileged to use him like a dog? Why should he, Bobbie, with more strength and adroitness in a minute than young master Tom had in a year, be forced to sit back and play second fiddle to the white boy? Other Negroes did not have to. They were free. They claimed a right to life, liberty, and property. They could swagger as boldly as any white. What was the distinction, then, between Bobbie and the rest? These were the thoughts of Bobbie, if not almost his words, and his grandfather responded with much deliberation, but smoothly, as one who speaks of that which he has long pondered.

"Bobbie," he said, "the difference between you and them is that they're growin' up to be fool niggers, and you is growin' up to be a wise one. I'll tell you a little story. You set down and rest yore feet and look at that slap-daddle water dog, lying off yonder on that stone."

"But, oh, Granddaddy," cried the little black boy, "why should we live like slaves?"

"How you go talkin', honey," said the old man, chuckling hoarsely. "Is settin' here, fishin' and squintin' at the sky through the trees, and watchin' of the ripples that come wigglin' on the bank . . . is that bein' a pore slave?" He shook his old gray head.

Here he launched into the body of his story that related how, in the old days when the Civil War passed across the land, he had remained with his master as a servant through the midst of the battling, and how he had fought at the side of the colonel, when it might be said that he was helping to tighten the rivets of the shackles that bound his own people. Afterward, when the war ended, and he and the colonel went back to the old place in Texas with their scars and their honors, he had served the bankrupt family for years after, years without a cent of pay, laboring and struggling night and day until at the last fortune changed. They moved into the western part of the state, and luck favored the colonel in the cow industry. He became wealthy. But he never could have crossed the dark hour of his life after the war had it not been for the devotion of the old Negro.

"Hisself was what said it," crooned that old toothless black man. "He said that I done help' an' saved him."

He continued his narrative with the growth to manhood of his only surviving child, Charlie—how Charlie came to maturity with his head full of ideas of independence; how he went to school and fought to distinguish himself; how he left the Texas ranch and journeyed across the country to New York; how he grew fat and well-to-do in that far-off city; how he married, and how Bobbie was born; how misfortune and sickness robbed Charlie of his wife and all his property; how he dragged himself back to the old ranch, sick and with his little son in his hand; how he died wishing that he had never stirred beyond the peace and safety of his home ranch in the dear old Lone Star State.

"He'd done gone and been a fool nigger," concluded the old grandfather. "And every nigger is a fool that tries to live like what a white man does. Let them lead, and we'll foller. Let them talk, and we'll work. They know, Bobbie. And them that know is a heap better and stronger than them that can only work."

Such were the opinions of his grandfather, expressed with a solemnity that amazed and subdued Bobbie. He had argued as well as he could, but it was like questioning a prophet. The old man felt he knew the truth, and he began to roar and thunder like a preacher in a church. So Bobbie had it worked firmly home in his brain that, no matter what chanced, it was better to stay faithful to a white master than to be free, because some people were meant for freedom and others were meant to be in service all their days. Such was the opinion of the grandfather.

"Them that looks high, stubs their toes and falls on their faces," he declared.

He had the glaring example of Bobbie's very own father with which to fortify his remarks, and from this example Bobbie could not escape. As for cruelty and injustice, now and again it was much better for a Negro to endure them than to strike out on his own behalf. For in the end woe and misery would be very apt to come to him. To endure the dangers of life required, said the grandfather, the adroitness of a snake and the fierceness of a hawk, and only the white man possessed these qualities of the brain. Far, far better to rest an arm upon him than to struggle for oneself.

Such was the opinion that he forced Bobbie to accept. But it was not a matter of one interview only. They talked the matter over time and time again. Little Bobbie had a thousand tests of the case. He could not reconcile himself to the manifest injustice of his grandfather's advice for a while, but in time he began to feel the weight of the old man's experience and will. In a year or so the creed had entered his mind as firmly as a religious faith, with a religious emotion behind it. If he were true to the Farnsworths, he felt, the Farnsworths would be true to him, and thus his happiness would be secured. More than this: to be faithful to the Farnsworths became more than duty and good sense. To have displeased them would have been to have committed sacrilege. Old Thomas Gainsborough Farnsworth, Sr., was a distant idol to be worshipped by Bobbie. But the immediate goal of his affections and his humble admiration was young Tom.

Young Tom grew into a slender fellow, with some wit, more sarcasm, and fists as free and ready as his tongue. He had a sallow skin and a lean, thoughtful look. In dress, like every Farnsworth, he was something of a dandy. Altogether he was a dapper young exquisite, with a cultivated taste for leisure, cards, and books. He read everything, digesting it as fast as it was devoured by his eyes, and filing it away in a memory that could forget nothing. He read, moreover, with tremendous speed. By the time he was fifteen he had crowded into his young brain more historical information of various and sundry sorts than the average college professor could boast. The result was that when he went to a great Eastern university, the first thing he did was to contract the bad habit of despising his instructors. At seventeen he could talk freely about *The Critique of Pure Reason*, for he had digested the thought of the difficult old German as readily as some children see to the heart of chess problems and bewilder older opponents.

Like most prodigies, young Tom soon promised to come to a no good end. He did not have to attend lectures in order to earn good marks. If he dodged classes, his examinations were always brilliant. His father, reading the flattering reports, decided that his boy was making a record for himself and acquiring a good and growing education. As a matter of fact, young Tom was letting his books take care of themselves. He was merely doing a little remembering from time to time, and his serious endeavors were lavished in winning the attentions of the prettiest girls in the college town. The only sport he favored was the old-fashioned and useless one—as far as newspapers were concerned—of fencing. Riding and fencing gave him his only exercise. His amusements were those of all prodigals, cards and drink, with other well known things in between.

The four years at college cost his father a small fortune, but the older man consoled himself with the fine marks that young Tom secured in his studies, and so the bills were duly paid. Tom came home, hating his prospective ranch life like so many days of threatened prison. He also came home bringing his manservant, Bobbie, who had been through the whole college career with his master. But where college had been wasted on the master, it had not been lost upon the slave. Where Tom sat up to finish a bottle, Bobbie sat up to finish a book. Where Tom lounged in bed till noon, Bobbie was swinging through his paces in the college gymnasium, or on the athletic fields. It was little that Tom himself could do for his *alma mater*, but at least he could lend the services of Bobbie, and this was enough. Bobbie was the standard in the school of the sprinters. He was the iron man against whom the star linemen of the football team tried their strength. And it was a thing of beauty to see Bobbie, playing on the second eleven, melt through the center of the line and stop the plunging fullback before he had well started to plunge. They used to say of him that he had the speed of a cat and the power of a horse, but he was always as gentle as a man playing with children. If he tackled a runner, it was done with an almost apologetic firmness; in the boxing ring, if he blocked a hard swing with a stiff counter, he was busy with apologies at once. Someone told Farnsworth that he would have been detested for his profligacy in the university had it not been that one and all admitted that a man who could inspire such a servant with such devotion must have a good heart and a clean one. Bobbie was the shadow, it might be said, that set off young Tom and made him seem a highlight.

Then they came back to the ranch together, Bobbie placid, as always, with that infinite good nature which was his, like continual springtime, and Tom surly and sullen because he faced the long exile away from his boon companions and the city he loved. He would have gone mad with discontent had it not been that he met Deborah Kinkaid and lost his heart to her at once.

She was not at all of a type that one would have selected as an enchantress to enthrall young Tom. She was a small, wiry little person, with a head of the brightest red hair, a nose rather too short, blue, lively eyes, and a world of animation. When she met the young college man, she refused to be impressed by his dignity and sullen reserve.

"Anyone can look like a blunderbuss," said Deborah.

That remark was carried to Tom. He was furious and interested at once. He formed a contemptible scheme on the spot of making desperate love to Deborah until he had broken her heart. So he called on her at once. She showed him her pet horse and her pet duck. With mischievous eyes she sang ragtime to him across her piano. She sat under the huge cypress tree by the river, with her arms tucked behind her head, and confessed that she didn't know a thing about books now, didn't ever expect to, and hoped that she never would.

Tom went home with his head reeling. He could not sleep. Before morning he knew that he loved her, and he knew that she was below him. Moreover, he knew that on account of this girl he would have to stay in the West and endure people he despised and a country and climate made 'specially to be his bane. It was to forget Deborah that he had ridden into Daggett, played and lost his money, and then taken out his spite so shamefully on the big person of Bobbie.

II

"THE CALL OF YOUTH"

No one carried to old Tom Farnsworth the tidings of how his son first beat Bobbie, but they could not help repeating how the big Negro had crushed Sam and Jud. Farnsworth made inquiry after that, learned the whole truth about the disgraceful fashion in which his son had behaved himself, and called young Tom before him—with thunder in his face.

"Tom," he said, "I'm ashamed of you and disgusted with you. And, by the eternal, unless you go this instant and beg the pardon of Bobbie, I swear I shall disinherit you! A Farnsworth to strike a servant . . . a Farnsworth! Thunderation, Tom, I see that you were created only to break my heart. This shame will never go out of the family."

Tom was brave enough. He dreaded nothing except the necessity of having to go to work. If he were disowned, he would have to labor with his hands. Rather than that, there was no humiliation through which he would not have passed. He went out, therefore, found Bobbie, and humbled himself before the Negro. But Bobbie would not hear him. It was not Master Tom who had struck him, he declared. It was simply a devil that had got into Master Tom for the moment, and which, he knew, would never come back again. But, no matter how much he said, he knew that young Tom would never forgive the servant, for the servant had been the means to this humiliation. He would far rather have faced the whipping again than to know that there was now a deep malice in the heart of young Tom Farnsworth.

Nor, in the meantime, were the results of that whipping ended. For, of course, the strange tale was carried straight to Deborah Kinkaid. She would not believe it at first, but, when the whole degrading fact was proved to her, she colored with shame and declared that, if she passed Tom Farnsworth again on the street, she would cut him dead. The very next day she did so straightway. To the amazement and the horror of young Tom, Deborah went by him with her head in the air, her eyes fixed on the enjoyment of some far-off prospect. He went home and lay all night in his bed, raging and tossing and twisting. First of all, he wanted to destroy the entire world and Deborah with it; then he wanted to perish gloomily. Eventually he resolved to go East at once. He even leaped out of bed, dressed, and started to pack. But, after all, he decided that he would see

Deborah again, even if his very heart had to bleed with the humiliation of bowing to her insult. For he could not go away before he had solved the mystery of why she was so hostile to him.

On the following night he went to see her. He slipped up behind the house and hesitated under the hedge for a long time. Young Jack Pattison was sitting on the porch, chatting with her, and the foolish laughter of the pair rattled and rang in his ears, tormenting him where he lay. Finally Pattison went away, and Tom got up to go to the girl before she entered the house. He must have a few words with her alone. If all did not turn out well, it must not be publicly known that he had so far debased himself that he had gone to cringe and crawl before this slip of a girl. For all the town of Daggett was repeating and relishing the story of how she had snubbed the rich man's son. He did not have a chance to see her in the dark of the porch, however, for young Jack Pattison had no sooner disappeared than she slipped into the house and ran up the stairs to her room. He saw the light flare in her window, and then he saw the shade pulled down, so that it became a dull rectangle, glowing. Then he decided that he must take one longer step in the adventure.

It was extremely rash. If he had been a thoughtful boy, he would never have done it, but Tom was not thoughtful. He followed the first impulse and went up the side of the house, climbing by means of the tree-like trunk and the sturdy branches of a great old climbing rose vine that had been planted when Mr. and Mrs. Kinkaid were married, and was, therefore, a year older than Deborah herself. It seemed a little wonderful to Tom, as he climbed, that creatures of one age should be so different—the vine, old and declining, Deborah in the very pink and flush of tender youth.

Now he sat on the ledge of her window, his heart thundering from the labor and the excitement of that climb. He tapped twice, cautiously. Suddenly it came to him with a shock that it would be a terrible thing if some other person should be in that room with the girl—if that other person—

her mother, perhaps—should open the window and look down into his face. What could he do? He had no time to decide, for now the window was raised. The shade lifted, and there was Deborah herself just before him. He had been wondering how she would address him. He could never have guessed the words she chose.

She said simply: "Tom Farnsworth, you idiot! Tom, you *crazy* boy! What are you doing here?"

And then, surprise and alarm both leaving her apparently, she dropped into a chair and burst into the heartiest laughter. He studied her the while with a sort of gloomy disgust. She was not lovely, certainly. When she laughed, and one saw the alarming width of her mouth, she was not even pretty. Yet, while his reason dissected her and decided upon fault after fault she most unquestionably possessed, his instinct was every instant saying to him: *How delightful, how rapturously charming this creature is. Oh, oh, that she could be mine!*

"Why are you laughing, Deborah?"

"Because you look so perfectly undignified and un-Farnsworthy on that window sill. Come inside, Tom."

"Good heavens, Deborah, you don't think that I would do a thing that might compromise you."

"Hush," said the girl, with a careless gesture. "Do you think it's any better for me to have you seated in my window where everyone within a mile can see you?"

This suggestion made him tumble hastily into the room.

"Why did you come!" asked Deborah, very curious, and not a little excited, but still smiling, as she looked at the red fragments of bark that littered his clothes and the scratches on his face and his hands. A modern Romeo was Tom!

"Because I'm such a weak fool," said Tom, crimson with rage and shame. "Because. . . ." He could not finish, but drew himself up and glowered down on her.

"Oh," said Deborah with a sudden change of tone. "I think I understand. You wanted to know why. . . ."

"Yes."

"Because they told me that you flogged Bobbie."

"In the name of heaven," cried Tom, "what's Bobbie to you?"

"A fine fellow, I understand."

"A nigger . . . and a fine fellow?"

"Certainly! Why not? He's a human being, Tom."

"Deborah, if such a thing. . . ."

"Well?"

He looked hopelessly at her. Every instant she insulted and defied him, made him pass through an agony of shame—and made him love her all the more violently.

"I'll say one thing," she cried suddenly to him. "I was a nasty cat yesterday. I'm really sorry for it. I shouldn't have passed you in that way. I apologize, Tom."

It was not a great concession, but it quite melted Tom and made the way easier for him. "Deborah," he told her, "I've been sick with it every moment of the time. Why the devil you did it, I can't make out. If you really mean that black rascal. . . ."

"Why do you call him a rascal?"

"He's a nigger, isn't he?"

"Tom, everyone in Daggett respects him, and everyone is a little afraid of him."

"I wish his bones were bleaching in the rain," cried Tom angrily. "But let's forget him. I've come here to talk about you and not about my valet."

She started to answer him with some heat, but then she changed her mind, after the fashion of one who feels that mere words are not tools sufficiently strong for the purpose at hand. "If you want to talk about me, I'm willing, of course," she said. "But you won't be silly, Tom?"

"You mean by that you hope I'll not be foolish enough to say that I love you. Is that it?"

"You have a nasty, sharp way of speaking, Tom."

"Frank people always hate frankness," he answered with equal testiness.

"Have you come to quarrel with me?" she asked, half angry and half smiling in spite of herself.

"I've come to make love to you," said Tom, "and I seem to be making a most awful mess of it."

"So you do . . . and yet. . . ."

"Well?"

"I like you better this way than with the grand manner, Tom. I'd rather see you blush and grow angry than looking like the grand duke of something or other."

"Be serious for two seconds, Deborah."

"I am serious . . . more than you dream."

"I want to say two or three short words that have been said a good many times before. I want you to know that I love you, Deborah. Confound it, I've fought against it. I've told myself that, if I have to stay out here to court you, I'll lose you anyway . . . but, even if I win, it means that I'm condemned to spend the rest of my life in the West, because you'd never move to the East, I know."

"Never, Tom," she admitted, glad that he had passed from his declaration into something else that gave her a chance to take her breath. "Do you know I'm astonished?" she could not help adding.

"Nonsense! You've seen me hanging about you, mooning like a sick calf."

"I've seen you now and then, drifting near me and looking me over with a sort of contemplative amusement, as if you wondered what sort of a watch ticked behind the queer case." She said this without resentment.

"Good gad, Deborah, are you using me for your amusement?"

"I'm not a bit amused. I'm terribly excited."

"Then tell me what to expect, and I'll bother you no more."

"Even when you tell me you love me," she said, with anger and curiosity commingled, "you speak more like a king than a suitor. I feel almost like crying . . . aye, aye, sir! . . . like a sailor aboard a ship when the captain calls."

"Deborah, this is an infernally embarrassing position. I'm in a torment. Tell me yes or no, and then I'll go."

"I'd like to be so certain that I could answer it in that

way, with a single word, and be sure that I'm right. Yesterday I was sure . . . but, when I heard how you'd treated Bobbie, I was convinced there was no man in the world so worthy of being hated. Today I'm beginning to doubt. Partly, it's because I'm immensely flattered that you notice me . . . partly, because I guess at all sorts of good things behind that cynical exterior of yours."

"You are a thousand times kind," he said coldly.

"There you are with your cynical touch again. Oh, Tom, confess frankly that you're carrying on this whole affair for a joke or a bet. Confess it, shake hands, and we'll part without malice."

A dull red burned up under his cheek, and, when he attempted to smile, his lips simply drew back in an ugly line. "That's your answer, then, Deborah?"

"It has to be. Let's be friends, Tom. Come to see me again. Let's grow to know one another."

"Every step I take toward you is an agony," he said. "The whole town of Daggett knows that you cut me, and the whole town will laugh and sneer when it sees me pursuing you."

"But you despise the whole town so much that you surely will not care a whit what it thinks of you."

He started at this and drew in his breath slowly, as though this were a new thought.

"It won't do, though," said the girl. "I think that I know how it is, Tom. You're one of those proud fellows who would sneer at the king of England to show your independence, but in your heart of hearts you care for the opinion of the smallest child and the poorest beggar on the street corner."

"Ridiculous!" Tom cried.

"I know I'm right."

He felt she had seen through him. He was partly relieved, partly amused, and in part he was very, very angry. It was just as if a strong man, in the midst of a passion of honest rage, should be tickled in the short ribs and forced to burst into laughter. What he wanted to do was to frown the opinion of Deborah into some other limbo; but what he did was to smile sheepishly upon her. "Confound it, Deborah," he said, "you turn me into a milk-and-water creature."

"Every minute," she said, "I see new things in you, Tom. Promise me that you'll do what I ask. We'll become friends. If the town of Daggett laughs at us, we'll laugh at the town of Daggett. And in the end we'll understand what's best to do. What's best right now is for you to go home . . . please. If someone should find you here, it would be mighty embarrassing."

"Shall I try to slip downstairs?"

"Dad is a wolf, when it comes to ears. You'd never get out that way. You'll have to go as you came."

He went to the window. "Deborah, I think that I shall go with hope."

"Of course you will."

She came up to him and took his hand, looking all the time into his eyes very earnestly, as though she were striving with all of her might to make out what might be going on inside his mind, guessing at the best, hoping for the best, but not quite sure. She seemed to Tom Farnsworth at that moment the loveliest and the best of women. He was so moved that he trembled—so shaken by her close scrutiny that he had to hide his face from her eyes by hurriedly raising her hand to his lips and then turning again to the window.

"Listen," she said, as he sat poised for an instant on the window ledge, "I'll ride down to the river tomorrow, near the hill with the three willows on the top. I'll go in the middle of the afternoon when everyone else is sleeping. Will you be there, Tom?"

"A thousand soldiers couldn't keep me from being there. Good night, Deborah."

"Good night, Tom."

She watched him swing into the darkness.

"Wild man . . . wild man," she whispered to herself, then closed the window, and drew back the shade once more.

III

"THE FARNSWORTH WAY"

As for Tom Farnsworth, he climbed down to the ground with a happy and reckless feeling growing in his heart. He had demeaned himself, of course, in going to her in this fashion, but dignity was one thing, and love was quite another, and they could not be near neighbors. She had despised him when he came; she had liked him well enough before he left. One more meeting might do much. He discovered that he no longer complained to himself because he was enchanted, as he had felt at first, without cause. Deborah became more and more one with his ideal of what a woman should be.

When he reached the earth, he was humming softly his content, and so, turning from the house, he saw a rudely outlined form in the darkness of the night, doubly black with the shadow of the house and the trees.

"What the devil . . . ," began Tom.

"This is Jack Pattison," said the other quietly. "I wonder if I may have the privilege of a short chat with you, Farnsworth?"

Farnsworth followed him among the trees, bewildered, hot with shame, angry. "Now," he said, when at last they had reached a plot of open grass, "tell me what you want, Pattison?"

"An explanation."

"Really?"

"This night I have asked Deborah Kinkaid to be my wife. As I left the house and went down the road, I stopped a while behind the hedge to moon at her lighted window, like a fool. Then I saw something work up the side of the house. The window opened. A man clambered inside the room. I've waited here, Tom, to meet that man when he came down again. I suppose you understand what's on my mind?"

An impulse of good-natured openness formed in the brain of Tom. He wanted to make a clean breast of everything—of all the shame and dread of the public voice that had kept him from going to Deborah openly by day or night. He wanted to explain it all clearly, as from one friend to another, but he changed his mind at the last instant. He had not the moral courage to humiliate himself.

"I neither know nor care what's in your mind, Pattison," he said. "But what I wish to understand is . . . how do you dare to spy on me and then stop me to ask what's in my mind?"

"Is that your attitude?"

"That's my attitude."

"Then I have to tell you that you're an overbearing, egotistical ass, Farnsworth. You've made yourself despised and hated by everyone in the county. I'm glad to have this chance to tell you my own opinion."

"You have a polished tongue, Pattison."

"As for Deborah, trust me that I'll have a full explanation out of you."

"In what way, Pattison?"

"If I have to beat it out of you, I'll do it!"

"Dear me," murmured Farnsworth. "You're a violent fellow, Pattison."

"Tom," cried the other, setting his grip on the breast of Farnsworth's coat, "you'll have to tell me everything I've asked, otherwise I'll go mad. I can't live and doubt Deborah."

The restraint with which Tom had held himself snapped. He struck off the hand of Pattison and leaped back. "Live or die and go to perdition for all of me!" he exclaimed. "Get out of my path, Pattison."

"Tom, this means a fight."

"As you please."

"Tom, I'm armed. For heaven's sake, be a man and a gentleman, and don't force us to do a murder here. I ask you for an explanation that you know I have a right to hear. Will you give it?"

"Not a syllable to any man on earth . . . by force."

"Then . . . God be on the right side!"

He jerked a hand for his hip pocket, but Farnsworth was much before him. He had already managed to shift his weapon to the deep pocket of his coat. He now dropped his hand upon it, found it lying already in line, and had merely to curl his finger around the trigger. Jack Pattison whirled around, throwing his revolver far into the brush, and fell on his face. The startling report of his own gun sobered and wakened Tom. He dropped instantly upon his knees beside the fallen man and turned him on his back. All that he could make out, in the dullness of the starlight, was the welling of blood from the very center of Pattison's forehead. Was he dead?

Tom stood up. Two birds, having been disturbed in their sleep by the roar of the gun beneath them, had soared a little distance into the air, but now they settled back to their roosting branch, with little sharp voices of complaint. The wind, tangling through some newly planted pine saplings, brought their freshness and purity of breath to Tom. Now he heard the outbreak of many voices from the Kinkaid house. A door slammed. Somebody ran noisily across the verandah.

"Who's there?" called Kinkaid. Then: "It came from yonder by the creek. Scatter, boys. Give a challenge as you go. If you meet anyone who won't speak, don't waste no time, but open up and. . . ."

Tom Farnsworth was already out of the grove. He crossed the lawn beyond it like a sprinter. He dove through a hole in the old hedge. He twisted to the left and found his horse, waiting at the place where it had been left, but not the horse alone, for a mounted man, very tall and on a horse of great size, sat his saddle nearby, holding the reins of Tom's mount.

"Who's there?" gasped Tom, snatching out his gun as he ran.

"Bobbie," called a guarded voice.

71

"Thank goodness . . . good boy." He flung himself into the saddle.

"What's happened, sir?"

It did not occur to Tom to keep back any secret from this man. "I've killed Jack Pattison."

"Lord, Lord!" groaned the Negro. "You're not sure, sir?"

"I shot him through the forehead . . . straight through the forehead, Bobbie. Can a man live after that?"

Another groan from Bobbie.

"What's to be done?"

"I'm thinkin' . . . I'm thinkin'."

"Best thing is to ride straight to the sheriff and give myself up. The sheriff would show me fair play."

"Master Tom, you're not very popular in Daggett just now. That was what brought me out after you tonight."

"What do you mean, Bobbie?"

"I mean that, when I saw you start for town, I guessed that there'd be trouble. So I came along."

"Start moving now. They're coming close."

The searchers from the house were beating through the garden, and now there was an outcry of horror. It could mean but one thing.

"They've found the dead body," said Tom. "Bobbie, this is my last minute as a free man. After this, I'm going to be a hound and run, and never stop running!"

"Mister Tom, wait and listen to me. I have a way out of all this. You ride straight home. Don't go to the sheriff and tell him what you've done. Don't do that, but ride straight home. If you go to the sheriff, you can trust that a mob will go to the jail to lynch you. Everybody loved Jack Pattison. People will go wild when they learn what's happened to him. But you go straight home the way I tell you. When you get home, go right straight up to your bed and turn in."

"You want me to put my head quietly into the noose?" asked Tom quietly.

"Mister Tom," said the Negro, "have I ever missed out on a promise I've made?"

"You haven't, Bobbie."

"Then just trust me this one time more to take you out of this trouble. I have a way all planned. Nobody will ever guess that you have a hand in what's happened tonight, unless Pattison wakes up and talks."

"I wish to goodness he would. If he'd talk again, I'd give them free leave to hang me. Bobbie, what can you do?"

"Just let it all to me, sir. I have a way in mind. But you have to go home first."

"Bobbie, God knows what devil got into me the other day when I struck you."

"I've forgotten what you mean, sir."

"You won't come with me, Bob?"

"No, sir."

"Good night, then, and good luck."

"Good night, sir."

Tom Farnsworth still hesitated for a little time, but now the noise from the Kinkaid house was growing more and more ugly. He could hear sounds from the stable behind the house, which was a very certain proof that they were saddling horses and making ready to pursue the murderer of poor Jack Pattison. Here was Bobbie, at whose side he somehow felt he should remain. But Bobbie was waving him away, and there the road stretched white and cool before him, twisting away into the pleasant darkness of the trees not far away. He let his long-legged bay mare drift softly through the silent dust that lay thick and light as feathers along the sides of the road. Presently, rounding the first turn and getting well out of the sight of the Kinkaid place, he gave the high-spirited creature her head, and she was away at once with a long, easy gallop. In the meantime, filled with a bitter concern, he wondered what could be in the mind of Bobbie.

"A nigger will show yellow sooner or later. Just give him time, and the bad streak will crop out," someone had said to him. He had never forgotten it. And he felt now an ugly premonition that Bobbie would use his knowledge of what had happened in order to get a full revenge for the beating he had received so lately. Indeed, he would be almost more than human, Farnsworth felt, if he did not make some use of that power now in his hands. He had merely to go to the men who were mustering at the Kinkaid house. A single word would send them thundering toward the Farnsworth house. So Tom drew up his horse and waited for a time to see what would happen, and in what direction the current of the pursuit would flow. He had not long to wait. There was a dim outbreak of yelling from the center of the town, which he had just left behind him. Then the voices began to recede rapidly, until he heard them no more, but only the hollow roar of hoofs, passing over a bridge. Tom gave this his own interpretation.

The cunning rascal, said Tom to himself, *he has told them that he saw the guilty man, and he has sent them on a wild goose chase. He's a handy fellow to have, is Bobbie.*

IV

"THE PURSUIT"

In the meantime Bobbie had waited near the Kinkaid house with never a thought of treachery, rising in his mind. His attitude toward his young master was a peculiar one. He did not love Tom. The blows that had been showered upon him lately had not been absolutely the first he had received. But, heretofore, Tom had been a little too much in awe of his gigantic servant to be free with punishment of a corporal nature. Yet he had taken Bobbie for granted from the first. They were almost exactly of an age. Bobbie was only a month or two older, but he had matured more quickly than the white boy, as Negroes almost always do. From the very first he had been little better than a slave to Tom. Never being without him, Tom had but a small value to place upon him. He heard other people make complimentary remarks about Bobbie, but he saw little reason for them. He accepted Bobbie as men accept pleasant weather with a sort of impersonal good nature.

Such was the attitude of Tom toward Bobbie, and of this attitude Bobbie was very well aware. For his own part he considered his master as a sort of limb of his own body. He could not separate himself from the thought of Tom Farnsworth. He had reached the age of memory in the service of Tom. He had continued in it all his life. He could not possibly think of his own comfort and happiness first.

What he thought of, when Tom confessed that he had shot a man, was of his own grandfather when that dusky-faced, white-headed old man should hear the tidings that a Farnsworth had done a murder. What a passion of grief and of shame the old man would fall into, not because a Farnsworth could have committed a crime, but because his grandson could have allowed the crime to be committed. Such was the stern fashion in which he would take Bobbie to account. In the early days, when Tom was whipped by his father for stealing fruit or for any other of a thousand mischiefs, Bobbie was punished twice as severely by his grandfather, simply because he had not been able to invent the means of dissuading his young master from the crime.

So it was that on this night, as he heard Tom speaking, he saw the stern face of the aged Negro and shivered with apprehension. He would rather have faced a thousand whips, a thousand guns, than his irate grandfather in a bad temper.

"Son," the old man had said when the tidings had come of how Bobbie had been publicly flogged by Tom Farnsworth, "niggers is niggers these days. They's dirt. They ain't no more what they used to be. Oh, Bobbie, I ain't got the patience to talk none to you. Ah'm sick inside. You've made Master Tom disgrace himself before the whole town."

This was only a small sample of the sympathy poor Bobbie received upon this and other occasions. He was like one of those ministers who served a monarch in the days when "a king could do no wrong." The guilt of the ruler meant the death of the minister who had executed his decrees. So it was with Bobbie. And, as he learned from the lips of Tom himself that he had shot and killed young Pattison, all that Bobbie could do was whisper to himself: "I've got to find some way to bring him off. I can't face Granddad, if I fail Tom now."

It was not, truly speaking, sheer love for the master; but it was that blind thing that sometimes keeps men marching and fighting and struggling to death, a thing divorced from love or even sympathy—the devotion to a cause. The Farnsworths were such a cause to Bobbie. Tom was part of the Farnsworths. So the servant marched resolutely ahead to take the risk upon his own head. He waited, first of all, until Tom was well out of sight down the thick gloom of the road. Then, sure that he could proceed without being recalled at a critical moment, he passed down the road slowly, keeping close to the fence, so that there would be the greater chance of his being seen from the garden. He was spotted almost at once.

"Hello!" someone sang out. "Who's there?"

Instead of answering, Tom ducked along the back of his horse and spurred away. This brought a shot, whistling above his head, and then a chorus of shouts: "I've seen him . . . a big man on a big horse . . . heading back through town."

Babel swelled up from the place. But already they had done much work and made many preparations. All that the people needed—they were saddling horses already—was such a stimulus as the explosion of that gun to make them leap into action. They rushed down the driveway from the stables and past Kinkaid's house. They spilled out into the street and spread out to keep from jostling, one against the other, until they saw in what direction they must next ride. So doing, they spotted the fugitive, moving swiftly down the street toward the very heart of the town. They raised a cry that would have done credit to a gang of Comanches newly riding on the warpath, with the blood appetite keen from long observance of peaceful ways. A score of men were almost instantly under way. For there were the men from Kinkaid's place plus neighbors who had heard the shot and happened to have horses standing ready—for it was not very late in the night. Still others rushed to stables and tossed saddles on their mounts when they heard that wild and long-drawn yell from many throats, serving as a signal to tell every man in town that the quarry was running, and that he was in full flight. So they stormed in pursuit of the hunted, eager to come up and lend a hand to the good work. And work it was, before the morning dawned upon them.

Bobbie went through the center of Daggett, twisting at every corner. He did not race his horse. In fact, the animal would not stand racing. It was a sturdily built roan, able to carry the two hundred and forty pounds Bobbie weighed in his clothes. No spindle-legged sprinter of a horse could be expected to handle Bobbie's weight, with the added pounds of a saddle that had to be made extra large and strong for the same reason. The result was that Bobbie had to be mounted on a thirteen-hundred-pound giant with sturdy ways and only an immense amount of endurance to rec-ommend him. He had the two points that mean toughness, as a rule. The one was his roan coloring; the other was his Roman nose. The roan could strike a long canter and keep to it though most of a day, even with the burden of Bobbie on his back. It was at this pace—or at only just a little more—that Bobbie went through the town. Every time he turned a corner, he could do it without drawing rein. Every time the pursuit foamed around the corner behind him, it swung wide. Racing horses crashed against one another. Men lost their tempers and blamed one another heartily. But they gained very little ground on Bobbie and the roan.

Then they drew out of Daggett. On the outskirts someone yelled, a boy's piping voice that could be heard half a mile away: "What's Bobbie done?"

"It's Bobbie!" ran another voice through the posse. And they repeated it with an oath: "It's Bobbie! There'll be dead men among us before we ever get that coon. If he's gone bad, he'll turn out a plumb lion."

They straightway settled down for a long hunt. Those who happened to be better mounted than the rest did not press rashly forward in the hunt—for every man of them had seen Bobbie take a Colt in either hand and roll two tin cans in differing directions, kicking them along with sprays of dust, as the slugs spat into the ground just in the rear. They had seen him do tricks with a rifle also. They had watched him box. For every man could well recall that historic occasion when the great black, who was battling upward among the ranks of the country's heavyweights, had paused at Daggett to astonish the natives with his prowess. Bobbie had taken a bet and gone in against him. They had fought mightily, and young Bobbie had at last struck that Negro beneath the heart and then beneath the jaw with all his force and sent him to the hospital to recover. They knew all of these things about Bobbie. If he could do so many things in sport, they could not help wondering what he would be able to do when he was fighting desperately for his life. At least they were unwilling to crowd him. When the daylight came, they would be prepared to open up their guns on him and bring him back to them. In the meantime they pushed steadily on, but made no endeavor to run him down suddenly. They wanted, if possible, a peaceful surrender, not a butchery. But that peaceful surrender, they knew, would mean a lynching for Bobbie when he was brought back to Daggett, for, as they rushed out of the town, the word had been whispered among them that poor Jack Pattison was breathing, indeed, but fast dying—that he could not possibly live until the morning light began the new day.

They stormed along behind Bobbie out of Daggett, down the dry course of the Pickett River, and to the rise of hills that had been dignified by the title of the Daggett Mountains. They might have served for mountains in Wales or Scotland, but here, where nature worked with a generous and a more hastily liberal hand, they were no more than hills. Into these they pushed Bobbie, who still fled fast before them.

Just before dawn he reached Milton Harrwitz's place. He spurred with all the might of his roan down the slope, leading to the ranch in the hollow. In the field he roped a muscular five-year-old gray gelding, pitched a saddle onto its back, and rode off like mad again, with the bullets beginning to whistle around his head. As he rode, he twisted on the back of the gelding and managed to pass the girths beneath the belly on the galloping horse, and so to cinch them up—a feat truly close to the miraculous. But in ten minutes all was settled, the gray had not lost ground, and the moment Bobbie settled down to the work of seriously jockeying him, the gray began to make a gap between the big Negro and the pursuers.

Mischief, however, had been born by that maneuver. Bobbie had forgotten something of the most vital importance, something that no one west of the Mississippi is allowed to neglect. There may be reasons why one man may kill another man; there are even known occasions when it is a desirable and highly honorable affair. But there is never any occasion when the theft of a horse can be overlooked. If the posse worked honestly to get at Bobbie before, it now worked in feverish earnest.

He fled all that day and into the next night. Then he was headed. The telegraph had worked against him in a round-about fashion. The wire had gone triangling clear up to Denver and then back again to Kiever City. From Kiever two score men and youngsters, who had nothing better to do, spread across the hills to find the Negro. They went in groups of three to five, well armed. Some of them had dogs—big hounds were popular in that district, being crosses of the mastiff and the greyhound breed. They had the burly shoulders and the fighting jaws and wills of the former breed and something of the speed and the endurance of the latter. Four men and four dogs fell across the trail of Bobbie. It is known through all the district, five hundred miles in any direction, that the men of Kiever City are like their dogs, strong and lean and swift and hard fighters. And their horses are like the men and the dogs. Yet Bobbie gave them the slip. As the four plunged on through the gray of the dawn, they heard one voice, of the four that bayed before them, grow silent. Then another ended, and then a third. The fourth dog raised a wail, and they rode swiftly up on him. They passed one huge brute with its throat slashed open, then another, and at the third dead body they found the fourth dog, the sole survivor, standing to mourn its mate. How Bobbie had done it they could not tell, but he must have found a way of swinging back in the saddle and meeting the leap of each hound with the slash of his long-bladed hunting knife.

They spread the tidings quickly to their companions in the hills. Such news travels without the aid of a telegraph wire. They learned that Bobbie was a dangerous man, indeed. The very next night he proved it. He had been flying for three days now, without rest or sleep. He had stolen and changed horses twice more on his way. But still the pursuers rose up out of the ground before him and clung in his rear, for the men of Kiever City and the Kiever Mountains do not give up a trail easily. Apparently he saw that straightway flight could not save him. He doubled straight down a narrow cañon, fell upon a party of three who were riding hotly after him, and went cleanly through them. He shot the first man off his horse, driving the bullet through the fellow's right thigh. Then he dropped his revolver and caught at the other two with his bare hands. He emptied two saddles with two gestures and left two writhing, stricken men on the ground behind him, as he cantered away, leading their horses. To those horses he changed. It was two long hours before they could spread the tidings of how he had broken through their ring, and by that time Bobbie was twenty miles, or thereabouts, away. He had this advantage: he had dodged all pursuit and could now hide and rest himself and his horse. He had this disadvantage: the men of Kiever City and the Kiever Mountains now felt it their duty and incumbent upon their honor to hunt Bobbie to the death.

V

"A SUMMONS"

On the second morning after the melodramatic flight of Bobbie, his young master, Tom Farnsworth, rode down the countryside and found the ranch of Milton Harrwitz. Harrwitz was a Russian who had lived on the Steppes in his youth, and he had learned how to ride and raise cattle from the Tartars when he was a boy, having been stolen and carried away by a group of wild nomadic marauders. When he was twenty, he was a chief, because his long legs could cling to a horse and his hands could shoot a rifle with great precision. At twenty-five he met a romantic American girl, won her heart by his wild, strange face and his horsemanship, married her, and came to the States. There he broke her heart, spent her money, left her dying behind him, and went West. The cow range was nearer to his heart and his liking than anything he had seen since Siberia. He took the remnant of his wife's money, bought a small herd, and ever since that time had slowly prospered. Now he was worth some hundreds of thousands. He was still a barbarian, but he had lived so long in the community that his neighbors were willing to overlook many of his faults. Like most Russians he was a good neighbor, true to those who trusted him, liberal with money to a friend, and, above all, an implacable enemy to those who excited his wrath. All of these qualities were highly admirable in the eyes of the men of the cow country. They were rather awe-stricken by the black squalor in which Harrwitz lived, by his swarthy, greasy skin, his bright eyes, and his smile like the hungry grin of a beast. But he had been a hero when the last forest fire swept the hills, and his other qualities had been proven. No one in the county would be more readily listened to.

Young Tom Farnsworth approached this formidable Russian with a good deal of trepidation and a good deal of disgust. He arrived just before noon, and he found a few

Mexican cowpunchers sitting about the door of the 'dobe hut where Harrwitz lived. They rolled their cigarettes and jerked a thumb to indicate that Harrwitz was inside. Tom Farnsworth entered and was staggered by the incredible filth of the room that was kitchen, living room, and dining room. It was odd that the Mexicans would accept such surroundings, but it was known that only the lowest of the low refugees from justice, brutes of a thousand crimes, came to Harrwitz who asked from them only hard work, and who gave them high pay and no questions. Tom pushed his way to an inner door, thrust it open, and found himself in a small, stuffy compartment, the one window of which was closed tight, so that the temperature of the air in the room had raised to almost blood heat. There was an old-fashioned four-poster bed, so big that it occupied nearly two thirds of the floor space of the dirty room. A few rags of faded cloth hung from the upper frame, all that remained of its canopy. The paint and the varnish had peeled away in the heat and had been worn away by the scraping of spurred heels and the scratching of matches. Harrwitz lay prone on the bed, face downwards, his face muffled in a mass of ragged old quilt whose colors were long since covered with dirt. He lay like a dead man, and Tom Farnsworth half suspected he had been murdered, until he saw the back of the man stir with deep, regular breathing. He was sleeping, exhausted. For Harrwitz had been up for three days and three nights, caring for sick cows. He was worn out by his work, but he had saved lives, which meant dollars, and now he slept the sleep of deep contentment. He was satisfied.

He wakened with a shudder of anguish and turned to Tom Farnsworth a haggard face, unshaven for a fortnight, with the result that long, black bristles thrust out sparsely here and there over his leathery countenance. He staggered to a corner of the room, lifting up a dipper of lukewarm water from a bucket, swallowed some, and poured the rest over the back of his neck and head, letting it drip and soak into his shirt and underclothes of thick red flannel. A shake of his head finished the work of clearing his senses, and he asked Tom what brought him here.

"My man, Bobbie," said young Tom, "stole a horse of yours. I've come to pay you for him."

"Ah?" said Harrwitz, and his face brightened at the mention of that welcome word, *pay*. He led the way to the outside. He did not make the Mexicans get up to give them stools, but he dragged out two staggering boxes in which groceries had been recently delivered.

"That gray hoss," said Harrwitz, "that gray hoss was one of the chosen and the choice ones, Mister Farnsworth. You might say I knowed the insides of the mind of that there colt."

"No doubt," said Farnsworth, too disgusted with the face and the smell of the man to prolong the conversation. "No doubt that the horse was an intimate friend, and that you have felt his loss very keenly. Perhaps he will one of these days be returned to you. In the meantime I wish to pay you for his full value, even for the loss of his companionship."

One would have said that Harrwitz accepted this sarcasm in all seriousness, for he began to nod, screwing the center of his mouth up and the sides of it down, while he turned out the palms of his hands with one of those eloquent gestures of his race. "But, Mister Farnsworth. . . ."

"Well?" asked Tom sharply. "Put the price high, if you wish to. Anything in reason, Harrwitz, or even a little more than reason."

"What you want is that I don't catch him for a thief!"

"That's it," said Tom.

"Ah, ah," said Harrwitz, sucking in his breath. "But what good is that? If they catch him, they hang him for killing Pattison . . . no?"

"Pattison isn't dead," said Tom. "He's still living. He's delirious. Has brain fever or something like that. May never speak sense again . . . chances are that he'll die . . . but, if he doesn't die"—Tom ended somewhat dubiously—"he'll live to clear Bobbie, perhaps. . . ."

Harrwitz grinned. "You make it funny, Mister Farnsworth. Why don't you laugh?" He looked up at Tom, boring him with little keen eyes that, it was said, had looked their way into many an important secret.

Tom trembled momentarily at his own secret. Yet, as he reflected, Bobbie had so perfectly covered the trail by taking all suspicion on his own shoulders that Tom presently regained his self-possession. He began to argue his point, even with this low fellow. "Consider this, Harrwitz . . . they were milling about in the place of Kinkaid. Someone saw Bobbie ride along the hedge. They shouted at him. He probably looked across the hedge and saw twenty men, walking about in the grounds. He may have become frightened. Sometimes Negroes get shabby justice from a crowd. Instead of waiting and answering, he rode away. Then the whole crowd of 'em took after him. He lost his head and rode like a mad man through Daggett. He knew he was innocent, perhaps, but he also knew that they were after him. He rode for his life. Reached your place, found his horse failing, stole another, and rode on. Then he may have reflected that he was a criminal, after stealing a horse, so the poor simple fellow has kept on running and fighting in order to get clear. If I can settle this horse theft, perhaps we can bring Bobbie back to us, while we locate the real criminal. What had Bobbie against Pattison? What would he gain by killing such a man?" His voice rose at the end.

Harrwitz considered this harangue soberly. "He stole a hoss," he said at last. "He stole my hoss. *He'll* have to pay for it . . . not you. I want *his* money, not yours." That was his way of seeing justice done.

"What was the price of the gray horse?" asked Tom, seeing that he could not talk of abstractions to a man with so much malice in him.

"Oh, maybe two hundred dollars."

That was about double a fair price, as Tom knew, but he pulled out his wallet at once.

"I have two hundred dollars for you, Harrwitz."

"Is it Bobbie's money?"

"Yes, because I'm using it for him."

"Let him come to pay it to me then. I want to talk with him." As he spoke, he fondled the butt of his Colt absently.

"I'll make it a shade more, Harrwitz, considering how much the gray meant to you. I'll make it two hundred and fifty dollars."

"Right quick . . . spot cash?"

"Yes."

Harrwitz ran the red tip of his tongue across his greasy lips. "I guess that I don't want your money. It ain't right," he said finally.

"Three hundred dollars, Harrwitz!"

The Russian stared at him. Then he pointed down the valley. "You see by the river bottom a hundred acres . . . that's worth two hundred an acre. Well, Mister Farnsworth, if you give me another hundred acres just like that for the gray horse, I take the hoss and leave you the acres."

"What *do* you want?"

"My rights," said the other.

Tom, meeting the glittering eyes for another moment, saw that there was nothing but wasted time in such a conversation. He rode back to Daggett and through Daggett to his father's ranch which he reached, with a staggering horse, at sunset. The old grandfather of Bobbie came out of the stable to take his young master's horse. Age had withered him without bowing his body. The lids were puckered around eyes that were still intelligent and bright. His step was short, but light and steady.

"Uncle," said Tom, "has any news come in?"

"There ain't goin' to be no news, Master Tom," said the Negro. "There ain't goin' to be no news till we hear that they've caught Bobbie and strung him up to a tree."

"That's a terrible thing to say."

"Books ain't for niggers," said the old dark man. "Bobbie read too much. He could talk too much. And the same bad streak in his daddy was a streak in Bobbie. I know."

"But suppose that he didn't do the shooting?"

The old Negro started at this suggestion. It seemed to bewilder more than please him. "If he didn't do nothin', but run just the same, then he's a fool. And a fool is pretty near as bad as a murderer, Master Tom."

Young Farnsworth went to the house. He had barely entered when his father came hurrying out to him with a note in his hand.

"Here's a letter from the town . . . it's from old Pattison. He's sent for you, Tom. His boy ain't any better, but his head has cleared up some, and he's askin' for you."

VI

"DEBORAH SPEAKS"

It was a thunderstroke for Tom. At first he put the simplest possible interpretation upon it, which was that young Pattison, recovering his senses, had denounced Tom as his destroyer and called upon his father to avenge him. Pattison, senior, had sent for him and would have the sheriff waiting when he came. To face a murder charge, as he now saw, would be a simple thing compared with the shame of having to confess that he had allowed his manservant to take the deadly burden of the suspicion on his shoulders and draw the vengeance of the law after him. He hesitated for ten seconds, revolving that thought in his brain. Then he determined that he would have to face Pattison, no matter what the consequences. If he did not come, and they indeed suspected him, they could apprehend him in his home. The only question in his mind was whether he would flee to the mountains and embrace outlawry, or else go to Pattison and meet whatever lay in wait for him there. To give up all that was pleasant to him in life for the sake of a roving existence in the wilderness was more than he was prepared to do. Hanging itself would not be much more bitter. So at length he had a fresh horse saddled, changed to fresh clothes after a bath, and in the dark of the evening, with his head high and the sweet aroma of an Egyptian cigarette in his nostrils, he rode for the Pattison house in Daggett.

It was the most gloomy and mysterious time of the evening. Across the fields a low-flying hoot owl pursued him, unseen, but with melancholy voice rolling about him now and again. He passed an old buggy, wheeling softly through the dust, with all the figures in it turned to shapeless blotches in the night. A man's voice and a girl's were singing and, as he passed into the acrid dust cloud on their back trail, the song floated dimly behind him. It stopped. The wheels of the rig rattled over a bump, then the horse pounded with hollow tread over a distant wooden culvert, and Tom was left alone on his path again. He went on with an empty heart, for that happy singing suggested to him such a picture of innocent contentment that his own crime seemed blacker than before. Being so sad of mind, he hurried on his way more quickly than ever. He reached Daggett and passed to the house of Pattison. Old Pattison met him in the hall.

"My dear Tom," he said, "I had no idea that you and my boy were such good friends. But he's been asking for no one else for hours."

"Poor Jack," murmured the hypocrite. "How is he now?"

"Very low . . . very low, indeed. God alone knows what will come to him. We pray, Tom, but we fear that the worst is about to come to us. The bullet passed through his head."

"I'll go in to him," said Tom hastily and, leaving the father behind him, he went to Jack Pattison.

He found Jack's face very pale, looking thinner and older by many years. The youngster's eyes were almost closed, and they were surrounded by great blue-black circles. Someone in white rose from a chair beside the bed. Tom had never seen her before, but the nurse apparently knew who he was. She leaned over the sufferer and took his arm gently.

"Mister Pattison, here is Mister Farnsworth to see you. You may talk with him if you will promise not to stir so much as a hand . . . and not to speak above a whisper." She stepped back, turning to Tom. "You may have one minute with him," she told Tom and, moving toward the wall of the room, she began to study the face of her watch, count-ing off the quick seconds.

"It's I, Jack," whispered Tom.

"Tom," murmured the wounded man faintly. "I wanted to tell you that I'll not let a soul know who did this thing. I've closed the door on it. In exchange for that promise I want you to tell me the thing you know I want to learn."

"I'll tell you frankly, Jack," said the other, immensely relieved, and now beginning to pity the wounded man, "I merely forced my way into her room the other night . . . or, rather, to her window, because I had to try to reinstate myself. She had cut me dead only a little while before, as you know. I was desperate, Jack, and I didn't dare to face her before other people, because I was fairly sure that she would cut me again."

There was a sigh of happiness from Jack. "I've been lying here in a fire of doubt," he confessed. "But now I know that you've told me the truth, and I think that it gives me almost enough strength to cure me. Tom. . . ."

"There is no more time," said the nurse, stepping up to the bedside. "The doctor's order was very strict."

Tom stepped away. He could have sung with happiness as he reached the door, and beyond it in the hall he talked for a moment with the father, who had been waiting anx-iously for him. It was not hard to explain the interview.

"Sick people get queer longings," said Tom to the father. "When I was a youngster, I had scarlet fever. I remember that the thing that haunted me was the desire for raw roast beef. Queer, eh? That's the way with Jack. He happened to fix his mind on me. And he kept it fixed for so long a time that he finally had to see me."

The nurse came out from the sick room with an excited, happy face.

"He's asleep," she said. "Send the message to the doctor, Mister Pattison. The moment Mister Farnsworth left the room he fell asleep. His pulse is steady . . . his nerves are better . . . his temperature is falling. Mister Farnsworth must have brought him good news!"

Pattison, frantic with happiness, hastened off to find the doctor, and Tom rode back to call on the lady of his heart. He was brought into the library of the old house and sat down to wait for her, feeling decidedly stiff and uncomfortable. The room was furnished after the pattern of thirty years before. The chairs were covered in glossy horsehair. There was a couch upholstered in the same material with a little round cushion on it. The carpet was blue, strewn with great roses. Gothic bookcases went around the walls. Behind the glass of the doors stood long sets whose glimmering backs betrayed that the volumes had never been frayed and worn by handling. Some of the doors, in fact, were closed tighter than with a lock because, being undisturbed for months at a time, the varnish had sweated and held like a stout glue. He had seen those same familiar faces in every library of the ranch houses of any pretension in the county.

The desk of Mr. Kinkaid was in a corner of the room with a swivel chair before it. It had a great broad blotter on the top, a rack of pens at hand, and a calendar in sight. But it was well known that Mr. Kinkaid never sat here. He carried his business in his head. He could tell you at any time just how many cows and calves were on his ranches, and what condition they were in, and how the market stood, and how the grass was looking in every corner of his places. His office was his saddle, and his office force consisted of his own strong, swiftly moving, accurate brain.

Such was the man, and such was the room in which Tom presently slid off the glossy seat of a chair and came to his feet, for Deborah stood in the doorway. She went straight to him, but, instead of shaking hands, she dropped into a chair and faced him, beckoning him to take an opposite seat.

"What have you come to tell me, Tom?"

"That Pattison is immensely better. I went to see him tonight."

"Really?"

"Why not? I've always liked Jack."

"Of course," murmured Deborah. "Everyone has always liked poor Jack."

"He sent for me, as a matter of fact."

"I didn't know you were such friends."

"Just a sick man's freak. I talked to him one minute, about nothing. Then I came away . . . but, before I left the house, we learned from the nurse that he had fallen in a sound, even sleep, and that his nerves were quieter . . . that he would awaken much stronger and better able to make a fight for his life."

"Good! Good! I'm so happy . . . so very happy, Tom! And now, what's the news of Bobbie?"

"The last we heard he was doubling into the Kiever Mountains. The Kiever men are wild over the hunt."

"And they're terrible people, aren't they?"

"They're supposed to be, but I've an idea that Bobbie will prove a match for them."

"Suppose he doesn't?"

"Well, a man has to take his punishment when he commits a crime like murder, Deborah."

She stirred in her chair, as though the thought pricked her to the quick. And Tom, staring hard at her, saw that her pallor had given way to a bright flush of excitement.

"Perhaps you're right, Tom. Murder will out, as people say."

She said this with a certain dryness of tone, such as people use when they have in mind a double innuendo.

"What do you mean by that remark, Deborah?" he asked her with a sick suspicion beginning to grow in him.

"I'll be franker with you than you've been with me. Tom, you were sent for by poor Jack because he was tormented with worries about me. He'd seen you climb up through the window of my room."

Young Farnsworth grew bolt erect in his chair. Something was born in him then that he had never felt in himself before in all his life. It was a consummate desire to destroy with his hands. He had not even felt it when he faced Jack the other night. On that occasion he had fought suddenly and shot to kill, but it had been because his back was against the wall. Now, as the girl struck at him, by sudden surprise, his first impulse was a red rage and a passionate desire to take her with his hands. . . . He controlled that impulse, marveling at himself, and watched the emotion die away in him, as an echo dies far down a cañon. Nevertheless, he felt that hot rush of blood to the head might come again, and, if it were any stronger, he would not be able to master himself. It filled him with awe. It also filled him with pride to know that he had in himself the sway of passions greater than his ability to control them. If he had made this discovery of new powers in himself, why might there not be other discoveries in the future? Anything became possible. He became a new country to himself. This was the attitude of Tom, and, as he faced the girl, he realized that she no longer meant to him what she had meant before. She had become a danger and a threat to him. Affection for her began to die at the roots of his heart.

"He wanted to know what brought you there," continued the steady voice of Deborah. "And he offered in exchange to keep it secret that you were the man, Tom, who shot him down." She faced him steadily.

He could not remain seated in the face of this attack. But, as he came to his feet, flaring at her, his cleared eyes looked through and through her, discerned all the glamour of her beauty fading from her, found her small, plain-faced, common, and he marveled beyond words that he could ever have wasted any time on her. He almost thanked God that all this tragic story had come about, if it could at least waken him to the truth about the lady of his heart. He wanted to laugh. Then he was disgusted by his own lack of taste. Last of all the hot anger that had gripped him just before swept over him again. She was assailing him, and he had to defend himself—with words.

"Deborah," he said at last, "I'll tell you the facts."

He considered another moment, made up his mind definitely that it was better to confess than to arouse her suspicions by lying. Still, it was strange that she could have seen their meeting, since her shade had been drawn, as he was sure it had been. Perhaps she had spied down at him through a crack at the side.

"I shot Jack," he said bluntly, "but it was because he forced the fight on me."

She started in her place and drew in a gasping breath.

"You didn't see it, after all?" he asked sharply.

"I only guessed," she confessed.

The hot wave came darkly upon his eyes once more. He had to clench his hands for a moment before his vision and his self-control returned.

"You are very angry?" said the girl curiously.

"You've made a fool of me."

"A fool?"

"You've set this little trap for me."

"Tom, I had not even a suspicion about you when you came this evening. But, while you were here, it jumped into my mind. I can't tell what had put it there. And still I can't believe it! You . . . you shot poor Jack Pattison?"

"In a fair fight!" cried Tom.

She waved her hand. "Frankly, I don't believe it."

"Do you accuse me of lying, Deborah? Is that what your friendship means?"

"I'm afraid that my friendship is dead."

"I swear to you, Deborah, that he started a hand for his gun before I stirred for mine."

"The real point of the matter," she said, skipping over what she was certain was the crux of the story and the evidence, "is that you shot Pattison and then allowed another man to take the blame for that work."

"How could I keep Bobbie from making a fool of himself?"

"Do you want me to tell you what I think? But no, I won't tell you that. It's too easy to speak too much about such things. I won't tell you. Only . . . you mustn't be surprised if men who hear this grow a little angry with you."

"That infernal fool nigger will be the destruction of me," said Tom Farnsworth gloomily. "Why didn't I tell him to go to the devil? As a matter of fact, Deborah, I knew nothing about what he intended. When he ran away and drew the rest of 'em after him, I was the most surprised man in Daggett. It was simply useless, foolish devotion on the part of Bobbie"

"I see," said Deborah, and smiled coldly at him.

He had been telling the truth on the whole. Now he flushed with rage. "You don't believe me?"

She rose and went to the door. "I suppose," she said, studying her words carefully, "that this is the last time I shall have an opportunity of talking with you, Tom."

"What does that mean?" Then panic succeeded his anger. "Good God, Deborah, it doesn't mean that you'd deliberately tell what. . . ."

"Go on."

"Tell what I've spoken to you in absolute confidence."

"When I'd wrung it out of you by a trick, Tom? No, I don't think that I'd be violating a confidence." Her eyes were impudent.

"You really mean, then, that you'll go to the sheriff with this rotten story? Don't you see that it'll make trouble for me, but that I can't be harmed in the end? Jack himself would testify for me."

"Poor, honest Jack. If anything happens to him. . . ." She controlled herself sternly. "Listen to me, Tom," she said, "what I firmly believe about you is what I'm going to tell you now. When I've told my story, I'm sure that it's what every other man and woman in Daggett will believe. You tried to kill poor Jack Pattison when he met you after you'd climbed down from my window."

"What will become of your reputation when you tell a story that has in it details such as this?"

"I thank God," said the girl quietly, "that my reputation is stronger than rock. I say that you shot Jack . . . probably through treachery, because he was known to be as good a shot as you are a bad one."

"Good Lord!"

"Be patient till I'm ended, please. You shot Jack . . . you

let your poor Negro take the blame on his shoulders . . . you let him run the danger of being shot as a murderer and a horse thief, and all the while you dared to pose as an innocent man in Daggett. It's a black, black story, Tom. And I tell you plainly this much . . . if Bobbie is not brought back to safety . . . poor faithful fool! . . . I'll tell."

"Suppose he's killed before I can reach him?"

"If that happens, it isn't your fault. Oh, Tom, even if you will make one great effort to save that poor black man, I swear that my lips are sealed forever. I'll never tell what I guess and what I know through your own confession."

VII

"A GAME OF CHESS"

How often one hears the remark concerning a patiently working horse: "If only it knew its strength!" The same thing is rarely said about a man, for the picture that fills the eye is of the great bulk of twelve or fifteen hundred weight of bone and muscle turned in revolt, smashing the wagon it pulls and the harness that attempts to control it, killing the driver with the blow of a hoof, or destroying the rider with a crunch of teeth stronger than a tiger's. If a man is wakened to lawlessness, his power is yet more terrible. He banishes with a gesture of the mind the load of duty at which he has been tugging. He annihilates the law by merely denying it. He trebles his strength by freedom that is absolute. He adds to the strength of a man the strength of a wild beast by casting himself loose from society.

Such was the case of Bobbie. He had started on this affair as upon a most perilous adventure to which he was compelled only because he loved his master far more than he loved himself. For the sake of his young master he had ridden through the midst of perils on that first night and through the days that followed. But now he was beginning to forget that he had started out for the sake of another person. The game was worthwhile on its own account. He could not recall another period in his life when he had enjoyed a tithe of this happiness. He was playing a game of chess. Upon his side there were only two pieces—himself and his horse. On the other side was a filled board, and only by the most complicated maneuvers could he escape them. He could not have survived for a single day had he not been among the Kiever Mountains, for they were created especially, so it seemed, to give a fugitive a chance to dodge away from his pursuers. The Kiever Mountains run from end to end through a distance of seventy miles, curving from northeast to southwest. The plateau in which they have footing is two thousand feet above the level of the sea. The loftiest peaks of the Kiever range are not more than three thousand feet above this point. The king of them all is a scant fifty feet short of a mile in elevation. In a word, they are small mountains for a country such as the great mountain desert, but they use every inch of their size for the greatest possible roughness. They are hewed across and up and down by great ravines, so that a picture from above would make the range look like a butcher's chopping block. There are not many trees, but there is sagebrush scattered here and there and a quantity of other small growths. Now and again, moreover, where there is water in a lowland or in a deep valley, one comes upon an almost tropical forest, for the soil is everywhere rich when it is deep enough to receive roots. This is not frequent in the range, however, and the majority of the upper slopes and of the mountain heads consist of junk heaps of stones and boulders and long slides of rock, still wearing the polish that was placed upon it during the glacial age. In this region of a myriad of rocks and a million hollows and gorges Bobbie found that he could hide so readily that it was even extremely difficult to find his own way. For two days he wandered in despair, appalled by the white-hot heat of the days, the cold of the nights, the lack of water, the scant provender that soon had the ribs of his horse thrusting out, and the difficulty of game. There were rabbits, of course, for there are rabbits everywhere, but there was little else. And the stomach of Bobbie revolted at his second day of fare consisting of only one article of diet.

His first exploit was undertaken purely with the view to recruiting his own larder. He had no higher motive, nor did he have the slightest desire to break away from the Kiever Mountains for, when he climbed to the central peaks, he could see out onto the wide sweep of desert and level plain beyond. In this covert he might prolong the game for some time. In yonder open he would receive a mate in the form of an ounce of lead planted skillfully among his ribs. So he contented himself with making himself in the first place master of his position.

This he did by spending some hours on the top of Old Kiever itself, as the highest of the peaks was called. From this point of vantage he could make out clearly enough and jot down in his mind the various landmarks up and down the length of the range. Keeping these firmly in his recollection, he had only to consult his mental notebook in order to tell himself where he was at any point in his later wanderings. He had reached this point in understanding of his environment when the delicately nurtured stomach of Bobbie demanded a change of diet and forced him out of his inner retreats, toward which the hunting parties had been laboring on both days with the dogs to lead them.

He stole down to the foot of the eastern mountains, and on the shores of a little pool he found a newly arrived party of a dozen honest citizens who had come out to join in this rare sport and to avenge the honor and fair fame of the town of Kiever. This was not a haphazard crew. Among them was the ex-sheriff, who secretly hoped to restore himself to the good graces of the voters in the county by rounding up the fugitive who had hitherto baffled both the regular and the irregular forces of the law in Kiever County. Accordingly, this well equipped and managed party went to sleep at the watering place only after all the horses had been well hobbled and a guard had been posted—the wariest and sharpest-eared member of the entire group, who could not conceivably doze.

Bobbie, slipping down among the shadows of the trees, took note. The watcher had placed himself on the top of a stone that sat on the edge of the pool. His back was to the water, since he was safe from attack in that direction. His eyes restlessly turned up and down the shore, sweeping over the sleepers and their effects. And across his knees, ready for instant action, lay a rifle with fifteen shots tucked into the magazine. When Bobbie had observed these things, he made his plan at once, skirted around to the other side of the pool, took off his clothes, and slid down into the warm water, a deep shadow among shadows. One who had learned to high dive from a springboard and enter the swimming pool with such oiled smoothness that hardly a ripple ran out around the point at which he entered certainly found no trouble in entering this pool without a sound. He melted into the black water and disappeared at once. For a moment he was out of view. Then a little ripple began to travel across the tiny lake. In the center of the ripple the nose of Bobbie projected to the air. Beneath the ripple his powerful arms and legs moved in a soft rhythm, sending him in slow pulses across to the other shore.

When he was near the spot, he sank deeper in the water, turned, dived, and came up directly behind the watcher on the stone. There was no struggle. Bobbie rose to his knees. He picked up the guard's own coat which lay neatly folded on the ground. That coat he flung like a net over the head of the unfortunate. Then, when he had stopped the noise of cries, he stopped the noise of struggles also, by discreetly tapping the padded head of the sentinel with a rock. Thus put to sleep, the watcher was laid behind the rock on which he had been sitting, and Bobbie proceeded with his work. He did not have long, but he did not need long. He gathered the food and the ammunition—of which he had run short— together with some tobacco and matches and other items required. These articles he made into a great parcel, wrapped in a tarpaulin. Next he went into the little glade adjoining where the horses were hobbled on the grass. He selected the toughest and best weight carrier—which happened to be the mount of the ex-sheriff himself—and led the animal away, while the pack was slung over his own broad shoulder. He had reached the farther side of the pool before the man he had left behind him, stunned, recovered his senses and his wits enough to raise an outcry. Then his shout brought every member of the party to his feet.

But Bobbie was in no great hurry. He changed saddles from his worn-out mount to his new one, arranged his pack behind the saddle, cast away a few non-essentials, and then mounted and jogged along on his way. As for the men on the farther side of the pool, they had hastily mounted and then bolted for the mountains, thundering threats of vengeance—all save the poor ex-sheriff, who stayed behind, cursing the thief who had deprived him of his best horse.

They found no track of Bobbie on that day or the next. He was well away and traveling in security by a route that none discovered. In the heart of the mountains he built a large fire, cooked a great quantity of bacon and flapjacks, warmed some tinned beans, made himself a great pot of coffee, stayed awake after his feast long enough to smoke half a cigarette, and then dropped into a sound slumber that lasted a round of the clock. It was the first real sleep he had enjoyed during his flight. When he wakened again, his head was clear, his stomach was again empty, his eye was bright, and it was now that he began truly to enjoy the game in which he was engaged.

After that, the hunters who worked through the Kiever Mountains led a wretched life. By nature Bobbie was two or three long strides closer to the soil than the white men who were now his enemies. His hearing was a little sharper, his sight a little more acute, and, above all, there was more keenly developed in him that indescribable sense which does not reside in any nerves of the flesh, but in the nerves of the soul—the power, in short, of premonition. After his long sleep he was ready for mischief, and straightway he had his fun.

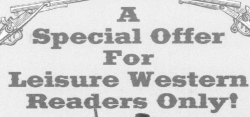

GET YOUR 4
FREE* BOOKS NOW—
A VALUE BETWEEN
$16 AND $20

Mail the Free* Book Certificate Today!

FREE* BOOKS
CERTIFICATE!

YES! I want to subscribe to the Leisure Western Book Club. Please send me my 4 FREE* BOOKS. Then, each month, I'll receive the four newest Leisure Western Selections to preview FREE* for 10 days. If I decide to keep them, I will pay the Special Member's Only discounted price of just $3.36 each, a total of $13.44 ($14.50 US in Canada). This saves me between $3 and $6 off the bookstore price. There are no shipping, handling or other charges.* There is no minimum number of books I must buy and I may cancel the program at any time. In any case, the 4 FREE* BOOKS are mine to keep—at a value of between $17 and $20!

*In Canada, add $5.00 Canadian shipping and handling per order for first shipment. For all subsequent shipments to Canada the cost of membership in the Book Club is $14.50 US, which includes $7.50 shipping and handling per month. All payments must be made in US currency.

Name _____

Address _____

City_____ State_____ Country_____

Zip_____ Telephone_____

If under 18, parent or guardian must sign. Terms, prices and conditions subject to change. Subscription subject to acceptance. Leisure Books reserves the right to reject any order or cancel any subscription.

Tear here and mail your FREE* book card today!

Get Four Books Totally FREE* — A Value between $16 and $20

Tear here and mail your FREE* book card today!

PLEASE RUSH
MY FOUR FREE*
BOOKS TO ME
RIGHT AWAY!

LeisureWestern Book Club
P.O. Box 6613
Edison, NJ 08818-6613

That afternoon three parties that had worked well into the hills glimpsed his horse, and at the same time Bobbie glimpsed them. They were coming in three different directions, and his chance of riding through was small. So he let his newly stolen horse remain behind him to keep the eyes of the enemy in focus, while he himself stole down a little gully and made off with his guns and little else besides. Half an hour later, as the baffled hunters closed on the horse and found that the master was gone, Bobbie discovered that a lone rider was jogging a fine bay stallion into the Kiever Mountains, hunting glory with his single hand. Bobbie tied that young hero's hands behind his back, did him no other harm, took his excellent mount, and made off blithely again.

He had no provisions again, however. So, on that very night, he dropped down on a party of his hunters. There were only three, and Bobbie used different methods here. He waked them up, herded them together with a few gestures of his revolvers, fastened them with two pairs of bridle reins, and then went through their belongings in the most leisurely fashion. He gained plunder enough. Hitherto he had taken only essentials. But now his eyes were caught and filled by a fine rifle, decorated with a little gold chasing. He took that weapon, while its owner groaned. Then he selected a fine hunting knife that belonged to another. Finally, though he retained the horse he was riding, he exchanged the saddle for another. He went through their stock of provisions, selected what he needed, cooked himself a meal, and then rode away through the night, singing in a rich and ringing baritone voice.

By the time the report of this affair had spread through Kiever County, the men of the district were half hysterical with rage and the desire for revenge. If forty men had been hunting the fugitive the day before, by nightfall of that day no fewer than fifty parties were laboring among the slopes of the Kiever Mountains. Still their task was not accomplished, and, indeed, it was not simple, for in every square league of the range there were enough hiding places difficult of access to employ the entire fifty hunting parties through a whole day's work. They had rushed out feeling that sheer numbers would now complete the net and make it perfect, but they saw that mere numbers would not avail them. Hard work and a little luck were what they needed.

In the meantime, to complete their anger, reporters began to ride in from various southwest cities. They wanted to have pictures of camera and pen to describe the range where the Negro was lurking. Kiever County snarled like a savage dog and quivered with rage. Then they read the stories of the reporters and grew more furious than ever. Bobbie was called a dusky-skinned Hannibal who now was showing the destructive talents of his race by setting at naught the efforts of the great odds that worked day and night against him. It was pointed out that he was a Negro with a sense of humor, and that he was not a sheer murderer, but really preferred to defend himself and leave his antagonists alive—so that he might have all the more to play with.

Such was the tone in which these articles were written. Kiever County, finding itself mentioned as giving "amusement" to a single fugitive by its combined effort to capture him, writhed in silence, and in silence it put forth fresh efforts. But still Bobbie was not taken. He was a little lean of face and a little grim of eye, but compared with his old self he was as one who has awakened from a deep sleep. He was finding himself, and what he found was all new to him.

It was now estimated that three hundred manhunters labored to find the trail of the Negro and run him down. There were packs of dogs of all descriptions. They were worked day and night. Even so, Bobbie was not caught, and even so Bobbie continued to descend upon the besiegers and prey upon them for his livelihood. All of this was noted by the merciless pens of the newspaper reporters. They talked with great and delicate sarcasm about the charity of the posses of the Kiever men, and they dilated upon the truly Christian spirit that, when men had been smitten, made them turn the other cheek to the smiter. But a new danger was drawing close to Bobbie.

VIII

"ON THE COUNT OF TEN"

When Tom Farnsworth left Deborah, his head was muddled, indeed. He had gone to see her with a high heart full of love for her. He left with his love cut off and destroyed utterly at the root. All of his hopes of happiness had been exchanged for a grisly threat that compromised his honor forever and even his very life. As he stumbled back to his horse after he left the house, he still could not quite understand how she had tricked him into confessing the truth to her. But now he could very well understand that he had made his case far blacker than it really was by his delay. If he had come before the people of the town the very night of the shooting and told them what had happened, they might have believed him. Certainly Jack had forced the fight more than he had. Jack himself would admit it. But now Jack was following a line that he thought would be most helpful to his rival, and with a mistaken sense of honor he was continuing to let Bobbie shoulder the blame he had taken up. That was not all. Jack was now fallen into a delirium again, and he well might die before he could awaken. In that case, either Bobbie must be killed before Tom could help Bobbie, or else, failing this, the girl would accuse him and damn him.

Such was the problem Tom Farnsworth now had to work out, and after half an hour of thinking and gritting of teeth he made up his mind that there was nothing for it. He had to find Bobbie and kill him.

To do young Farnsworth justice, his head spun, and he grew sick when he thought of betraying that long-suffering servant. Yet, being by nature an opportunist, he balanced matters back and forth and argued in the following manner:

Max Brand

If Bobbie had not foolishly ridden away that night, I would have told the truth about the affair. As it happened, he rode away, took the blame, kept me from confessing, and now it is so late that, if I confess, I shall not be believed. Bobbie, in short, is at the root of all the mischief. And he has himself brought this matter to such a point that now I have to procure his death and make it seem as though a third person dropped him. This is all very difficult and close work, and I shall have to be more adroit than I have ever been before.

This may seem cold-blooded reasoning, and in fact it was, but Tom was working for his life, and on such occasions even generous men with warm hearts are apt to change a little from their better natures. He went home, surprised himself by being able to sleep well, rose early the next morning, took a good horse, and started out on his journey. He went through Daggett and let his errand be known. He had gone to find his truant servant and learn what had happened to the usually sober brain of Bobbie. He had to make that announcement in Daggett in the hope that the tidings would roll before him and come to Bobbie among the Kiever Mountains, via some of the guards whom he was now harrying daily with his descents from the fastnesses of the peaks. When Bobbie learned of it, he would instantly do his best to throw himself into the path of his coming master.

Before Tom left, he heard other news. Just as he had dreaded, young Jack Pattison had grown worse almost immediately after his interview with Tom. The sweet sleep into which he had fallen had been the result, apparently, of having wrought nerves that now had snapped. The sleep changed to a nightmare. Jack Pattison wakened in a shrieking delirium, begging for Deborah, and Deborah went to him. She quieted him, but she could not bring him back to reason. She had spent the rest of the night leaning over his bed, and on this day she and the doctor and two nurses were fighting gallantly to save the youngster from death, but it seemed to be a losing fight.

It means that I must hurry, said Tom to himself. *If Bobbie and Pattison are both disposed of, the girl will tell herself that enough men have died on account of this affair. But if Pattison dies, and Bobbie is still at large, she'll speak out, and then I'm a ruined man.*

He rode furiously forward after that. On the second day he saw the Kiever Mountains, drawing out of the horizon like great blue-gray clouds. That evening he reached the mountains themselves, pressed into them until he found a camping place, and then, having unsaddled his horse, he sat down, lighted a cigarette, and waited. He was as certain that Bobbie would come to him at once as he was certain that an eagle can see what a man cannot. He looked forward to that meeting with a disagreeable shudder. He decided, finally, that he would have to kill Bobbie from in front. That meant that he would have to murder his man while looking him in the eye, and even the iron nerves of Tom Farnsworth trembled at such a prospect. He must shoot Bobbie from in front. Probably he had better shoot through the head. Then it could be explained as an accident that had taken place while Bobbie himself was handling a gun.

In the midst of these black meditations he was aware of something stirring in the black of the night behind him. He turned sharply, and there was Bobbie. But how changed! He saw first a streak of red where a huge red silk bandanna was tied like a turban around the head of the Negro. Beneath that red was the gleam of eyes and the white glimmer of teeth, as Bobbie grinned delightedly down at his visitor. He wore a canvas jacket without sleeves, and his trousers had been cut off at the knees. On his feet were rudely made moccasins. About his waist was no cartridge belt—there was only the holster for the Colt, dangling from his right hip, and there was no rifle behind his shoulder. The Colt was his only weapon, and the whole outfit of the Negro seemed invented and adapted for great activity in flight rather than power to stand and give battle. But the appearance of Bobbie was not the only wild thing about him. He danced like a wild man when he saw his master and broke

103

into frantic protestations of delight. That very morning he had come down in the gray of the dawn upon a camp, taken a supply of coffee that he needed, and carried away with him a young cowpuncher from whom he had extracted all manner of information about the number of his assailants, the plans of the sheriff, and, above all, the tidings that his master, Tom Farnsworth, was on the way to take a hand in this matter and bring the fugitive to justice.

As he reached this point in his narrative, Bobbie rocked back and forth in his place in an ecstasy of silent mirth. He made Tom Farnsworth think of a big, sleek-muscled panther.

"Where's your horse?" he asked the big Negro.

"In the hollow," said the other.

"Your rifle?"

"I don't use one."

"Nor a coat?"

"I travel light. I can't fight three hundred men, but I can run away from them. A rifle is heavy. I carry six shots in a revolver and a few more in a pocket. That's enough. I only fire one a day at game and another one for practice. And so far I haven't had to use guns on men very often."

"Bobbie, you seem happy!"

"As a king, sir."

"You haven't lost much weight or sleep, I see."

"Not a particle."

He has gone back to nature, said Farnsworth to himself. *The rascal has reverted to his old and true type. He has turned from a perfect servant into a perfect devil. And why*, he added to himself, *should I keep my scruples when I'm dealing with this wild man?* He said aloud: "Let me have that gun."

He could hardly believe his eyes when he saw that Bobbie hesitated nervously before he surrendered the required weapon, as though a slight suspicion of what his master intended may have flashed across his mind. But he shook his head, shrugged the fear away, and passed over the Colt.

Now, said Farnsworth to himself, *I have him in my hand*

. . . I have only to press this trigger. . . . He looked up squarely and suddenly into the man's face. "Bobbie," he said, "do you know what's in my mind?"

The mirth and the recklessness had faded out of the face of Bobbie. He stood very stiffly erect with his arms folded high on his breast. "I've a sort of an idea, sir," said Bobbie dryly.

"Your idea is right, let me tell you."

"I hope not, sir."

"Have you ever worked for me simply because you thought I was a good man, Bobbie?"

"Good, sir?" echoed Bobbie, rolling his eyes, as the thought struck him for the first time.

"No," concluded the master, "of course, you haven't. You've always known in your heart of hearts that I was a rascal. Yes, you've always known that, Bobbie, and the reason you've kept true to me and my needs is simply that you'd had the old example stuffed down your throat by your granddaddy. Am I right?"

"Maybe you are, sir."

He saw the hand of Bobbie slide down. The thumb hooked into his belt. The fingers disappeared into the side pocket, and into the mind of Tom flashed understanding. The Negro had curled his fingers around the handle of the hunting knife, and, if he fought for his life, it would be by throwing that heavy and deadly weapon at Tom.

"I know," said Tom, "a knife is good for close work like this, but it's hardly fast enough. A bullet beats it from the start so far that it really hasn't a man-sized chance. You understand me? Here I am with your gun in one hand and my own"—drawing it—"in the other. I think that I have you fairly at my mercy, Bobbie. Let me tell you, in the first place, why it's necessary for me to do this. It isn't a matter of careless wish. I'd rather lose a leg than lose you, Bobbie. But matters have come to such a point that I have to lose you or myself. I'm very fond of you . . . far fonder than you really dream. But, much as I like you, I confess that I prefer my own life. Matters have come to such a point,

105

Bobbie, that I have to choose between us, and my choice is myself. If you die, all is well. If I die, there will be one less rascal in the world. As for the shabby treatment I'm giving you . . . well, I'll answer for that in hell, where I suppose I'm tolerably certain to pull up. So, to make an end of the talking . . . Bobbie, good bye. If you've got a prayer to say, say it, because this is the end of your time."

The Negro merely stiffened in his place. "Shoot straight, Mister Tom," he said quietly. "Don't let that gun pull to the right, the way you mostly always do."

"Curse you!" gasped Tom Farnsworth.

The bright, black eyes glittered back at him as steadily as the light along the shining barrel of his Colt. So, with an oath, the white man threw the revolver down on the ground at Bobbie's feet.

"I can't do it," said Tom.

"Thank God!" cried the big Negro. "I knew you couldn't, sir. I. . . ." He made as though to throw himself at the feet of Tom in an excess of his joy, but the white man repulsed him with a sharp word.

"I'm not through. I've simply changed my mind about you, Bobbie. I find that I haven't as steady a nerve as I thought I had. I can't murder you in cold blood. But I'll fight you with an equal chance between us."

The Negro frowned. "Mister Tom, you've seen me use a gun."

"I've seen you chip twigs off trees and knock the heads off ground squirrels at thirty yards . . . I've seen you do all the tricks, Bobbie, but there is no trick in this. And I'll put myself against yourself in this manner of fight. There's your gun at your feet. Pick it up!"

Bobbie stooped, grasped the revolver, and stood straight again.

"Are you ready, Bobbie?"

"Yes, sir."

"Don't call me sir. Damn me . . . curse me. I'm trying to steal your life, Bobbie. I'm trying to take that on top of twenty years of slavish service for me. I'm trying to take your life after I've beaten you before strangers . . . like a dog. Remember these things. Now, Bobbie, are you ready?"

"Ready, sir."

The white man scowled, then he shrugged his shoulders. "Shoot to kill, Bobbie," he warned the other. "If you only wing me, I'll keep blazing away until the last spark is out in me. Now, Bobbie, stoop with me and put your gun down at your feet once more. So! Now we stand once more and consider what we have to do. I begin to count ten. When I hit the last count, we dive for our Colts and open fire. You understand? Is that fair to you as it is to me?"

"Yes, sir," said Bobbie.

"For pity's sake, man," broke out Tom, "is there no malice in you? Have you nothing to say about this life of yours, which I'm trying to waste after you freely put it in such danger for me, Bobbie?"

"I've nothing to say, sir."

The master swore to himself, first very softly, then very loudly, as though he needed all that violence to waken his own courage and bring it hotly up to the point of swift action. Then he began to count. He tolled out the words, as regularly as a bell strikes. He reached nine and trembled with eagerness. He reached ten, snatched up his Colt with one frantically swift gesture, and fired without lifting his hand from the ground. His finger was already closing on the trigger when he saw that Bobbie had not stirred in his place. His arms were still folded stiffly and high across his chest, and he had not stooped an inch toward the gun at his feet. Too late Tom strove to check that curling of his finger. But his whole hand had gripped at gun butt and trigger, and he groaned as the revolver exploded.

"I've missed," cried Tom, hurling his gun far away from him. "Thank heaven, I missed you, Bobbie!"

For Bobbie had not stirred in his place. "A mighty neat shot, sir," said Bobbie. "But the head is the thing to aim at, even with a snap shot. The body will do only once in a while." He pushed open his canvas jacket and thrust his hand into his bosom. He brought it out again with the fingers stained crimson. "This time," said Bobbie, "I think that it will do very nicely."

Then he crumpled, as though the force of the bullet had torn into him at that moment. The arms of Tom caught at him, but that huge bulk of solid bone and muscle glided through his hands like an avalanche and came to rest heavily against the earth. The canvas jacket was ripped away. The jet-black chest was exposed, arched like a noble dome, and splashed with the thick red.

The white man beat his hands together and then dashed them against his face. He tore off his shirt and started to tear it into strips for bandages. Then he stopped to take the big head of the Negro in his arms and groan: "Bobbie, Bobbie, I've killed you! It was the devil, Bobbie, not I."

"Steady," whispered a faint voice from the ground. "Tell them that you were cleaning your own gun . . . they won't care, except that I belonged to you, and they'll wonder why you threw me away."

IX

"TOM TURNS MAN"

"No talk," breathed Tom Farnsworth. "Save your strength . . . save your strength, Bobbie."

"Yes, sir," murmured the Negro.

Farnsworth was working like mad, twisting the bandages into place, stripping his body for that purpose, shivering not with the cold of the mountain night but with the icy fears that were whispering at his shoulder. For, as he worked, he was looking deep, deep into the truth about himself and the truth about the man he'd shot. *What if Bobbie died?* At that thought a thousand pictures leaped across his mind. There was time for many memories in every fraction of a second. And every recollection was of Bobbie in some other day, and in each one of those other days Bobbie was serving him more faithfully than any brother, more humbly than any slave.

He finished the bandaging. He rushed down the slope to the brink of the little spring and brought back a canteen of water. When he returned, the eyes of the Negro were closed, and the heart of Tom Farnsworth sank in him. But he recalled that men in death open their eyes for the last time. It was only a fainting fit. So he poured some water down the throat of Bobbie and had the sad gratification of hearing Bobbie groan and seeing his eyelids flicker.

Then he was up on his feet again and working like a madman. There was a growth of young pine saplings near the spring. He fell upon them with his hatchet, which he carried behind his saddle, and felled them one and all. With some he built a roaring fire, partly to keep away the cold and partly because he felt that he needed light and warmth to fight away death, which had stolen close to his servant in the darkness. With the tips and the needles of the saplings he constructed a deep and soft bed, over which he spread his tarpaulin and then fell to the labor of moving the big, wounded man to this new position of comfort. There followed five minutes of agony of effort, for Tom was not strong, and the inert bulk of Bobbie almost baffled all of his pulling and straining. There could be no roughness. All must be done smoothly, easily. When it was accomplished, he looked frantically at the bandage, fearful lest it might have shown a new spurting of blood. But the bandage showed only the one dark spot.

He now covered Bobbie with a saddle blanket and moistened his lips with a dram of brandy from his pocket flask. Bobbie opened his eyes again, sighed, and looked with a faint smile upon his master. The white man took advantage of this glimmer of returning consciousness to make a desperate appeal.

"You're not nearly gone, partner," he said. "Keep on fighting, Bobbie. Don't let it get you. Here we are, shoulder to shoulder, fighting the same fight. Can it beat the two of us when we are making a hard fight, old man? Good old Bobbie. Don't answer me with a word. Just lift the forefinger of your hand to let me know."

"Yes, sir," whispered Bobbie, and his smile broadened to an ecstasy of happiness. Then his smile died, and his eyes closed once more, while his face wrinkled in a spasm of pain.

"He's dead!" gasped Tom Farnsworth.

He looked wildly about him, but what was there he could do? He had felt, up to this point, that he had been fighting valiantly and successfully against death. He had felt that he was almost as strong as death itself in this great battle. But now there was no longer anything with which he could employ his hands. He could only sit and look about him at the greatness and the blackness of the night and up the brawny sides of the mountain, so utterly indifferent to this trifling human misery. There was nothing he could do except to throw more wood upon the fire. That light might prove a beacon which would bring in the hunters upon them both. But he desired nothing more. Let them come, and he might find among them a doctor who could be of direct help in this emergency.

He started up and threw more fuel on the blaze. The pitchy needles cast towering masses of red fire high into the air. The wood itself caught and flared grandly. Then, troubled with a new thought, he turned and knelt beside Bobbie to shield his eyes from the play and shaking of the columns of light. Once the Negro opened his eyes and looked up calmly with no dimness of faded strength.

"Bobbie," whispered the master, "will you forgive me, my friend?"

Before even an assent of expression could cross the face of Bobbie, the life had died in his eyes once more, and he passed into an utter faint. Farnsworth was furiously at work over him in a trice. There was another taste of brandy and water, then chafing of the Negro's temples—not that he really expected that this would help, but because he must either do something, or else go mad with the suspense.

As he worked, he felt barriers broken down, one by one, in his heart. He began to remember a thousand instances of cruelty on his part and of bitter neglect of Bobbie. He began to recall the gentle dignity of Bobbie in all the years of service that the Negro had poured out like a slave in service to the Farnsworth family. And then shame, grief, the deepest remorse for what he had done, and what he had been, swept over him. He looked upon the thing that he had been yesterday with a sort of horror, as though these had been the doings of strangers, and unworthy strangers at that. That he could have allowed this worthy fellow to ride away, carrying the burden and the danger of a charge of murder on his shoulders, was now incomprehensible, though then he had no more than shrugged his shoulders and called Bobbie a fool to himself.

When the doors of self-knowledge are once opened, we are too apt to see far deeper into our souls than we had intended or ever guessed. He saw a great deal about himself in the first glance, and nearly everything was damning. His college career, of whose dissipations he had been rather proud, he now looked back upon as a wasted season of foolishness in which he had prided himself merely because of the difference that had existed between himself and other people. Such were some of the reflections of Tom Farnsworth. But worse than this and coming nearer to the present, he could now see that the reason Deborah Kinkaid had been so attractive to him was simply because she had refused to be awed by his presence. She had kept him at arm's length, and for that reason she had at once seemed to him far pleasanter than any girl he had seen. He thought of this grimly, then with something of a shudder. Suppose that he had married her and awakened later on? Yet it was presumptuous to suppose that she would even have considered accepting him as a husband. But to learn all these things he had had to bring poor Bobbie to the gate of death. The second man within a few days. He sat up straight as the thought drove home in him. *Was the very instinct of murder in him, then?*

That thought faded into a reality of forms that stood before him. One—two—three—sneaking up toward him, with guns in their hands. He turned his head another way.

There were twenty men circling in upon him. He raised his hand.

"Any one of you fellows a doctor?" he asked.

Then they came hurrying in. They looked at him. They looked at Bobbie. Then they cursed softly, eyeing him as though he were a leper.

"You did this, Farnsworth?" asked one gray-headed man with a young face. "I thought that Bobbie was your servant?"

"Friends," said Farnsworth, "I came here to meet Bobbie, and, while we were looking over a gun, it exploded."

He saw faint smiles of contempt and derision in their faces. In the old days—that is to say, an hour before that— he would have scoffed at such expressions from the boors of the cattle range. But now every man was a man, no matter what his breeding or his manners. And their opinions stung him like so many whips. A doctor was brought forward. He was a veterinary in practice, but much more a rancher. He had some knowledge of anatomy, and his hands had taken care of scores of wounded men in his day. Therefore, he was soon beside the unconscious figure of Bobbie. While he worked to give an opinion of the nature of the hurt, the others stood around and rolled their cigarettes. They made few comments, but those were to the point. One man, noting the long, rounded, smooth-muscled arm of the Negro, swore that he could not understand why Bobbie had handled grown cowpunchers as though they were children. Another, staring at the unconscious face of the wounded man, said that there was only one black thing about him, and that was his skin.

"What's more," said the 'puncher with the gray hair, "we'd never have taken him except for. . . ." He turned with a gesture to Tom and an ugly look to complete his thought.

The doctor now rose to his feet, dusting his hands together and frowning down at the victim. His eyes were keen. "He's dead."

There was a mutter and a sharp exclamation of pain from Tom Farnsworth, so real, so ringing, that the cowpunchers, who had made up their minds about him, it seemed, now stared at him with a new interest.

"Dead?" cried Tom.

"I say he's dead," barked the doctor. "Anyways, he ought to be dead. That chunk of lead carved right straight through him. Why he ain't foaming blood at the mouth I dunno . . . why he ain't dead right now, I dunno. But here he is, living and calling me the same's a liar. And if he ain't dead or dying right this minute, maybe there's a hope for him. He's got to be treated plumb careful."

"He'll have all the care in the world!" exclaimed Tom.

The sheriff yawned. "We got to get him to jail," he said.

"For horse stealing?" asked Tom.

"That's part."

"I'll pay every man's claim."

"Will you pay the claim of poor young Pattison, dying over to Daggett?"

"There's no blame on Bobbie for that."

"Are you aiming to tell me my business, young man?" said the sheriff, who like most of the men on the range had heard of the eccentricities of young Farnsworth and greatly disliked all that he knew of the latter.

"I'll tell you what Bobbie did," said Tom. "He took the blame of another man on his shoulders."

"That sounds likely. Run his head into a noose for the sake of somebody else, eh?"

"I mean it, Sheriff."

"Look here, Mister Farnsworth"—and those the sheriff called by that formal title could be sure they rested under his disapproval—"your pa is a smart man. I've knowed him well and thought a lot of him. But even your pa couldn't have me swallow such bunk as that. You been to college, Mister Farnsworth, which is an advantage that I ain't never had, but I thank my Maker that I can use the few brains He give me better than to believe any yarn like that."

"Sheriff," said Tom, "I can name the man who shot Jack Pattison."

"So can everybody west of the Mississippi. It's Bobbie."

"It is not."

"Let's have your guess then, son."

The others waited, and the sheriff smiled wisely upon them, and they smiled wisely back upon the sheriff, for it would be pleasant to have this youth with his superior airs brought to time.

"I did," said Tom.

The smiles wavered and then went out, like candles snuffed by a rudely unexpected wind.

"Are you makin' a joke out of me, Farnsworth?"

"It's the truth, Sheriff. I shot Jack. He's kept the secret for my sake."

"Look here," muttered the sheriff, "you mean to say that you shot Pattison and then let your man here ride off with the blame for the killing?"

It was exquisite agony for Tom, but he swallowed the medicine and felt it burn home in him. "I did," he answered.

"I'm a tolerable reasonable man," said the sheriff, " but I got to admit free and quick that this here plumb beats me. Which I aim to hear you talk some more about, Farnsworth. You let him go, but then you come after him?"

"I did."

"Wanted to change places with him, maybe?"

"No."

"Why didn't you let well enough alone?"

"I wanted to get more out of him," said Tom bitterly, and all at once, as he found in himself the strength to confess, he found the strength, also, to lift his head and look around on those grave, weather-chiseled faces.

"More than what he'd done?"

"Yes."

"What was it, Tom?" asked the sheriff. His gentleness was amazing.

He's trying to draw me out, thought Tom. He said aloud: "There was still one more thing that Bobbie could do for me."

"And that?"

"Die, as Pattison was doing, and take my secret away with him."

The sheriff gasped. "You admit then . . . ?"

"Everything," said Tom.

"You're under arrest, Tom!" cried the sheriff. "For the Lord's sake, man, mind that everything you say now can be used against you."

"I mind it very well."

"You confess that you shot Jack Pattison?"

"I do."

"That you let Bobbie take the blame of it?"

"I do."

"That you come out here to get rid of the man that had risked his head for you?"

"I confess it," groaned Tom.

"And that, when you met him, you shot him down?"

"God have mercy on me," replied Tom solemnly, "as I expect nothing but justice on earth . . . I confess this, too."

The silence of the men weighed upon him like lead. He turned desperate eyes upon the wide circle of their faces, and he saw with amazement that they were looking upon him rather with surprise than with horror or anger.

"Tom," said the sheriff slowly at last, "dog-gone me if I quite make you out. Being and talking like a white man this hour, how could you have played the skunk one hour back?"

And that, on the whole, was the general opinion of the entire cattle range. It was freely expressed that day and the next, while Tom Farnsworth was being brought to Daggett to sleep in the jail.

X

"TOM TURNS AGAIN"

The news came like a bomb to Daggett. It affected people with one emotion—astonishment. They could not believe that the son of Thomas Farnsworth was guilty of a shooting scrape. When they heard it confirmed, they could not understand how Tom Farnsworth had been induced to confess to his double crime. They heard of other things also. On the way into town he was not moved to mention his own welfare once, but he was thinking and talking every moment of ways in which the comfort of Bobbie could be increased while he lay on the mountainside. In the first place, he had furnished an ample supply of cash to buy all sorts of provisions. They had secured enough tarpaulins from the cowpunchers to erect a little tent for the wounded Negro. Then the veterinary and two cowpunchers were hired to act as nurses until more aid could be sent out from the town, together with bandages and all manner of medical necessities, for it was beyond question that it would kill Bobbie to move him. So young Farnsworth planned to build a house over him, so to speak, and turn that spot on the mountainside into a little hospital.

As for his own trial, he refused to speak except to say that he had confessed everything and would confess it again. He felt that he had downed Pattison in a fair fight, and, as for Bobbie, nothing could save Tom if the Negro perished. He wished to have the law executed to the letter upon his person.

These were the strange sentiments that were expressed by Tom on his way back to Daggett. His father met him at the jail, throwing himself off a foaming horse and rushing into the building in spite of the sheriff.

"You have disgraced your family and me forever!" he had cried to his son.

"Farnsworth," said the sheriff, "you're wrong. He's just proved that he's a credit to you all. By the Lord, Farnsworth, I wish he were my boy."

This was much quoted around the streets the next day. Still more repeated was the interview between Bobbie's grandfather and young Tom the next morning. The ancient Negro had hobbled into the jail, supporting himself on a cane with one hand and fumbling his way along the wall with the other. He had been straight as a string the day before. He was bent as a bow now. He had grown decrepit overnight. When he saw his master's boy behind the bars, he fell on his knees and burst into pitiful sobbing.

"Marse Tom! Marse Tom," groaned the old fellow. "Lawdy, Lawdy! I knowed that Bobbie would be a trouble and a harm to you."

"Hush, Uncle," said the prisoner, coming to the bars of his cell. "Bobbie has done more for me than all the rest of the world together could ever have done. He's taught me what men are."

"He's brought you to ruin, Marse Tom."

"Let me tell you what he has done, Uncle," said the other. "He's taught me that a man who thinks that he's worthy of being a master is not fit to be even a slave. He taught me that he is a far better man than I am."

Tidings of this odd conversation were brought to Deborah Kinkaid, where she labored night and day at the bedside of Jack Pattison. She had made up her mind, at last. Jack was to be her husband, if she could win him back to life. She had told him so, and he was fighting with his whole strength to aid in the battle. The doctor said that it was being won from a reluctant enemy, step by step. She heard that report and turned straightway to the window and looked out at the morning sunlight, glistening on the roofs of Daggett.

"I half guessed it before," she murmured, "but only half. I didn't know he had such a thing in him."

And she sighed, but, if it were with a regret, Jack Pattison was never to know. He began to recover rapidly. By that night he was out of danger. Still another week passed before word came from the Kiever Mountains that the big Negro was also recovering slowly. All of Daggett came down to give Tom Farnsworth a cheer in the jail. He listened to the noise with amazement, and the sheriff came in to explain.

"When a man shows that he's white," said the sheriff, "all the black things that he's ever done before are washed away and forgotten. That's the way with you, Tom. I'm going to bust the law ten ways from Sunday. You're free this minute. Go outside. Your father is waiting to take you home."

Outside, Tom walked into an ovation. He received it with his head bared and bowed, and he rode all the way out to the ranch at his father's side without answering a word to that fine old gentleman's exultation.

"Now," said Thomas Farnsworth, Sr., "when you have all the fool nonsense worked out of your head, you can settle right down on the ranch and get ready to take charge when I'm ready to step out, which will be plenty *pronto.*"

It was not until the next morning that Tom, Jr., came to make his reply at the breakfast table. He was dressed not for the ranch, but for travel, and he explained this condition at once.

"Father," he said to the old man, "I've decided that I don't want the ranch, and that the ranch doesn't want me."

"What the devil sort of talk is this?" roared the rancher.

"Straight talk."

"What do you intend to do, then?"

"Start with these clothes on my back and fifty dollars in my pocket and see where it takes me. Then buck my own way with my own hands."

"You learned that out of some fool book."

The son smiled and said no more.

"You mean," shouted his father, "that you're not coming back?"

"I don't mean that. I'll come back when I can tell you something that I've done besides spend your money."

"The ranch is to go to pot, eh?"

"You don't need help, and you know it. If you do, I can give you a proved man to take my place and do better than I could ever have done."

"Who's that?"

"Bobbie."

With that the talk was brought to a sudden close. That very day young Tom rode away from his home. He avoided

Daggett, simply because he did not want to be run after and congratulated. He felt a warm shame and a weakness in his throat when he thought of the average goodness of human beings who could overlook and forget the harm he had done. He set the head of his horse toward the Kiever Mountains, far north and west, for one last talk with Bobbie. And he wondered, as he went on, what he would find in the big Negro, when he looked on him as a free man and not as a slave, and what would Bobbie find in him, now that he was no longer the master?

Lake Tyndal

Faust's final Western serial, "Dust Across the Range," was published in The American Magazine *(11/37–2/38) when he was working in several other genres, notably in the fields of crime and historical fiction. His splendid novel of the French Revolution, "The American," was serialized in* Argosy *(2/27/37–4/10/37). Yet, as "Lake Tyndal" proves, he had not yet abandoned the shorter Western tale. He wrote this story in the summer of 1937, and it appeared in* All-American Fiction *that December. Ex-con Pete Harrison is an unsavory killer, cast in the same self-destructive mold as Dick Durante, protagonist of Brand's most famous Western short story, "Wine on the Desert," published in* This Week *(6/7/36). Both men operate out of greed and both pay a bitter price for their obsession. With a sure feel for character and situation, Faust presents another sharply realized vignette of the Wild West.*

The mule lasted all the way across the alkali flats, through the wind-carved badlands of the Mallikaw Valley, and up the stubborn eastern slope of the Tyndal Mountains.

120

Strange to say, it was on the easy downslope that Harrison rode it to death. For when he reached the summit and looked into the southwest over the deep, narrow valley of the upper Tyndal, he saw a spreading gleam on the valley floor, steel bright, unlike the blue of mirage water. The heart went out of him, then, in a sort of gasping prayer made up of curses, for he knew that what he was seeing was no dream in the desert, but the actual sheen of water, backing up behind the new Tyndal Dam. In that first moment of agony he made sure that the rising lake already had covered the place where he had buried the money.

That was why he raced the mule all the way down the slope to get a closer view. When the knees of the poor beast began to buckle, he paid no attention to the telltale sign, for he was too busy cursing the state board of pardons for not giving him the parole sooner. He was reddening his spurs deeper and deeper in the flanks of the mule as he passed the elbow turn of the trail where he stuck up Monte Parons. His lawyer had been quite right. He had intended his bullet to be a mere settler for Monte. He had not dreamed that the fool would bleed to death. After all, it was only gambler's blood, just as the ten thousand he took from Monte had been only gambler's money. Nevertheless, they had given him ten years. The buck-toothed prosecutor had talked about "a spirit obdurate in crime." Four long years of that term he had served before the parole arrived. Now the parole lay broken behind him and could be damned. He had gone that far in his journey and in his own thoughts when the mule dropped headlong under him and sent him rolling.

He climbed to his feet, spitting blood, frightened, hurt as though by the sudden pang and hammer stroke of a bullet wound. But then he saw that no human enemy was near him. The mule lay on its side with its long pale tongue thrust out above the bit and blackening in the dust. Pete Harrison was surprised. He always said that a horse is like a woman—jittery, silly, and likely to play out on you in the time of need—but a mule is money in the bank. Now he noticed the red flank of the dead beast and said: "Why, you poor worthless critter, I guess I rode you right some, at that." But he had no time for pity. The dread of what he was to find in the valley drove him to snatch up the pick and shovel, the rifle, the canteen, and go forward at a run, a dog-trot, a stagger, until he came through tall brush to the verge of Tyndal Valley's floor.

There he dropped on his knees and with his lungs on fire gave thanks with one upward look. The dust of his running overtook him in a lazy cloud and thickened his breathing, but he paid no attention to that, for though the impounded waters behind the dam had spread back past the site where his treasure lay buried, threatening it on either side, the place stood up against the black margin of the flood like the rising prow of a ship. He knew it by the three mesquite bushes. Once the water covered them, all token of the spot would be gone, but still the three showed like flags, in line between Mount Buford and Calamity Peak. Sometimes a man builds better than he knows, and by the divine grace of chance Harrison had cached his money in high ground.

He shouldered his tools and went out slowly across the burned, naked desert where even the three mesquite bushes showed on the flat like three tall trees. As he came toward them, he was stopped for a moment by the trail of a jack-rabbit such as it leaves when it hops along very slowly with a dainty print of forepaws and long, squatting marks where the hind legs touch the sand. The sign made him think of the day of his arrest. He would have got clean through the line of the extended posse, except that a sudden rustling in the tall grass made him think that a man was rising behind him. The gun in his hand had exploded almost of its own volition, and that was why they had closed in and found him. So, in a manner of speaking, a jackrabbit had scared him into prison.

Pete Harrison believed in tokens and foreboding symbols. He was scrupulous about the manner in which he first looked at the new moon. And now he stepped big to cross this unlucky trail. A moment later he forgot about it, for he was standing inside the mesquite triangle and felt that he was walled about by good fortune. From this island of security in life he looked upon the outer world.

The southward turn of the valley took the lake out of his view, but there was a whole mile of open water in sight, silver bright toward the edges but darkening with wind riffles in the center, as though a current flowed there. He shook his two-quart canteen and made sure that it was almost full, for it was plain that it would be hard to get water from the lake unless he crossed the valley floor and went far down the verge of it to where clear water rose along the rocky hills. In the valley itself a thick black margin of mud extended ahead of the rising lake as the sand drank up the water, sand hundreds of feet deep, perhaps, and now turning quick with moisture. The sound of the dry earth drinking was a crinkling sound, a delicate rustling like soft wind in grass, or the falling of a light rain. He looked to the mountains, their heads and shoulders loaded with snowbanks that were melting fast, now. The thunder and groaning of cataracts in the upper gorges and the chime of a thousand waterfalls made the music and the tremor in the air which came echoing out and entered Harrison's mind. He looked down from these pictures to the valley again and noticed how the black of the mud was creeping up past the mesquites on either hand. Suddenly the place where he stood seemed to have motion, downstream.

He fell to work with a hearty good will. Between the southwest and the northwest mesquite, he remembered clearly, he had dug the hole exactly in the center. He stepped off the distance now, found the center, and thrust the shovel into the ground. He worked fast, for he was a strong two-hundred pound engine, hardened by prison labor and prison temperance. The careful living had taken away ten from his forty years. He was six years up on the state, if he looked at it that way. There were other benefits from that long withdrawal from the world, he considered as he dug, changing shovel for pick and pick for shovel. Best of all, he had been away so long that certain enmities had had a chance to cool. Some who hated him were dead—Josh Payson had lost the trigger-finger of his right hand; Marty Malone was a lunger down in Arizona; and the booze had softened young Steve Holliday to a worthless pulp. Some day he would look up Steve and kick the pulpy remains of him into strange shapes and attitudes. He laughed as he thought of this. Then his laughter stopped, for he realized that he had dug at least a foot beneath the level at which he buried the little canvas packet of money. It was gone!

He jumped out of the hole and looked wildly about him. He never had known a fear, even for his very life, that was equal to this dreadful fear of loss. And then he felt that he remembered. It was not between the southwest and the northwest shrubs that he had dug the burial hole, but on the other side of the triangle. He measured the line, found the center of it, and began to labor more furiously than before, so that pain appeared in the small of his back and his lips turned salty with drying, and running, and drying sweat

He almost had finished the canteen when he realized that here, also, he had dug beneath the necessary level. He got out of the hole and tried to think. All he could remember was the leering smile of that desert rat, old Dan Weston. Old Dan, who often followed him as a coyote will follow loafer wolves, to pick up fragments from the feast. If old Dan had trailed him and seen him digging, from the distance . . . ?

Pete Harrison looked up at the sun-faded sky and said aloud: "God wouldn't do it to me. He wouldn't do it to *me!*"

He forced himself out of the darkness and the weakness of despair. Had he not, on that day four years ago, thought first of digging between two of the shrubs, and had he not afterward decided to dig in the very center of the triangle? Coldly, with deliberation, he tried to spot the center of that triangle, but it was hard to do. He paced and repaced the ground until he had found a place equidistant from all three of the mesquite bushes. Then he thrust the shovel into the sand, remained for a moment, leaning on the handle of it, looking about him. In each of the holes he had dug something seemed to be hiding, crouched down out of his sight. This preconception troubled him so much that he went and took a reassuring look into each hollow. He looked north and saw that the black of the mud had spread incredibly far even during the brief hours of his labor, leaving only a narrowing road of white sand in the center, leading toward his bit of high land. This sense of having found a place favored and chosen by nature itself gave him a sudden heartening of the will. He flung the first shovelful right at the face of the sun, that was now halfway down from the zenith, and sank a wide-mouthed hole rapidly.

The bigness of the hole delayed him, but he dared not narrow it toward the center. It was his third gesture in the dark, and it must not fail him. As he dug, he remembered the smallness of the package. If he had had any brain about him, he would have made the bundle a whole armful. But life is full of small things and narrow margins.

The panic that overtook him in Tyndal Valley was simply an intensification of the long, cold fear that had risen in him when he heard about the building of the Tyndal Dam. He had begun then, two years before, to make himself the most model prisoner, the most trusted of trustees, building a good reputation bit by bit, stone by stone, block by block, as they were building the dam. He had not troubled the senator, then, with any foolish requests for help with the pardon board. He had waited, heaping up good deeds that would tell in his behalf, until at last, six months before, he had called, the great man had come, and he had poured forth his promises. Five thousand dollars—on trust. And the senator had trusted him. That had been heaven's first act in his behalf. The second had been the chance that kept him from lingering by the way for so much as a single drink, so that he had reached Tyndal Valley in time.

Then a cool wind struck his face, and he realized that the sun was almost down. He could not force his arms to act more quickly. They were numb to the shoulders. His back, from constant bending, was about to break like a bit of rusty tin. He dared not look into the west, but he felt the shadow wash over him and lift over his head like water as the sun sank behind the western peaks. And then the next pick stroke went home into something soft as flesh. His heart shriveled up in his chest then, and a sigh that had the ring of terror and a prayer left his twisting lips.

Suppose it were the canvas—suppose the pick tore the bills to shreds? Such a shuddering weakness ran through his blood that his knees buckled under him. He hardly had power to work the pick loose and to begin chipping gently at the ground, raking the earth away with his hands. And then his fingertips ran over the rough of a canvas seam. He had the bundle out at once. He began to lay back the flaps and the wrappings, and suddenly the face of the money looked up at him—the old, worn face of George Washington, flabby under the chin, receding in the brow. Joy was too great to take him at once between thumb and finger and give him the real pinch of delight. He had time to wonder at that great dead man for a moment, and then laughter began to bubble up from a bottomless well in his heart. It reached his throat. It overflowed. Tears blinded him and then washed his eyes clean. He looked up. The sun had dipped from view long ago, but only now it was sinking below the true horizon, and the conflagration in the sky seemed to Pete Harrison a bonfire built in honor of this glorious moment.

It was when he looked down from that exaltation that he saw the rabbit. He stared at it dully for a moment, as if it were more than a beast, as if it had a meaning in itself that he couldn't for the life of him understand. Sunburned to the pallor of the desert itself, it crouched flat, the long ears laid right back along its sides, and the yellow oval of its eyes fixed upon Harrison.

In his amazement, he forgot the ten thousand dollars he was holding in his hands, for he was seeing a thing no other human being, he was sure, ever had beheld: a great Western jackrabbit—that most fleet and timid of creatures, armed by nature with nothing but speed and with wings of fear ever ready to lighten its way—now actually confronting a man eye to eye with no movement toward flight.

He remembered the rabbit in the grass four years before. He remembered the rabbit trail that had crossed his path this day, but he cursed the fear that jumped up in him and reached out his hand for his supper. The wind touched the soft, light fur of the jack. There was no other movement of its body as the hand of Harrison took it by the scruff of the neck and lifted it up. A good, fat jack—a full meal even for a hungry man. It was not dead with its eyes open, either. Under his fingertips Harrison felt a heart, racing with incredible speed. Terror might be killing it, but it was not dead. It seemed sound in every part. What in heaven's name, then, had made it sit down beside its enemy? Why . . . why . . . ?

Then Harrison saw the hind legs hanging down—the big, muscular legs that carry it, flying far faster than fox or coyote ever could dream of racing. He saw that the fur was caked and wet with fresh mud. Understanding opened the door of Harrison's mind and entered him with one long stride. He dropped the jack. It fell solidly, without feet to break the shock, for now it was actually near death with fright. And Harrison, looking with terrified eyes to the north, saw that his dry road of retreat had vanished. No, there was still a swiftly diminishing strip of dry sand in the very center. Why had not the rabbit found it when it tried to flee from the higher ground? Because the rabbit is of all creatures the most brainless. It has no wits at all, except in its feet. Harrison thrust his money almost unregarded into his shirt pocket and fled up that glimmering way. He had not taken three steps before his feet were plunging into something softer than dry sand, something pulpy, a bottomless yielding to his weight. The faster he ran, the less his feet would have a chance to sink. So he rushed with a more frantic speed that sent him to floundering suddenly knee-deep, thigh-deep into an unexpected bog. Only a film of surface dryness overlay the quicksand through which the water had been seeping during his hours of digging.

His bit of high land was the only salvation for the moment, even though it was sure to melt into mud long before morning. He turned back toward it and, in turning, sank to the waist. The bog had him with flexible, patient hands about the feet and the knees. He made one vast, blind, screaming effort to tear himself free but succeeded in sinking only his body to the chest. Then he stopped. Water was collecting faster and faster in the place he had churned up with his efforts. He felt the increasing cold of it. He shivered helplessly.

The racing of his heart kept him from thinking, just as a great knocking at a door stops the speaking voices inside the house. It was better to die quickly than to endure the frightful sickness of fear. Then hope found him in the great dark wilderness of his despair. If he did not sink himself with emotional struggles, it might be that the rising water would loosen the mud that held him, turning it thin and powerless. Afterward, if he could not wade, he might swim to the shore. He could hear the waterfalls, singing faintly in the darkening mountains, as they hurried the streams down to Tyndal Lake.

He still could see the little spot of high land where he had worked, and he understood now that, if he had not given way to the blind panic, like a frightened rabbit, he might have built up a high, high mound and simply sat upon it until the water rose and was deep enough for swimming. Or, by tying the mesquite branches in large bundles, he might have given himself such large footing that he could have walked the surface of the bog without sinking.

Still, with a strange clearness, he could see the jackrabbit like an almost shapeless lump. When he looked up, the darkness was filling the valley to the brim, like water rising far above his head.

The Two-Handed Man

Nineteen Thirty-Two was a peak year for Faust in Western Story Magazine. *Using five pseudonyms, he churned out fiction for all fifty-two weekly numbers, often appearing under three names in a single issue, with a complete short novel and two serial segments. In that one incredible year, for this magazine alone, Faust produced the mind-boggling total of 1,600,000 words, equal to twenty-three full-length novels. Has any writer ever written more in a twelve-month period? Under the pen name of George Owen Baxter, "The Two-Handed Man" was published in the issue of* Western Story Magazine *for December 3, 1932. The story's protagonist, Jimmy Bristol, a two-handed man with knife and gun, is yet another example of Faust's "good badman"—driven to the outlaw trail by false charges, these characters always redeem themselves by heroic action. There is, of course, the pure-souled young woman, the swift-galloping wonder horse, and the larger-than-life villain. To this standard mix, Faust brings his flair for dynamic action, his gift for colorful dialogue, and his glittering poetic style in creating another highly readable, entertaining Western adventure.*

Max Brand

I

"FLAPJACKS AND COFFEE"

When Jimmy Bristol reached the top of the hill, the wind and rain came at him across the valley with such a roar that his horse turned, cowering. Jimmy squinted his eyes against the stinging and beating of the rain and stared down into the hollow. Like water, the pale evening and the storm filled the ravine. Through the twilight he could see the glimmer of a town down there, and suddenly a craving struck him mightily for hot cakes and maple syrup, and coffee with real milk in it.

He knew that he would be a fool to go into the town. Its name might be unknown to him, but he was probably well enough known to it. Men with a money reward hanging over their heads are quickly enough recognized. The newspapers see to that, and placards in post offices and other public buildings. When money is hard to come by, why shouldn't the active fellows who are quick on the trigger look out for the odd chance? A bullet costs very little. In the case of Jimmy Bristol, it would bring home a reward of just over five thousand dollars, to say nothing of the fame.

That was why Jimmy Bristol waited there with the rain volleying to smoke against the rubber face of his slicker. He dreaded the force of the law. He feared the many hands that might serve it down there where the lights were twinkling. But his craving for hot cakes and syrup, and coffee with real milk in it, was altogether too much for him. For three months he had cooked his own food and boiled his own coffee. A good deal of that food had been toasted rabbit and mountain grouse. Tempting fare, you say. But that's because you have not been forced to live on it.

Now he turned the chestnut down into the valley and jogged it into the town. The ruts were full of water that was flung up from the cup of a forehoof now and then and splashed as high as the knee. Once a pair of riders went crashing by him, suddenly appearing and suddenly disappearing through the penciled grayness of rain that filled the air. He passed windows that were covered with ten thousand little starry eyes, where the lamplight inside was broken up by the drops that adhered to the glass panes. It was the supper hour, and many odors of cookery came out to him. Far away and long ago, centuries distant from him, he had known the sweetness of ginger cookies. He knew how they breathed forth fragrance from a deep tin pan where they were kept in the pantry. It made him think of the taste of them as he sensed the odor again now. Tell me, what is so good as cold, fresh milk and ginger cookies? There was many a flavor of bacon on the air, too. There always is, in Western cookery. Bacon runs through the kitchen work more than prayer runs through the air of a church. And he knew the smell of frying steaks, too, with some of the grease burning, and the rest bubbling in the hot pan. Other scents were strong, such as cabbage boiling, onions frying. They all drew out in the heart of Jimmy Bristol various stops of emotion and great crashing chords of desire. Well, the safe, honest men, they could remain at home and enjoy such delicacies as liver and bacon—strange how he always had hated that estimable dish—but he, Jimmy Bristol, had time in this town for no more than hot cakes and coffee—with real milk in it.

He found two desired opportunities close to one another—one was a livery stable, and the other was a lunch counter. So he rode straight in through the big double doors of the stable and heard the hoofbeats of his horse sound muffled on the floor, made pulpy by the treading of countless iron shoes. The rain roared on the roof, high up and far away, and the rain crashed in the street, nearer at hand. When he dismounted, the fall and the upsplash of that rain made a shining mist before the eyes of Jimmy Bristol.

A stable attendant came toward him, wearing rubber boots, a shirt with the sleeves cut off at the shoulders, and the suspenders holding his trousers were worn outside the shirt. He held a big sponge in his hand, as though he had just come from washing down some buggy or buckboard. Jimmy Bristol looked curiously at him. He never could quite understand what made men work for wages—certainly he never could comprehend how a fellow would be willing to take on the night shift in a livery stable.

"Yeah?" greeted the man with the sponge.

"This horse of mine is tuckered out a little," said Bristol.

"Yeah." The stable man nodded.

"And I've got to be moving on before long. Got any good horses for sale here?"

"Yeah," said the stableman.

"Show me the three best, beginning with the best of the three," said Jimmy Bristol.

"Yeah," said the stableman.

He led the way to a box stall and opened the door. There was a brown mare inside, with dark points all around. But Bristol did not even step into the stall to make a closer examination. His knowing eye had looked for and found the faults immediately.

"That's a good mare," he said. "That mare can carry weight, and she can run fast. But she can't go far. There's not much room for a heart in her under the cinches."

The stableman looked askance at him. He started toward the next box, but Jimmy Bristol called him back.

"If that's your best, I'll take your word for it and not look at the second best. You can start in working on this chestnut, will you?"

"Yeah," said the stableman.

"I'll be back here in about fifteen minutes. Give her a swallow of water, put her in a stall, and pass out a feed of oats. You have some good clean oats?"

"Yeah," said the stableman. He hooked a thumb under his suspenders and snapped the elastic against his swelling chest.

"While she's eating those oats, never stop working on her. Rub her down. Do you know how to rub a horse down?"

"Yeah," said the stableman.

"And really work your thumb under the muscles?"

"Yeah," said the stableman. And this time there was a faint glint of interest in his eyes.

"Well, start working now, and keep on working," said Jimmy Bristol. "Peel the saddle right off her, and start in working hard on her. Here's a dollar for your work. I'll pay the other bill when I come for her."

"Yeah," said the stableman.

Jimmy Bristol went out into the rain and let it whip on his face. He smiled at the cold and the wet and the sting of it. There were few places where the water had not already soaked through to his skin, but that made small difference. Better to be wet by rain than by the melting snow and hail of a blizzard, as he had been three days before this.

He walked in to the lunch counter and leaned on the rail. There was nobody else in the place, but it was an old-established eating house to judge by the greasy, battered look of the bill of fare that was written against the wall, and to judge, also, by the way the linoleum on the floor was worn into paths with holes in them.

"Have you got some hot cake batter all mixed?"

The cook was a man of importance. The lower part of his body and the lower part of his face bulged out into dignified curves. He had a drooping mustache, too, and he caught hold of one glistening, steam-dampened end of this mustache as he answered: "I got hot cake batter mixed."

"I don't mean just dough. I don't mean self-rising, either. I mean honest hot cakes, not leathery flapjacks."

"You mean something that comes apart in your mouth, eh?"

"That's what I mean."

"Look at that," said the cook.

He pulled out a deep crockery bowl and showed to the eager eyes of Jimmy Bristol a yellowish, liquid mass whose surface was roughened by many bubblings of effervescence, a slow and sticky working of the whole.

"That's it," said Jimmy Bristol.

The cook smiled at him, and he smiled at the cook.

"Slap a dozen of those on the fire," said Jimmy Bristol. "Is that stove clean?"

"Look," said the cook. He swabbed his steamy hand over a part of it and offered the tips of his fingers to Bristol's eyes—and nose, for that matter.

"All right. It's clean," said Bristol. "Cover that stove with flapjacks. *Pronto!* But wait a minute. Have you got some maple syrup?"

"You mean maple syrup or *maple syrup?*" asked the cook.

"I mean maple syrup."

"It's ten cents a plate extra."

"That's the kind of maple syrup I mean."

A positive fire of enthusiasm came upon the cook. "Taste it first," he said. "Let the taste of it start working in on you while I start them flapjacks cooking."

He offered a battered can. Jimmy Bristol took it, uncorked it, sniffed it as though it were a wine of vintage, and set it down with a sigh.

"It's real," he said. "One more thing."

The cook was ladling out hot cakes all over the stove. "You bet it's real," he said.

"And maybe," said Bristol tenderly, "maybe you have some real coffee here? I don't mean that mocha and Java that costs twenty-three cents a pound. I mean *real* coffee."

"What kind? What brand?" asked the cook.

"The kind that *you* like," said Jimmy Bristol.

It was an inspiration. The cook smiled a coy and greasy smile over the shoulder. Then he winked. He said: "All right, brother. You'll have it."

"And maybe," went on Jimmy Bristol, "you've got real milk from the inside of a cow instead of from the inside of a can?"

The cook turned around on him. "Me," he said, stabbing his breast with his thumb, "I keep cows. I keep *Jersey* cows. You know what I mean?"

"I'm trying to believe you, brother," said Jimmy Bristol.

"Look," said the cook. He raised a large glass pitcher. At the top was a yellow stain of cream that ran through the upper strata of the milk. But, even so, there remained a rich tinting of yellow through the whole mass of the liquid.

Before Jimmy Bristol could speak, however, a boy who looked like the cook without the curves of the face and the stomach came running in and gasped across the counter: "Pop, the sheriff's been looking in through the back window!"

II

"THE SHERIFF'S IDEA"

When the cook heard this, he put his lips all on one side of his mouth and then bit the hard-drawn opposite corner. "Whatcha mean?" he asked of the lad. "Get out of here. Whatcha mean?"

"I mean, I *seen* him," said the lad. "Jiminy, and didn't I! I seen him give the glass a swab with his hand and look through." Saying this, he fled out of the room the way he had come in.

"Thunder," said the cook, "what would that mean?"

Jimmy Bristol saw that the hot cakes were apt to be spoiled. He said: "The sheriff is looking around the town, and maybe he's looking for me."

At this the cook leaned suddenly nearer across the bar. He leaned so near that his glance was able to reach down across the farther edge of the counter, and so find the big holster that was strapped to the thigh of Bristol's right leg. It had been black leather once, but now it was worn in many places to a slimy gray.

"Ugh!" grunted the cook, and opened his eyes.

"My name is Jimmy Bristol," said the outlaw. "There's five thousand dollars on my head. I came into this town, not to shoot it up, but to get hot cakes and maple syrup, and coffee with real milk in it."

135

The cook licked his lips. Slowly, color began to return to his blanched face. Although as a flapjack maker he was a man of parts, it was evident that he had no ambition to become an outlaw catcher.

"How long you been out?" he asked finally.

"Three months," said Bristol.

Suddenly the cook grinned. "I was out once myself. It wasn't nothing much . . . but I had to leave a town once. I was only out three days . . . but it was the biggest half of my life, them three days was."

He turned, suddenly twitched back to the stove by a sense of duty, and at that moment the sheriff entered—the very moment when the cook began to shovel the first hot cakes onto a platter. For such a patron as Jimmy Bristol he disdained to offer a mere plate.

The sheriff of that town was almost as fat as the cook at the lunch counter, but under his puffy body extended a pair of long, wiry legs that looked capable of mastering the toughest broncho on the range. He wore a gun on each side of him. His hat was on the side of his head.

The cook saw him coming as he shoved the platter before Bristol, between the half roll of butter and the can of syrup.

"That's him," whispered the cook.

"All right," said Bristol. "It's not time for me to move yet."

The sheriff came up and paused four feet away. "I'm Tom Denton," he said. "I'm the sheriff."

"Hullo, Sheriff," said Bristol. "Anything biting you?"

He turned his young, handsome face on the sheriff and smiled straight into his eyes. The sun had burned Bristol to a golden brown, and that color set off the blue-gray of his eyes. It was only now and then that too much light crowded into the pupils of those eyes and made them blaze without any color.

"Nothing's biting me," said the sheriff. "I just wondered what your hurry was?"

"You mean, getting on through town?"

"That's what I mean," said the sheriff, running his eyes

slowly over the big shoulders of Bristol and then down to the spoon-handled spurs that arched out from the heels of his boots. "You only got fifteen minutes in town, eh?"

Bristol smiled and hooked a thumb over his shoulder. "That dummy in the stables had an idea, did he?" he asked.

"Yeah," said the sheriff. "Maybe he did, at that."

"Well, I'll tell you," said Bristol. "I've been working on the Jerry Comfort place, and Jerry laid me off the other day. I've got a cousin up country, working on the other side of the Kennisaw Gap, over near Milton. He wrote me a long time ago it was a good layout, and they fed well. So I thought I'd ramble up that way. I aimed to get up closer to the Gap tonight and stop over at some ranch house. Tomorrow they're taking on three new men where my cousin works, and I aim to be one of the three, but even if I put on ten more miles tonight, I'll still be forty miles short of Milton. Isn't that about right?"

"But why the fifteen minutes? Why not an hour?" asked the sheriff.

"And let the chestnut get cold?" asked Bristol, smiling and shaking his head.

"There's something in that," agreed the sheriff, pursing his lips in doubt. Then he added: "Stand up and turn your back to me."

Rather slowly Bristol obeyed.

"Now," said the sheriff, "pull a gun with your left hand and aim it at that doorknob . . . that back doorknob."

Bristol hitched up the holster on his right thigh, reached across his body with his left hand, and drew out the revolver. He balanced the gun carefully, but still the muzzle of it wavered from side to side. He did not squint down the barrel with his left eye, but with his right eye, holding the gun well toward that side of his body.

Suddenly the sheriff laughed. "All right," he said. "Put up that gun and feed your face. Sorry I bothered you, son. But I had an idea."

Bristol put up the gun and buckled down the flap of the holster over it again. He sat down on the stool in front of the lunch counter and began to lay slabs of butter between the strata of the pile of hot cakes. "What idea did you have?" he asked.

"There's a fellow named Jimmy Bristol that's riding not a thousand miles from here," said the sheriff. "From what I hear, I guess that he's a bigger man than you are. But just the same . . . well, I thought I'd see."

"See how big I am?" asked Bristol, apparently amazed.

"Jimmy Bristol's a two-handed man," said the sheriff. "He's a little faster and a little better with the left than he is with the right. But it's easy to see that *you're* no two-handed man." He laughed again. "You took hold of that gun with your left like an old woman," he added. "Well, so long. It's all right, son. I just had an idea, that was all."

He left the place, and the cook sighed. He seemed to be deflating, though his dimensions grew no less. "My Jiminy," he said, "and you *are* Jimmy Bristol?"

"These," said Bristol, "are the best hot cakes that I ever set a tooth in. And this," he added, raising the cup of coffee and hot milk, "is the best coffee and the finest milk that I ever laid a lip over. Brother, here's to you and bottoms up."

He was as good as his word. When he put down the cup, he saw that the cook was mopping his forehead with a towel, and still the perspiration gleamed again and again on his brow.

"You've finished that platter of hot cakes," said the cook. "Maybe you'd better drift along, son. I wouldn't want. . . ."

"It's not time to go," said Bristol. "It's nowhere near time to go. Let's have some more. The next row of 'em are beginning to smoke. Look at the beauties puff up, will you?"

"Yeah. They're made, that's what they are," said the cook. And he stacked them on the platter once more. He laid his hands on the edge of the counter and smiled with a frightened admiration at Bristol. "You got the cold-steel nerve," he declared. "I never seen nothing like it." He added: "What they want you for?"

"Not much," said Jimmy Bristol. "There was a fellow in Tombstone who felt like four of a kind when he was only holding three tens, and so he borrowed one out of his sleeve. When I saw it, he started to draw, but I beat him to it. I took the pot and went away. But a lot of people at the burying of that *hombre* didn't know about the cards up the sleeve or him going for his gun, and they thought that they'd better inquire into the business. So they came and asked me a few questions, which I answered over my shoulder as I was cutting the wind, because I saw too many guns and too many ropes in that crowd, and I've got a right tender neck when it comes to stretching hemp. When my own horse wore out, I borrowed another. And that made me a horse thief. You see how the landslide starts?" He laughed a little. "That was three months ago," he said.

"My Jiminy!"

Jimmy Bristol looked at a far corner of the ceiling. "I'll tell you, partner," he said, "I've spent too much time learning how to shoot with both hands. I was riding for a fall, and I got it. Besides, these three months have been fun. The best in my life. Except that I got pretty hungry for hot cakes and maple syrup."

The back door of the room opened, and there entered a quick-stepping fellow with a set face and with blazing eyes. The cook saw that and saw the flash of the man's gun. But he hardly followed the whiplash movement by which Jimmy Bristol produced a gun from inside his slicker. With his left hand he produced it and fired. The stranger dropped his own gun and caught at his right shoulder with his left hand.

"I'm sorry, Bob," said Jimmy Bristol. "I only trimmed the wick, though. I didn't put out the light. The cook, here, will put a bandage on you."

"Damn you!" said the wounded man. "You murdering hoss thief . . . you . . . !"

"Tie up his shoulder, cook, will you?" requested Jimmy Bristol.

"You better get out," said the cook in a hoarse whisper.

"There's still time," said Jimmy Bristol, putting up his gun. "I can finish this platter. Fill up my cup again before you start working on him, will you?"

He continued eating, while the cook ran around to the wounded man and made him sit in a chair.

"Go raise the town, you danged fool!" shouted the stranger. "That's Jimmy Bristol, and there's five thousand bucks on his murdering head."

Bristol continued to eat. "The fact is, Bob," he said, "that your friend, McNamara, borrowed a card out of his sleeve that day."

"You lie!" shouted Bob. "There were three others at the table. They didn't say nothing about that."

"Sure, they didn't," answered Bristol. "They all had reasons for getting me out of town. That's why the game was started . . . to squeeze me out of Tombstone. So long, Bob."

"Help! Murder! Jimmy Bristol's here!" yelled Bob.

Bristol rang a ten-dollar gold piece on the counter and stood up. "Here's to your health, Bob," he said. And he drained the coffee.

A stream of men poured through the front door as he walked toward it.

"Get a doctor," said Bristol. "There's a fellow back there raving, and he needs help. He's tried to kill himself." He passed into the street.

III

"THE GRANEYS"

He reached the livery stable, walking close to the wall of it, and suddenly stepped into the open doorway. There was the man with the sponge, gaping round-eyed and listening to sounds of excited shouting that streamed out of the lunch counter not far away. Bristol took him by the fat of his chin.

"I told you to keep working on that chestnut," he said.

"I was working . . . only . . . except . . . ," the man with the sponge defended himself.

"Get the saddle and bridle back on it," said Bristol.

Standing in the doorway, he could watch the liveryman saddle the chestnut. He could also watch the street, and, as the horse was led up, he saw a sudden rush of men boil out from the front of the lunch counter, like steam out of the spout of a kettle. He knew that in every one of those men there was a passionate hunger for five thousand dollars' worth of Jimmy Bristol.

The chestnut was led up to him on the run by the stableman. "I kind of thought . . . ," he began.

Bristol looked him fairly between the eyes. Then he exclaimed: "You're a poor devil! Here's another dollar." He flung the money on the floor, leaped into the saddle, and raced the chestnut up the street. He heard shots behind him.

The shooting ended as he turned a corner, and half a minute later he was out of that town and heading again toward Kennisaw Gap. The loneliness of the rain, which is only less than the loneliness of the sea, gathered around him and cupped him in with his own soul.

He got off and ran when he reached the sweep of the hills and the grama grass that covered them. The chestnut was tired, and he needed to put miles between him and that town. In a while he mounted and rode again at a steady jog until, far away, he saw the shattered starlight of a lamp shining through a wet windowpane. Presently, he was in front of a small ranch house. The roof sloped down over the shed-like back of the house where the lamp was burning from the kitchen window. Dismounting, he looked through that window. The rain had fallen away to a thin drizzle, and through the misted window he could see the details of the small kitchen and the girl, washing dishes. She was as brown as the back of a cowpuncher's hand, and the darkness of her sunburned skin gave an extra flash to her teeth and her eyes. She was washing dishes and singing, and the words or the music of the song, which he could scarcely hear, kept her laughing.

Jimmy Bristol began to smile in turn. In fact, he had ridden all the way from the last town with a smile on his lips, fed from a source of upwelling inward contentment. He led his horse past the back of the house and out toward the looming shapes of great barns. He pulled open the door of the first one. The moon had risen behind the rain, and, since Bristol was looking east, he was able to see the naked skeleton of the barn, the huge beams, and the joists. There were no animals here. There was no hay in the mow. Through a gap in the roof he could hear the patter of the lonely rain inside the building. He closed the door and went on to the next barn gloomily. There were four of these huge barns dimly outlined through the rain and lying about a great corral. Beyond the corral there was a forest of entangled fencing, such as one finds on a place equipped for the handling of thousands of cattle. When he pulled open the door of the next barn, he heard a jangle of tin close beside him. He guessed that it must be a lantern hung on a nail. When he lighted a match, he found it.

By the light of the lantern he looked upon a barn whose interior was as vast as the other, which he had dimly beheld in its nakedness against that pale moonshine that made the rain luminous outside the great upper door of the hay mow. In this mow there was a small stack of hay at the farther end. Tethered to the manger and lying down were an old gray mule and a brown mustang.

He tied his chestnut to the nearest stall. Then he stripped saddle and bridle from it and held the lantern close. The knees of the chestnut were trembling.

"I thought so," said Bristol to himself.

He ran his fingers under the belly of the horse and found the muscles drawn hard. The gelding was badly gaunted by the long labor it had passed through. He took wisps of hay and fell to work, laboring earnestly until the horse was dry and glowing. Then he put out the lantern, left the barn, and went back to the house.

The girl was still in the kitchen. He looked through the dining-room window and saw an elderly man in his shirt

142

sleeves, reading a newspaper. He held the edges of the sheets between thumb and finger of one hand and between the first two fingers of the right hand, for the good reason that his right hand lacked a thumb. By the red of the scar, Bristol judged, that the wound was not many years old.

He went to the door that opened from the dining room onto the little back verandah.

"Come in," said a voice.

He pulled open the door and stepped in. The girl came to the open door of the kitchen and looked at him.

"Hello," she said.

"Take off your coat and sit down," said the elderly man.

Bristol had pulled off his hat, and the water from it leaked in rapid drops onto the floor. "I've tied a horse in your barn out there," he said. "Is that all right?"

"Sure, it's all right," said the host.

He stood up and extended his thumbless hand. Bristol took it.

"I'm Joe Graney. Here's my girl, Margaret."

"I'm Jimmy Bristol." He waited for that name to take effect, like an acid, but there was no shadow of a response on their faces—merely a polite interest. He shook hands with the girl, too, and saw that her eyes were pure, unwatered blue. She used them not like a pretty girl, reaching for admiration, but straight and true, as a man does who knows what hard work means. And she, like a man, measured his height, his shoulders, his weight.

These are honest people, he said to himself, and he felt a little uneasy. Graney was ordering him to sit down, telling the girl to put some food on the stove.

Bristol said: "Never mind. I had two platters of hot cakes in a town not more'n eight or ten miles back."

"Richtown?" asked Graney.

"I don't know the name."

Graney took off his spectacles and looked at his guest, not offensively, but with open curiosity. "You say you didn't know the name?"

"I was passing through fast," said Bristol. He hung his

slicker on a nail. Water still ran from it to the floor as Bristol sat down. "I'll go out and tuck myself up in the hay," he suggested.

"There's an extra bed here in the house," said the girl.

"Sure. You'll sleep in here," said Graney. "Won't you take a cup of coffee?"

Bristol shook his head. He felt more uneasy than ever. It seemed to him that these people would hardly be able to afford even as much as a cup of coffee to a stranger. The house was clean. So were the clothes they wore, but faded and patched to the last degree. Good people who had fallen in the world, who had missed their chances. He half wished that he had ridden on and left the place, for he could feel a silent and insistent demand being made on his conscience. He said suddenly: "Look here . . . not long ago those barns were filled with hay."

"How long ago would you say?" asked Graney.

"Two years. I saw the bits of hay high up on the sides of the walls. And the spiders haven't built many cobwebs. Those barns have been in use not so long ago."

"No, it's just two years," admitted Graney. "Two years ago Dirk Van Wey stepped in, and everything stepped off the place except the two of us." He smiled faintly and nodded.

"Who's Dirk Van Wey?" asked Bristol.

"Dirk Van Wey? You don't know him?"

"I come from pretty far south," said Bristol.

"Dirk Van Wey," said the girl, "liked the look of Kennisaw Gap and decided to settle in it two years ago. But he didn't like to have neighbors too close to him. So little by little our cows began to wander off . . . hundreds of 'em. There's only a handful left now. And when they're gone, I suppose that we'll move along, just as Dirk wants us to."

"No," said Graney calmly, steadily. "You know that I'll never move along, Margie. I'll eat grass first."

"Van Wey is a rustler, is he?" asked Bristol.

"Van Wey is anything that makes money without work."

The lips of Bristol twitched, and not with mirth. He felt

the eyes of the girl on his face and knew that she had seen him wince.

"Van Wey," said Graney, "lives in an old house of ours up in the gap, and there he'll stay, like an eagle on a rock, king of everything in sight."

"Why doesn't the sheriff take a hand with him?" asked Bristol.

"One sheriff did, and he never came back. Then a deputy sheriff took a big posse up there. They found the house empty. They scattered through the woods and the rocks. And three of them never came back. Since then, hunting down Van Wey hasn't been popular. Eh, Margie?"

The girl did not answer. Instead, she remarked: "You're tired. You'd better go to bed. I'll show you the room."

She led the way before Bristol when he had said good night to the broken rancher and ushered him into a small room that had a clean rug on the floor, a bed of enameled iron, and the first big mirror he had seen in three months. She pulled back the curtains and opened the window.

Outside the rain had stopped, but he could hear the crinkling sound of the soil, still drinking. "Look," said Bristol, "is anything going to be done about Van Wey?"

"Nothing," said the girl.

"And your father's going to stay here with his lost cause?"

"It's a horse that keeps him here. I'll tell you more in the morning, if you want to know. Good night. Sleep well." She smiled at him from the door and closed it softly after her.

She sees through me, he said to himself. And he sat down in a chair with his head bowed, regardless of the clammy cold that began to steal slowly through him from his wet clothes.

IV

"DIRK VAN WEY"

In the gray of the morning Jimmy Bristol was at the barn, where he found the chestnut in a cold sweat, with knees still trembling. He rubbed down the horse again, but it was clearly folly to take the gelding out for another journey that day. He stood for a time in the doorway of the barn, looking across the great tangle of fencing, wondering how many hundreds of cattle could be worked with ease with such accommodations. Then he went back to the house, remembering during every step of the way that Tom Denton, though he might be a fat sheriff, had the lean legs of a good rider. And how long might it be before Sheriff Tom Denton picked up his trail?

When he came to the house, he found the girl up, with a white streaking of smoke in the kitchen air. The half-thin, half-choking smell of burned paper dominated. But the stove was already humming. The draft was open. The chimney trembled with the strength of the flames that were shaking their heads inside it. Margaret Graney was swiftly rolling out a slab of biscuit dough. He went out to the wood pile, split some chunks into size for the firebox, and brought the load back to fill the wood box. Then he retired to the pump, filled the granite washbasin, washed, and shaved.

He came inside once more with a face somewhat red and tender from the quick work with the razor. Leaning in the kitchen door, he said: "Let's have it, will you?"

She was cutting out the biscuits, dipping the round cutter in flour every time. Then she began to lay the limp little rounds of dough rapidly in the greased pan. "It's not a long yarn," she said. "Father was doing well with everything until two years ago, when Dirk Van Wey appeared and asked to rent the old house in the Gap. He took the house, but, of course, he never paid the rent. It's now headquarters

146

for his gang of thieves. They've cleaned out Father, but he won't leave."

"There was something about a horse, too," Bristol suggested.

"Father had bought a stallion called Pringle, a long, drawn-out, shambly sort of a creature to look at, but Pringle can carry weight all day long and go like the wind. Father's idea was to build up the quality of the horse herd for the ranch. He wanted them all half-bred, or three-quarter-bred, or still better. He was ambitious. That was just before Van Wey came, and, of course, Pringle was the very first animal that Dirk Van Wey stole from us. The thought of Pringle sticks in the mind of my father. He doesn't mind so much the empty barns and corrals. He doesn't mind the loss of the thumb that one of Dirk's men shot off a year ago. It's the loss of Pringle that really matters."

Joe Graney came out, smiling, cheerful, and talked until breakfast was ready about deer hunting in the Gap. But all during breakfast Jimmy Bristol was silent, trying to lift from his mind the weight that lay redoubled upon it every time he looked at Margaret Graney. She had the calmness of one who understands. He felt that, above all, she understood Jimmy Bristol and had put him down for a rascal.

So he said suddenly, at the end of the meal: "Give me the right, and let me ride up through the Gap, and try to get Pringle and the back rent."

"Yeah, that would be a joke," murmured Graney. "A whole posse has tried that trick, partner."

"Crowds are not much good with fellows like Dirk Van Wey," said Jimmy Bristol. "Let me try my own hand and my own shuffle with him, will you? I'll have to trade my chestnut horse for your brown one to get there. That's all."

He saw the girl frown, very faintly, and saw her eyes look with warning at her father. And, for that matter, it was true that the chestnut was a stolen horse. So were all the horses he had ridden during the last three months, except the first one, the best one of all. As for Graney, he seemed more irritated than suspicious of the offer, as though it angered him to have a young braggart attempt the impossible.

"You can start now, if you want to," said Graney, frowning.

Yet it was chiefly to escape the cold, clear eyes of the girl that Bristol hurried from the table. There was neither disgust nor contempt in her face, but an amused understanding that was more humiliating than anything else could have been. It made Jimmy Bristol want to slay armies or cleave mountains. And always that newly awakened sense of guilt worked like a poison in him.

In two minutes Bristol sat on the brown mustang before the small ranch house, waving good bye to the faint smile of the girl and the gloomy frown of Graney. Then he turned and rode over the wet hills toward Kennisaw Gap, an axe cleft between Kennisaw Mountain and Downey Peak. He found a creek lined with cottonwoods, and the valley lifted to lodgepole pines, then to big trees, until he came into the gap itself.

It was a place of the utmost confusion. Vast boulders had dropped from the mountainsides above, and here and there were groves and clusters of big yellow pines to show that the soil was deep and good. Through the middle ran a trickle of water, flashing and dodging here and there among the rocks. That lonely mountain quiet gave him second thoughts. He camped for half the day, telling himself he was a fool to go on. But in the late afternoon he was in the saddle again.

Bristol heard the occasional tinkling of a bell, the sound growing louder and louder. Then he saw a smattering of sheep, but not the goat or the wether that carried the bell, when a voice said, close beside him: "Hello, partner!"

He turned and saw a little man seated in the lap of a great rock that offered a natural seat. He was a fellow of middle age, wearing old, battered leather chaps, and he had a rifle across his knees. His face was very thin and brown, but he had the smooth brow of a mountaineer as distinguished from the puckered forehead and the squinting eyes of a man of the desert.

"Hello," said Jimmy Bristol, reining in his horse. "Looking for something?"

He nodded toward the rifle. "Yeah. Wolves . . . and coyotes," said the other. "Seen any?"

"You're the shepherd, eh?"

"That's me. The damned coyotes, they'll be down among the rocks and trees, trying to sneak a lamb, if they get a chance. The coyotes make more trouble than the wolves."

"You're the shepherd, eh?" repeated Jimmy Bristol, hooking his right leg over the horn of the saddle and making a cigarette.

"Yeah. What are you, brother?"

"I'm an ace full on a pair of kings," said Jimmy Bristol, smiling gently.

The little man did not smile. "That's a pretty big hand," he said, "but you can lose money on it in some games."

"It takes four of a kind to beat it," answered Bristol.

"They can be found, brother . . . they can be found," said the shepherd. "Did I see a streak of yellow over there?"

He stood up, the rifle at the ready. And, turning his head a little, Jimmy Bristol actually saw the yellow-gray fur of a coyote as it flashed among the rocks, some fifty yards away.

"There's a coyote over there," agreed Bristol.

"There's more than one coyote in this Gap," said the other man. "And they know how to use cover and sneak up close on the sheep, too, day or night. There. . . ."

He jerked the rifle to his shoulder and fired. The coyote, either that which Bristol had just seen or another, had appeared suddenly on top of a rock that was not far off. It had barely pointed its head into the wind when it saw the flash of the rifle. At the clang of the gun it made a leap into the air and, landing, sprang for safety among the boulders.

This had taken a full second, perhaps, and a full second was a very long time for Jimmy Bristol. His revolver exploded. The coyote twisted sidewise in the air and disappeared.

"That was pretty smooth," said the little man, calmly as ever. "Maybe you been up here in the Gap before?"

"No, it's my first trip," answered Jimmy Bristol. "But I like the scenery and the air. I wouldn't mind staying a while in this neck of the woods."

The little man walked away among the rocks and came back, carrying by the scruff of the neck the limp body of a dead coyote. "Right behind the shoulder," he said. "You nailed him clean. He didn't suffer any. He must have died in the air. Want the skin?"

"No," said Jimmy Bristol. "I'm heading for Dirk Van Wey's place. Know where it is?"

The other stared earnestly at him. "You know Dirk Van Wey?" he asked at last.

"By reputation. Not by sight."

"There's quite a lot to know about him, take him either way. Well, I'm about ready to go in. I'll take the skin off this coyote and go in with you and show you the way. I'll introduce you."

Bristol did not offer to help in the skinning of the dead coyote. There was little need, for the mountaineer seemed to know perfectly how the skin was fitted over the supple body, and the edge of his knife seemed to have eyes and a separate sense of touch. All in a moment the skin was off, and the slender, naked little carcass lay on the ground, white, streaked with slashes of red. The pelt was folded, the knife cleaned, and the man of the rifle walked away, with Bristol riding behind him.

"What about the sheep and the coyotes?" asked Bristol.

"What about 'em? The coyotes'll keep away when they see their pal, lying dead there. What's your moniker, brother?"

"Bristol. Jim Bristol. Who are you?"

"I'm Dan Miller."

"Been in the sheep business a long time?"

"Quite a spell."

"That's what I guessed," said Bristol, "by the look of the chaps."

Dan Miller turned his sharp brown face and spoke over his shoulder. "It's easy to see too much up here," he said gravely.

"Because of the altitude, eh?" asked Jimmy Bristol.

"Yes," said Dan Miller. "A lot of fellows get up here and find it so high that they think they can see over the whole world, pretty near."

"That must make 'em dizzy," suggested Bristol.

"It does," agreed Miller. "And a lot of 'em get bad falls, too."

After these cryptic remarks he led the way through a tangle of trees and rocks until they came out suddenly into a clearing where a rambling house of rough stone masonry and logs stood beside a blue pool, into which the sunset was beginning to drop embers of red and gold. A big spruce grew before the house, and under the tree stood a table built up from the ground, meant to stay there in all weather. Tin plates and cups had been laid out on it, and one man already sat at the head of the board. On a blanket in front of the door of the house sat a broken-nosed, swarthy fellow, rolling dice with a handsome, golden-haired youth of twenty.

That pair at the side would have taken the eye ordinarily, but they were nothing compared with the fellow who sat at the table. Dark by nature and still darker from exposure to all weather, he sat with his great arms folded on top of the table, the might of his shoulders thrown loosely forward, and in the wide slit of his mouth a pipe was gripped savagely, as though he intended to bite through the stem at once. That was the air of him, at once brooding and ready for instant action. There was such a bright spark in his eyes that Jimmy Bristol could hardly conceive of eyelids that could cover and shut out entirely that uneasy light.

Dan Miller, the pair who rolled the dice, the ragged old cabin, the big mountains around them, the flaming western sky, all became a blank before the mind of Jimmy Bristol, and he saw only the face of this man. It was Dirk Van Wey, he knew at once.

"Here's a fellow wants to see you," said Dan Miller. "His

151

name is Jimmy Bristol . . . and he snagged a coyote down the way. I missed with a rifle, and he snagged it with his Colt."

"That's the right kind of a Colt to have," said the big man at the table.

"Hello, Mister Van Wey," said Bristol, and held out his hand.

It was seized with a pressure that turned his arm numb to the elbow and made him into a helpless child.

V

"BRISTOL'S CHOICE"

Jimmy Bristol was aware that the two who rolled dice had turned their heads to watch him. From the corner of his eye he saw that they were grinning and knew at once that the grip of the giant must be a famous thing among them.

"How d'you know my face? I never saw you before," said Dirk Van Wey.

Jimmy Bristol maintained his smile. The quality of it had changed a little, but it was still a smile. "When you see the cubs and the father together," said Jimmy Bristol, "it's very easy to pick out the old bear."

The mouth of Van Wey widened on either side of the pipestem, but the grimace was not a smile. He did not relax, but freshened his grip, and, though Bristol strove with all his might, until his arm shook with the effort, he could not make an impression on the iron grasp. Yet he managed to continue his smile and to keep his face unexpressive of pain.

"You can pick out bears, eh?" said Van Wey. "Well, to know that is a lot better than to know nothing. You know a Colt, too, do you?"

"I know it partly."

"Lemme see how well you know a gun," said Van Wey.

"There's a fool of a squirrel over there at the edge of this pool. Pick it off for me."

He relaxed his grip. The right hand of Jimmy Bristol was as white as a stone and his wrist crimson. It was his left hand, however, that flicked out the shining length of a revolver and fired. The red squirrel, that had been sitting up on a small stone at the edge of the glowing water, disappeared. A splash of blood remained on the stone for a sign of the life that had been there the moment before.

Dirk Van Wey puffed on his pipe and let a stream of smoke squirt out from each corner of his mouth. "You're a two-handed man," he said. "Or are you a lefty?"

"I have two hands," agreed Jimmy Bristol, putting up the gun.

"Two hands are better'n one," reasoned Dirk Van Wey. "Sit down."

There were immovable stools of stone or wood driven into the ground around the table. Jimmy Bristol sat down on the nearest one and faced Van Wey. He saw the golden-haired youth leave the dice game, step to the edge of the standing water, and pick up from the margin a pitiful little rag of blood-stained fur. He looked at it, then tossed it toward his gambling companion. Last, he turned and stared steadily at Jimmy Bristol, as a cat stares at a bird.

"What brought you up here?" asked Dirk Van Wey.

"I was sashaying through the country," said Jimmy Bristol, "and I ran into a ranch down the valley that's owned by Joe Graney."

"Yeah. He's an old friend of mine. He's my landlord. I got no complaints about him for a landlord, neither." A flash came in his eyes.

Dan Miller began to chuckle.

"Shut up, Dan," said Dirk Van Wey. "Ain't Joe Graney a fine landlord?"

"Sure he is," said Miller.

"Then shut up, and lemme talk to this two-handed man. Bristol, go on. What happened at the Graney place?"

"My horse went lame," said Jimmy Bristol. "And when

Graney heard that I was aiming for the Kennisaw Gap, he told me that he'd keep my horse and let me have a fresh one if I'd do him a favor."

"Aye," said Dirk Van Wey, "and what was that favor?"

"Just to drop by here and ask Dirk Van Wey for the rent he owed and to bring back with me a bay stallion called Pringle, which is on pasture with you here."

"How much is the rent?" asked Dirk Van Wey.

"A thousand dollars for the year."

"And how many years?"

"One year's rent is enough for me to take away."

Dirk Van Wey puffed steadily at his pipe and, by the trick of his mouth, still squirted out the smoke in two separate streams. Around the stem of the pipe he spoke, as before: "How'll you have the money? Gold or bills?"

"I'll have it the easiest way," said Jimmy Bristol.

"All right," said Dirk Van Wey. "Take it in greenbacks."

He pulled out a wallet, thumbed some bills in it, and then rapidly counted out a stack of ten hundreds.

"There's a year's rent. Times are kind of hard, Bristol. You tell Joe Graney that."

Bristol fingered the money for an instant. "It's a fair joke, but bad money," he said.

"Why is it bad?"

"The stuff is all queer."

Van Wey stared, then snatched up the money, and held one of the bills toward the western light. He grunted suddenly, balled the apparent greenbacks in his hand, and hurled them at the head of Dan Miller.

"That's what you bring in . . . counterfeit!" said Van Wey.

"It ain't possible," groaned Miller. "Nobody could make a sucker out of me like that."

He had put up one of the bills to the light in his turn by this time, and now he broke off his talking and began to curse in a subdued rumble.

Van Wey silently unbuckled a money belt. In the pause,

Jimmy Bristol heard the golden-haired young man saying: "I'm tired of this dice business, Lefty."

"All right, Harry," said the man with the broken nose. "Anything you please."

"I'll bet you there ain't a bill in this lot of the queer that Dan Miller is swearing at that has a corner torn off."

"That's a fool bet. There's always a corner torn off."

"If I'm a fool, I'll bet you a hundred bucks on it."

"All right. Or two hundred."

"Make it five hundred and be danged!" exclaimed Harry heartily.

"Five hundred it is. Dan, come let us look at that stuff."

"Take it and eat it, for all I care. I'm going to have the hide of the gent that shoved that queer on me!" exclaimed Miller, balling the paper into a wad again and tossing it to the pair on the blanket.

Dirk Van Wey had stacked up fifty twenty-dollar gold pieces in two piles.

"Here's the money," he said.

There was something electric in the air, and Jimmy Bristol felt the prickling of it down his spine. He took up the money, counted it with a rapid clinking of the coins, and pocketed the gold. Only now was the circulation returning to his right hand.

"About the hoss," said Dirk. "Come along."

He led the way into a wide shed where half a dozen horses were tied to the mangers on either side of a mow in which the hay had sunk lower than breast-high. Van Wey pointed at the animals on the farther side of the mow. "Pringle is over there. Pick him out," he said.

Again that sense of electric suspense swept through Jimmy Bristol. Something very important depended on the correctness of his judgment, something more than the mere possession of the stallion.

The light was dull. The sun was down, and, though both the western doors of the shed were open, only a reddish haze was flowing into the shed. Big Jimmy Bristol shaded his eyes and stared. Of the six horses, three were bays that faced him. The high mangers shut them off at the breast. One was a big, noble creature, with the gloss of polished bronze. That could hardly be Pringle, the stallion, that had been described as a lean and ugly horse. There were two of the bays, in fact, that looked, from the head, like long-eared, long-legged, ramble-shacks. The temples of one were rather sunken, as though by many years.

Jimmy Bristol hissed suddenly like a snake, and every horse in the shed jumped and threw up its head. All, that is, except the bay with the sunken temples.

"I'll take that fellow to be Pringle," said Bristol.

Dirk Van Wey grunted. "All right," he said. "You picked him. And you picked a good one. He can carry a ton all day long, and I need a hoss that can pack a ton."

He did, in fact. He was hardly taller than Jimmy Bristol, but he was a square chunk of power from head to heels. When he moved his arms, his muscles filled his shirt sleeves.

"It's a pile better for you to pick out Pringle than to pick out . . . bad luck," said Dirk Van Wey suddenly. "Know that?" He clapped his hand on the shoulder of Bristol and let the grip of it remain there, bruising the flesh against the bone.

"I know something else," said Jimmy Bristol, "that, if you don't take your hand off my shoulder, I'll split your wishbone for you. And if you ever put a hand on me again, I'll do the same thing!"

"Will you?" said Dirk Van Wey. And he kept his grip intact.

VI

"OUTLAW HOSPITALITY"

In the pause they stared solemnly at one another. Fear leaped like a cold snake up the back of Jimmy Bristol as he saw the eyes of Dirk Van Wey apparently drawing nearer to him. But suddenly the hand that gripped his shoulder was withdrawn.

"It's all right, brother," said Van Wey. "I won't lean on you ag'in unless I have to. There's the dinner bell. Let's go." It was the roar of the cook, bellowing—"Come and get it! Come and get it!"—and banging on a tin pan.

Van Wey led the way back to the table, where a fellow with a ship tattooed on one arm and the rather blurred face of a pretty girl on the other forearm, was shoveling fried steaks onto the plates. In the center of the table rose on a platter a great mound of potatoes, fried to a golden brown. That and pone and black coffee were all of supper.

As they settled themselves around the table, the cook began to pour coffee into the cups, and golden-haired Harry said: "I want two hundred bucks, chief. I've just lost a bet."

"*I* ain't got two hundred bucks," said Van Wey. "Dan paid me with some queer . . . and Bristol, here, has just collected the rent for the landlord. I'm pretty near cleaned out. You had better go fishing for that two hundred bucks, if you want it, Weston."

"And me pulling out in the morning," said the man with the broken nose, "it kind of rushed Harry a little to raise the money."

"You pulling out in the morning, Parr?" asked Van Wey.

"Yeah. You know I got an engagement over the hills and far away."

Dan Miller said nothing. He lowered his head, until his sharp nose was almost touching his food, and ate in a thoughtful silence. For some reason Jimmy Bristol felt that the thoughts of Dan Miller were fixed firmly upon him.

"It's a darkish sort of night for a ride through the Gap," said Van Wey to Bristol. "You better put up here tonight."

"Got an extra blanket?"

"Yeah. *And* an extra bed. *And* an extra room," said Van Wey. "There's a lot of space in the old shack. It was built by a man that had a big family. What's his name, Dan?"

"Gresham," said Dan Miller. "Oliver Gresham built it. He had three thousand head of cows, running here in the

Gap and down in the valley. He done pretty well for a long while."

"Yeah," said Van Wey. "He done pretty well. He kind of went to pieces before the end, though."

As he finished speaking, his mouth stretched. Bristol at last recognized the grimace as a smile, or the nearest that Van Wey could come to an expression of mirth.

"What happened to him?" asked Bristol.

"His girl married Joe Graney. The cows still grew fat. But then the rustlers, they sort of edged in and skimmed the cream off the pan. There's been a terrible lot of rustlers around these parts," said Dan Miller solemnly.

Lefty Parr rubbed his broken nose. His eyes shone. At last his mirth grew greater than his self-control, and he burst into hearty laughter.

"Whatcha laughing at?" demanded Van Wey.

"Nothing. I just thought of a joke. Nothing much to tell," said Lefty Parr, and concealed his face behind the upward tipping of his tin coffee cup.

The cook came to the table and took a place, reaching his greasy hands for what he wanted. They called him Rance. He looked like a low-grade Scandinavian with a great flat slab of a face, a mouth that was a brother to the mouth of Van Wey, and a pair of faded-blue eyes. He never looked a man in the face, but always askance. When he talked, he kept turning his head from side to side, as though he were searching for a hidden thing in the background.

Van Wey filled and emptied his plate three times, poured a fourth cup of steaming coffee down his throat, filled, lighted his pipe, and rose from the table.

"Where you going, chief?" asked Harry Weston.

"For a walk," said Van Wey.

"Far?"

"Far enough," answered the chief, and, turning his back on them, he strode away, letting the rumble of his voice come back over his shoulder. "The three of you and Rance can take care of Bristol. Make him mighty comfortable, I hope."

There was an odd accent on the last words, and Bristol heard it. He did not need to see the glances that were covertly exchanged between Harry Weston and broken-nosed Lefty Parr in order to understand that the mode of their entertaining might be distinctly original.

"What about a game?" Weston asked gently at the end of supper.

"I'm flat broke," said Jimmy Bristol. "I haven't a penny on me."

"I told you he was a high-stepper," said Lefty Parr dryly. "He don't call a thousand bucks a penny. He's one of those gents that picks his teeth with diamonds maybe, and washes his hands in rose water, eh?"

He leered across the table at Jimmy Bristol, and the quiet, steady smile of Jimmy Bristol answered him.

"We'll play for fun," said Harry Weston. "I'm broke, too. We'll play for matches. Poker, eh?"

"I'm tired," answered Jimmy Bristol. "One of you fellows tell me where to find a blanket and a spare bed?"

They looked at one another.

"I'll show you," said Rance, the cook, who was shoveling the last of the fried potatoes into his vast mouth. He rose, took a swallow of coffee, while standing, and then led the way to the house. Behind him, Bristol felt three pairs of sharp eyes, following and probing.

By the door hung a lantern that the cook lighted and led the way through the open door and across a big room with a low ceiling. The flooring was broken. Some of the masonry of the fireplace at the farther end of the room had fallen down on the hearth. And it was plain that, for Van Wey and his followers, the house was no more than a strongly protected camp, a place to sleep in rather than a place to live in.

Rance led the way up creaking stairs, humming a song in the guttural depths of his throat. Down the upper hall he turned until he came to the end of it, and kicked open a door.

"How does this sound to you, brother?" he asked.

It was a good-size room, with a single cot stowed in a corner, and a tousled blanket heaped on the foot of that bed. There was no other furniture, not a washstand, or a chair, or any rag of a rug.

"Regular Palace Hotel," said Jimmy Bristol with his smile. "Bath with every room, telephone, hot and cold running water. A regular home, eh?"

Rance held up the lantern and slowly turned around.

"It's better than a forecastle on an old hooker off the Horn, laying her nose ag'in' the westerlies for six weeks, like I've seen," he said.

"It'll do for me," agreed Bristol. "Can you leave me that lantern?"

"Sure," said the cook. "I can find my way around by dark in this place."

"Makings?" asked Bristol, holding out a battered little sack of tobacco and wheat-straw papers.

The cook hesitated. Then, with an almost imperceptible shrug of his shoulders, he accepted the makings, tore off a paper with his greasy fingers, and built a smoke. He returned the makings to Jimmy Bristol and was fumbling for a match when Bristol held a lighted one before him. The faded blue eyes of Rance shifted up uncomfortably toward Bristol's face. He nodded a little apologetically, as he used the proffered flame. And then, standing back with a worried frown on his fleshy forehead, he puffed on the cigarette, turned toward the door, and now turned back again.

"What's the matter, Rance?" asked Bristol. "Anything on your mind?"

"No," muttered the cook.

He came a stride nearer to Bristol and looked earnestly into his face, as though seeing him for the first time. "Well," said Rance, "what I was just wondering was . . . er . . . I dunno. . . . It's all right, I guess."

He went back toward the door. His baffled eyes stared again at Bristol, but in another moment he had stepped out and closed the door with a grunted: "Good night."

Bristol listened to the muffled tread of the footfalls going down the hall. He heard the squeaking of the stairs as the cook descended. A lonely feeling came over him, as though a friend had just departed.

"Murder," whispered Bristol to himself. "Murder is what it means."

VII

"THE CAT'S WARNING"

The heart of Rance had been touched by the small courtesies that Jimmy Bristol had showed him. Rance had been stirred to the very verge of speech—yet he had not spoken. He had gone as from a death chamber.

It seemed to Jimmy Bristol that he had been the greatest fool in the world to allow himself to be herded into the house, when all the while he had known that the money which Dirk Van Wey had given him was not intended to be kept in his pocket for long. It was simply a jest on the part of Van Wey, a brutal jest, to appear to give merely for the sake of taking away again. He said that he had gone for a walk and did not know when he would return. In the meantime his inference was perfectly clear. He had four men here. If they were worth their salt, they would handle Jimmy Bristol in a manner that he would never forget, and either bury him or send him packing as fast as he could go. To a brute like Dirk Van Wey such a scheme would be a very clever way of testing his men, keeping them up on their mettle.

Bristol went to the window of the room and looked out. The wall of the house dropped sheer down without a break. Below the foundations a steep bank continued the fall. It was a full sixty feet from the sill of his window to the level. Suppose that he made a rope out of the blanket and his own clothes, still he would never be able to get to the ground without broken bones. As for going out the door, not even a ghost could walk down that hallway or those stairs without making the warped boards creak like an empty wagon on a rough road.

A scratching sound made him jump. It was an old gray tiger cat that was reaching up from the floor to sharpen its claws on the edge of the canvas tick of the bed. Bristol sat down on the edge of the bed, picked the cat up, and let it stretch out on his thigh. The cat accepted the position at once, closed its eyes, and, purring with content, began to work its claws into the tough cloth that covered his knees. The cat was very old and very ill cared for. Its whiskers were white as silver. With the tip of a finger he could count its vertebrae from behind its ears to the root of its fur. Plainly the animal was not fed, but had to hunt for its living, and increasing age made this more and more difficult. He could see it waiting for death at last under the lee of a southern bank, its paws tucked under its body, purring for gratitude because of the warmth of the sun.

But the cat was a poor beast, incapable of reason, and therefore trapped by circumstance. Jimmy Bristol was a human creature with a brain, yet from the moment he had met Dan Miller in the Gap he had allowed himself to drift on from one point to another until he found himself closed in this impasse. He had done such things before. He was a wine taster, and danger always had been the wine that he loved. The danger that thickened around him in the Gap had been a glorious delight to him. There had been only one moment of real fear, and that was when Dirk Van Wey gripped his shoulder in the barn. Now there was fear again, real fear. The breath of it was in the cold damp of the room.

He had one consolation. If it were impossible for him to get out of the room unnoticed, it would also be impossible for the men of the house to get into the room without waking him. There was a key in the door. He got up and turned that key, and felt the rusty bolt slide home. They would have to beat down that door to get at him. And they were not apt to do that. Morning might bring him new ideas. So he pulled off his boots, opened the window, blew out the lantern, and lay down in his clothes to be ready for any alarm. The old gray cat curled up against his breast, and the hoarse music of its purring put him to sleep. The last he remembered was the secret voice of the wind through the foliage of the big tree outside the house.

He wakened with a start and in another world. Pale moonlight streamed before him, and a monstrous tiger with dim, gray stripes was before him. Only gradually he realized that he was lying in the bed in the house of Dirk Van Wey, and that the moonshine was streaking through the window. The huge tiger, that stood with ears laid savagely back and with tail lashing its sides, was no other than the old gray cat that had awakened him by its sudden start, and that now stood on the edge of the bed, staring toward a corner of the room.

Bristol turned his head in that direction and almost exclaimed aloud. For a whole section of the ceiling hung down, a big square section of the boards. And now, into the dimness, dropped what seemed to be a swaying rope ladder. It began to swing and sway more violently. The boots and spurs of a man appeared, then his knees, his hips, his head, and shoulders.

Bristol drew a revolver and leveled it. Having reached the floor, the intruder waved his hand. The rope ladder gradually ascended. The trap door closed on soundless hinges. Peering through the gloom, Bristol made out the profile of that broken-nosed man, Lefty Parr.

The head of Lefty had turned only once toward the bed. Now, as though perfectly assured that his victim slept, he raised his face and watched the soundless closing of the trap. In that moment the gray cat couched itself as if for a spring, and big Jimmy Bristol glided from the bed and across the floor. Moonlight bathed him to the knees, and, as though the flash of it struck the corner of Lefty's eye, he whirled suddenly, gun in hand.

The leveled Colt in Bristol's hand made his own weapon waver. Then it hung at his side at the length of a limp arm. Yet there was little or no fear in his face.

"Walk over to the bed and put the gun on it," said Jimmy Bristol.

Lefty Parr obeyed. He laid down the gun with a sort of reverence and, straightening, turned to Bristol again.

"Now stand over in the moonlight," said Bristol softly. "And take care of your hands. No quick moves, Lefty."

"All right," said Lefty.

He stepped into the moonlight until the bright current of it cut across his face at the sag in his nose. Still he seemed perfectly calm.

"Now, what's up, brother?" asked Bristol.

Lefty made a gesture with both hands, palms up, inviting Bristol to see for himself.

"A thousand bucks is a whole lot of money. Is that it?" asked Bristol.

"Yeah," said Lefty, "it's too much to throw away."

"On rent, eh? Van Wey left it up to you fellows to get it?"

"Something like that," muttered Lefty Parr.

"Where are the rest of 'em? Who elected you? I mean, for the dirty work."

"We drew for the first black ace. I collected it," said Parr. "I wasn't going to bump you off. I was just going to stick you up and take the dough."

"Tap me on the head, maybe, for a settler?"

"Well, maybe. I dunno." His casual attitude remained.

"Where are the rest of 'em, Lefty?" asked Bristol.

"I dunno. That's their business."

"I like a man that talks up," suggested Bristol. He crossed the floor. The muzzle of his revolver he laid on the square chin of Lefty Parr.

"That's no good," said Parr. "It wouldn't buy you anything to blow my head off."

"It would make me a lot happier, though," said Bristol. "It's worth dying for, Lefty, to put away a rat of your size."

Lefty considered him with a sudden squinting of the eyes. He said nothing.

"Tell me where those fellows are . . . all of 'em."

Lefty moistened his lips. The tip of his tongue glistened in the moonshine. "Dan Miller was up in the attic, handling the trap and the ladder for me," he said. "And out in the hall is Harry Weston."

"Where's Rance?"

"I dunno, exactly. Maybe outside the house."

His tone inferred that the whereabouts of Rance did not greatly matter.

"Has Van Wey come back?"

"Maybe. I dunno. I ain't seen him."

"You lie," said Bristol.

The first real sign of fear was the shudder of Lefty's body. "I'm telling you straight," he gasped.

Bristol considered for an instant. It might well be that Dan Miller was still working his way quietly down from the attic. In that case, it was time to move at once. He merely paused to ask: "Ever use this room this way before?"

"No," said Lefty Parr.

"That's a louder lie than the rest," said Bristol. "You keep the hinges of it oiled. That shows it's always ready for use."

He saw the Adam's apple work up and down in the throat of his captive as Lefty swallowed. It was confession enough.

"Walk to the door," commanded Bristol.

Lefty obeyed. He stood at the door, whispering, "What's the idea going to be, Bristol?"

Bristol laid the muzzle of the Colt against the small of Lefty's back, reached past him with the other hand, and turned the key. Then he fastened the grip of his left hand on Parr's neck from behind.

"Pull the door open and walk out," he ordered.

"Hey, wait a minute," argued Parr, still whispering. "If I walk out, you know that snaky devil of a Weston is out there."

"That's all right. You'll be walking first."

"He wouldn't let up because I went first. He'd shoot me

165

to get at you. He ain't human. He'd do a murder for ten dollars. He'd do it for fun."

Bristol remembered the handsome, cold face of Harry Weston and knew that what he heard was true. He merely answered: "Better take your chance with him. You've got no chance with me. If I have to leave the room without you, I'll leave you dead behind me, Lefty. Killing snakes is not murder, Parr. Open that door."

Lefty Parr's head dropped weakly back with a groan. But he pulled the door open, nevertheless, and before them was the velvet blackness of the hallway.

VIII

"GUNS IN THE DARK"

The voice of Lefty Parr went before them, whining, appealing, with the same shiver in the sound that there was in his body. "Harry, don't shoot. Harry, you ain't going to shoot, boy. He's got me. He tricked me, and he got me."

Out of the darkness down the hallway a voice laughed softly. "You used up all your luck tonight, Lefty. I'm sorry for you. Are you walking ahead of the big boy?"

"I'm right ahead of him," said Lefty Parr, stepping slowly into the blackness, with his arms stretched out before him. "He's got me by the neck. He's got a gun rammed into the small of my back. Harry, don't shoot, for God's sake."

"No, I won't shoot," said Harry Weston. "I'll let the big shoemaker walk right out of the house and never try to stop him. I'll let him walk away with the coin just because I don't want to hurt your feelings, eh?"

Bristol, straining his eyes through the blackness, could make out nothing, but the hallway was so narrow that few bullets could fly at random. Besides, since Weston had been in the hall for some time, his eyes had probably grown accustomed to the blackness.

"He's going to do it. He's going to kill me," breathed Lefty Parr to himself. "Bristol, you see how it is. It ain't any good . . . it ain't going to help you. . . ."

"The best way with rats is to let 'em kill one another," Bristol said. "Stop squirming and walk straight ahead. Faster."

Lefty cried: "Harry, will you listen?"

"Yeah, I'll listen, if listening will do you any good."

"I always liked you, Harry. You was always about my best friend. It's going to be a murder if you shoot me. Harry, if things was different, I never would pull a trigger on you. You know that, don't you?"

"I know what you'd do," said the voice of Harry Weston. "Stop your whining, and take it like a man."

"Then shoot low!" screamed Lefty. "Don't shoot breast high or head high. Shoot low. Maybe you'll snag his legs as well as mine. Don't go and murder me, Harry. Don't shoot for the breast."

"Shut your mouth, you cur!" snarled Weston. "You've never been a whole man. You never been more than half a man. Now you take your chances the way you find 'em. This ain't a pack of cards that you can stack."

He laughed as he said it, and suddenly big Jimmy Bristol could endure the thing no more. The direction of that voice seemed to him to come rather high and to the right, as though Weston were standing with his back to the wall, thus giving greater clearance for bullets to go by him. As for poor Lefty Parr, he was squeezing himself to nothing against the left-hand wall.

Now Bristol tried a snap shot in the direction of his guess. The gun raised a thunder in his ears. There was an instant flash and report in response. By the flash he saw that all his guessing had been wrong, for the golden-headed youth lay flat on the floor of the hall with his gun stretched out before him. As Weston fired, Parr shrieked, then doubled up in the hands of Bristol. Bristol let the writhing body fall and bounded ahead. He could thank his stockinged feet and the screeching of the wounded man that made his coming silent.

Again the gun flashed, this time not from the floor, but higher up and to the left, for Weston had moved between shots. He was kneeling, and, as the flash of his gun showed him, Bristol fired at the dimly revealed body, the white glimpse of the face. He knew that he had missed, but he was not a stride away, and through the darkness he reached out and struck with the length of his Colt. The weight of the blow fell on metal, and the sudden force of that shock knocked his own gun out of his hand. He was disarmed!

Then sinewy arms were cast about him. It seemed that a lithe python had cast a coil around him and was striking his body with sledge-hammer blows. Yet this was that slender fellow, Harry Weston. Amazement stunned Bristol's brain. He would have given his word that he could break the man in two like a brittle stick, and yet he found himself fighting in the darkness for his life.

"Lemme have some light. I don't wanta die in the dark. Lemme have some light. Gimme a candle, even. I gotta have light!"

Jimmy Bristol heard the groaning clearly. He was working for a proper hold or a place where he could plant a telling blow, but still it was like struggling with an active snake that continually shifts his grip. A fist like the steel face of a hammer struck the side of his head. It struck again, lower down, and thudded against his cheekbone. He ducked his head down and struck. His blow glanced from a muscular body, and his fist hammered against the wall, numbing his arm.

Footfalls were racing up the stairs. The voice of Dan Miller shouted: "Where are you? What's up?"

"I got him here. I don't need you. I'm going to tear the big hunk of cheese in two," gasped Harry. Weston. "I'm going to strangle him. Leave me alone!"

It seemed to big Jimmy Bristol that in fact he soon might be helpless against this tigerish fighter. The fellow had the strength of a wildcat. He never paused for a breathing space. Then, hooking his left hand down and striking hard, Bristol felt his fist drive between Weston's arm and the ribs. He jerked his arm up until it fitted under the other's armpit. Then, bending his hand over the shoulder, he reached Weston's face. He was promptly bitten through the palm of his hand. That agony did not matter. He fumbled lower down and curled the steel-hard tips of his fingers around Weston's chin. Golden-haired Harry cursed. For now, with a mighty leverage in his favor, Bristol put forth all his strength and felt Weston's head go back by jerks, little by little.

"What's up, Harry?" cried Dan Miller through the choking darkness.

"Dan! Oh, Danny!" screamed Parr's voice. "He murdered me. Harry murdered me! Gimme water! Gimme a light! Oh, please, don't let me die in the dark like this!"

"He . . . he's got me" gasped Weston.

Bristol, with a desperate effort, snapped back the head of Harry Weston at that moment. The whole body of the man gave, and into the body Bristol struck with all his might. The expelled breath of Weston gasped at his ear. He raised his head and struck three hammer blows against the side of Weston's head. And at last Harry Weston dropped like a limp rag to the floor of the hall.

Bristol was free barely in time. Dan Miller, bewildered by the darkness, had fired a bullet over his head to give himself one flash of light. That flash, however, found Bristol with his hands free. He saw Miller clearly, and the slanting well of the stairs behind him. At that thin wedge of a face he struck with all his might. His fist struck a glancing blow. The revolver exploded again, and the bullet ripped through the wall beside Bristol as he sprang in, reaching for the gun.

He found the wrist that held it, lurched on, and toppled down the slope of the stairs head over heels, with Dan Miller's arms and legs entangled in his own. They regained footing for an instant almost at the first landing, but they fell again. The head and shoulders of Bristol struck against the closed shutters of the window that was meant to light the stairway and knocked those shutters wide, so that for an instant a blinding stream of moonlight poured over them.

The grasp of Bristol luckily found Miller's gun hand and closed on it. He lurched forward to tear himself free from Miller's clinging grip. But the little man was almost as tenacious as Harry Weston. In the effort that Bristol was making, he merely sent them both staggering down the lower flight of the stairs. Strangely enough, they did not fall until they struck the level of the big room beneath, and above them they could hear Lefty Parr screeching: "Boys, don't leave me! Don't leave me! Don't lemme die alone!"

Then they hit the floor and tumbled head over heels across it. The shaft of moonlight followed and fell upon them and the large form of Rance, the cook. He had an axe in his hands, and he came toward them with the weapon gripped and held high over his head. His face was convulsed. Jimmy Bristol could see the desperate crime in it by the moonshine.

And little Dan Miller, with incredible strength, was grappling at the hands of Bristol, snarling the while at Rance: "Strike, Rance! Sink the axe into him! Kill him, the big devil! Now, now, now!"

For an instant, as they rolled and struggled, Miller was on top, and Bristol's head was clearly exposed for a blow. To that purpose, Rance sprang closer and swung up the axe again. Death glimmered on the chisel edge of it, and Bristol, looking up in an agony, clearly saw the glimmering of the danger. But something staggered Rance as though a club had struck him. His whole body wavered. The axe shuddered wildly back and forth in his grasp. Prison shakes! Bristol had heard of them before, but never seen them—the terrible and utter unnerving of a man who has felt the grasp of the law too long. In the last emergency, in the moment of utter need, strength goes out of those poor victims, and fear takes its place. So Rance shuddered now, helplessly.

That moment of delay was enough for Bristol. Above him he heard the wounded man, groaning in the sickness of his pain again. He heard the voice of that wildcat, Harry Weston, calling hollowly: "Hold him, Danny. I'm coming!"

Now Bristol managed to tear the gun from Miller's hand at last. He struck with the barrel. The warding hand of Miller checked the blow. He could pull the trigger, of course—but that was a killing almost in cold blood, and he had no appetite for such a slaughter. He struck again, harder, and part of the length of the steel barrel rang on the skull of Miller. That game little man twisted his legs together, kicked out once, and lay still.

IX

"THE STRANGER"

There was Rance, the ex-sailor, still between him and the door as Bristol came to his feet, charging. The axe was raised again on high, but, when Rance saw the leveled revolver, he shrank back against the wall with a groan and threw up a hand before his face. Bristol, disdaining to touch a man so helpless, ran past him into the open. Dirk Van Wey—where was he? The rest had fought hard enough, but where was Dirk Van Wey? It seemed to Bristol that the giant was about to step out from behind the trunk of the big tree. Then as the door of the horse shed was torn open, surely Dirk Van Wey would spring upon him with his irresistible hands—or a straight tongue of flame would dart at him from the muzzle of Van Wey's gun.

He reached the place of the stallion and found Pringle just lurching to his feet, the last of the horses to rise. A saddle and a bridle hung from the peg on the wall. There was no time for the saddle. Even the seconds used for pulling the bridle over the head of the horse were moments in which all the blood in Bristol's heart seemed to flow away. He blessed the stallion for parting its teeth to receive the bit and, with the throat latch still unfastened, he ran toward the door of the shed again with the horse trotting willingly behind him.

He saw the form of Harry Weston come running through the doorway of the house, opposite him, with a rifle in his hands. As Bristol swung onto the back of the stallion, he saw the rifle go to Weston's shoulder. Twice the gun barked, but the bullets sang nowhere near Bristol. As he straightened out the stallion to full speed up the Gap, he saw Weston rub a hand across his forehead, as though trying to wipe away the cloud that hung over his eyes. No doubt he was still more than half stunned by the blows that he had received from powerful fists. Again and again the rifle barked, and this time the bullets stung the air close to Bristol's head. Then the maze of trees and great rocks received him and shut him off from danger.

But where was Dirk Van Wey? That question haunted him on the way down the pass. Every moment he seemed to hear the beating of the hoofs of horses behind him. The wind rose and howled through the Gap, and to Bristol it was the voice of the giant. Yet no Van Wey appeared!

The stallion went under him like silk. One hardly needed a saddle. For though withers and backbone thrust up, the gait of this daisy cutter was like the motion of a boat down a smooth current. Leaving the steep descent, he opened up Pringle to a sweeping gallop that poured the hills behind them like moving waves of the sea. With hardly a break, the tall horse maintained that gait until, far before them, Bristol saw the old, squat outline of the ranch house of Joe Graney. The moon was far up the sky now, whitening the hills. When he came close to the house, he saw the hoof-marked dust in front of it as bright as water under that steady light, with little shadows as black as ink, outlining the hollows where horses had stamped at the hitch rack. There he dismounted and threw the reins. At once the ugly head of Pringle dropped low. He pointed a back hoof and seemed instantly to fall asleep on his feet.

At the door of the house Jimmy Bristol paused and looked over the sweep of the landscape. The hills marched away in steady succession, and the mountains were half hidden in the moon haze. It seemed impossible that he had started not many hours ago toward the Kennisaw Gap. That must have been in another life, or in a dream. Yet he could feel a lump on the side of his head and another on his cheek where the hard fists of Harry Weston had gone home. His whole body was bruised and sore from that tumble down the stairs, and, where the grip of Dan Miller had lain in his flesh, it burned as though it had been scorched.

Then he tried the latch, found the door open, and walked into the darkness of the house. It was not like the damp cold of the stone-and-log building in the Kennisaw Gap. A faint, half stale odor of cookery hung in the air of the hall. There was a gentle hush as of sleep. He could almost hear the breathing of the sleepers. He thought of the girl, then, and smiled. Weariness could be permitted to come over him now. He could relax for a few moments—though not for long.

Dirk Van Wey by this time must know what had happened to his money, his horse, and his men. And Dirk Van Wey would follow him around the world to be quits for the defeat. It was only the first trick of a long game that Bristol felt he had won.

In the meantime he was hungry. He would get to the kitchen, start the fire, and heat some coffee. After that, he would have to waken Joe Graney. It would be worthwhile to see the face of the rancher when he looked again on Pringle. He was almost at the end of the narrow hallway when a door opened. It was the girl.

"Hush, Margaret. It's Bristol," he whispered.

"Ah, thank God," he heard her answer softly. "This will make Dad the happiest man in the world. Look!" She pushed open the door to the dining room. A lamp was burning and, through the doorway, big Jimmy Bristol saw the rancher, sitting with his head bowed upon one arm, asleep. His mutilated hand was extended before him, palm up. It was like the last act of one in despair, asking alms from an unheeding world.

Something pinched the heart of Jimmy Bristol.

"He wouldn't go to bed," said the girl. "He was in mis-

ery. He wanted to ride after you and make you come back.
I told him it was too late . . . that he'd never overtake you.
And here you are . . . safe." She called: "Father!"

He groaned in his sleep. To Bristol's ear it was like an
echo of the sick moaning he had heard from the wounded
Lefty Parr on that same night. The girl rounded the table
and touched the shoulder of Graney. He wakened with a
start, jumping to his feet, exclaiming, still half in his dream:
"Don't go, Bristol! Don't. . . ."

"He's back. He's safe," said the girl.

He rubbed his eyes in confusion, and she began to laugh
with such a happiness in her eyes that Bristol seemed invited to join in the mirth. Joe Graney came to him and
gripped him with that deformed hand of his. "Well, this is
pretty good! This is pretty good," he said. "I half thought
that I'd never . . . Margie, she thought that you wouldn't
have the nerve to go right on ahead . . . but I was sure you
would. I'm glad that she was right. I kind of thought that
I'd sent you off to be murdered. That was the way I felt
. . . like a murderer. And here you are back, son."

He blinked his eyes, and there was moisture in them that
stung the heart of Bristol again. But he muttered: "Margie
thought I wouldn't go, eh?"

He looked at the girl, and she frowned a little, shaking
her head.

"No one man could do it. No one man could walk in on
them. I knew that, Jimmy."

"Anyway," said Jimmy Bristol, "I brought back some
luck for you, Graney. Here's a part of it."

"Hush," said the girl, "or you'll wake him. The stranger."

"Who?" asked Bristol, with his hand in his pocket.

"A man dropped in last evening. We put him up, of
course, for the night."

It was on the tip of Bristol's tongue to ask what man it
might be, or a description of him, but the act he was engaged in was too important for that. He pulled out the gold
pieces and spilled them on the table.

"That's only one year's rent," he said. "Van Wey didn't

seem to be able to spare any more than that for the moment."

Joe Graney picked up one of the coins, turned it in his hand, and stared helplessly at it. Then Margaret Graney caught Bristol's arm and shook it a little. Her eyes were starting out. There were white patches of fear in her face.

"You went . . . into the Kennisaw Gap?" she breathed.

"Sure," said Bristol, "and Dirk Van Wey was glad to see me. I suppose he'd been anxious to pay that rent for a long time. He forked it right out. And the horse, too."

She looked carefully into his face. "There's been a fight!" she gasped. "You've been hurt. Father, do you see that?"

"Wait a minute," said Graney. "Did you say the horse, too?"

"Yes."

"You brought back Pringle with you?"

"He's out at the hitch rack in front of the house."

"Great Moses," murmured Joe Graney. He shook his head, but could not seem to clear the cloud of astonishment that possessed it.

"We'll go out and see the horse," said the girl.

There was no joy in *her* face—only trouble and anxiety. That was the woman of it, thought Bristol. The terror of the unknown was on her and would take many words to dispel.

"We'll go out and see Pringle. I don't know how you did it, Bristol. I can't even ask yet. But maybe it's the turning point. Maybe it's the beginning of a change. . . ." He turned, as he spoke, toward the door into the hall but paused. "We've waked him up. That's too bad," muttered Joe Graney. "Here he comes now."

All that Bristol saw at first was a dim shape that moved among the dense shadows of the hall, obscure as a fish that stirs in dusky waters. But now the form of the man crossed the doorway into the light of the dining-room lamp, and Bristol recognized the battered face of Sheriff Tom Denton, who stood there with a gun in his hand.

X

"ON THE ROAD"

What Jimmy Bristol was aware of later was that neither the girl nor her father uttered a single exclamation. All he was conscious of at the time was the thunderclap in his own brain as he saw the sheriff emerge from the shadows, carrying the gun that was pointed at Bristol's body.

"Just stick 'em up, Jimmy," he said.

Jimmy Bristol, inch by inch, fought with his hands to make them rise as high as his head.

"Is this right?" said Graney suddenly. "It's in my own house, man!"

"It's in your house, but it's in my county," said Denton. "I'm the sheriff, Graney. I didn't tell you, when I came, because this gent is the kind that makes friends and keeps them. It's a good thing for the law that I didn't talk too much, either, by the look of things. Bristol, turn your face to the wall."

Jim Bristol obeyed. In the despair that came over him, he pressed his forehead and the flat of his hands against the wall, while he felt the muzzle of the sheriff's gun lodge against the small of his back. All was of the recognized procedure. A large revolver was taken from Bristol's person, to say nothing of a very capable jackknife. The sheriff stepped back a little.

"Turn around, Jimmy," he ordered.

Jimmy, turning, saw the revolver still covering him closely, while in the sheriff's left hand dangled a pair of manacles.

"Hold out one wrist," commanded Tom Denton.

Jimmy Bristol did not move. Now the color was gone from his eyes, and they were a blaze of light.

"You're helpless, and the sheriff means business," said the girl calmly.

He looked suddenly at Margaret Graney and saw that the

white of her face denied the smoothness of her voice.

"I mean business, all right, son," said Tom Denton. "I don't wanta do you no harm, but you know what you're wanted for."

Jimmy Bristol held out his wrists, and the handcuffs were rapidly snapped in place.

"That's that," said the sheriff. "Now I guess you're as good as in the death house, Bristol, and God help your soul. I'm sorry for you."

"Death house?" cried Joe Graney.

He reached for the arm of the sheriff, who exclaimed: "Don't touch me, Graney. I can see that the boy's done you a good turn. But don't touch me. I belong to the law just now, and so does he. I've got my job to do, and I'm going to do it."

"Yes," said Bristol bitterly. "Five thousand dollars' worth of a job, at that."

"It ain't the money so much," answered the sheriff, flushing, "but it's the way you made fools of us back there in town. Beginning with me, you made fools of us all. You might have known that we'd do some riding to get onto your trail."

"I knew. I took the wrong chance," admitted Bristol.

"You knew," said the girl, "and yet you came back here, when you might have ridden on?"

Bristol made a sudden gesture that caused the manacles to clank musically. "Sooner or later my sort of a trail comes to this wind-up," he told her. "I'm not so sorry."

"That's what *you* say," said Joe Graney. "But what I know is that I've been the bait in the trap for you. And God forgive me. Sheriff, what's this boy charged with?"

"Murder," said the sheriff bluntly. "The shooting of a gent in Tombstone about three months ago. After that, stealing a few hosses to help him along his way. That's about all." He smiled sourly and added: "Winged a fellow back in town yesterday. Fellow that had trailed him all the way from Tombstone. And made a fool of me, too. The biggest fool that I've ever seen. How come you to drill that gent in Tombstone, Bristol?"

"Poker," said Bristol. "The deck of cards on the table wasn't enough for him. He helped himself to extra deals out of his sleeve."

"That so?" murmured the sheriff. "Well, in this part of the world shooting comes to folks that fool too much with the deal in a poker game. Too bad for you, Bristol. But maybe the jury will do some considering."

"Maybe," said Bristol shortly. "But I'll tell you who'll have to do the considering for all of us if we stay here long."

"Who?" asked the sheriff.

"The coroner," answered Bristol. "That money comes from Dirk Van Wey. And outside the door is the horse that Dirk likes better than anything else in this world. Dirk left me to be trimmed by some of his boys. He was testing the lot of 'em. But the test went bad, and I had the luck. He won't let the stuff go, though. If he can guess my back trail, he'll be here before long, and he won't be alone."

"We'll see that horse," said the sheriff.

The whole group moved out into the moonlight. Bristol walked at the head of the line, the sheriff at his back. So they came into view of the stallion that stood with hanging head still and pendulous lower lip.

"That nag?" said the sheriff.

"It's Pringle!" exclaimed Joe Graney. "Pringle, d'you know me, boy?"

The stallion lifted his head, tilted his long ears forward, and actually whinnied a faint greeting to his master. Joe Graney began to laugh aloud.

"He knows me, Margaret!" he called to the girl.

"Aye," said the sheriff, standing at the side of Pringle and looking over the long lines, the whipcord muscles. "I can get the idea of him better, now. No wonder that Van Wey liked him."

"He's ridden nothing but Pringle for two years," said Graney.

"If Van Wey's in danger of coming down here, we gotta move," said Tom Denton. "Graney, will you saddle that chestnut and that mule in the barn and my horse? You'll have Pringle, here, and Bristol can take the mule."

The girl ran with her father toward the barn, and the sheriff muttered to Bristol, "I'm sorry about this, son. A low hound of a yaller-toothed coyote that cheats at poker deserves being salted away with lead. I'm mighty sorry. Never heard anything about the crooked poker at the start of your trail."

"There were four of them framing me," said Bristol calmly. "Nothing can be done about it now. They'll all swear that black's white. They have to, to save their own hides."

"If you've been up and fronted that thug, Van Wey, it'll tell in your favor."

"Of course, it will. Life instead of the rope. That's about all the good that it will do me."

"You saw Van Wey face to face?"

"I shook hands with him."

The sheriff whistled. "How many went with you?" he asked.

"I went alone."

"Well," said Tom Denton, "either you're a cut above the rest of us, or you're a little light in the head. I've tried three times to get a posse together and clean out that devil of a Van Wey. But I never managed to raise three men at a time. It's because everybody knows that Van Wey isn't in the game for the money he makes, but for the number of his killings. It's hard to go ag'in' a fellow who kills for the fun of it. Here come the hosses. Maybe we'll all be glad when we reach town, eh?"

Bristol looked up at the brilliance of the moon and said nothing. He was considering that the moon already had moved forward in the sky since he arrived at the house of Joe Graney. If Dirk Van Wey was the man and the brain that Bristol felt him to be, the outlaw might ride over the nearest hill at any time.

"How many men would he have with him?" asked the sheriff.

"Three, I suppose, or perhaps only two. One of his crowd is sick, and another one has the prison shakes. Here are the horses."

They mounted at once, Bristol on the mule, whose bridle was tied to the horn of the sheriff's saddle, and Graney on the back of the stallion. The girl rode the chestnut, and the sheriff his own low-built, powerful mustang.

The girl passed close to the side of Bristol and whispered, "Do you want to face a trial or to escape tonight on the way?"

He looked closely at her. There was hardly a chance to answer, unless he had been able to think like lightning. So he merely replied with a shake of his head. Whatever happened, he wanted her hands to remain clean.

They went off at a canter, from which the mule continually broke down into the sort of a trot that comes from straight shoulders and the stiffness of age, so that Bristol was continually lagging to the rear. The sheriff kept beside him and urged the mule along with an occasional lash from the quirt. The two Graneys rode ahead on the dim trail. But the whole party had not gone two miles when Bristol felt, rather than heard, a vibration of hoofs in the distance.

"Somebody's coming, and coming fast," he told the sheriff. "Keep your eyes open. Not many people are likely to be in the saddle at this time of the night."

They dipped from the top of a low hill into a wide hollow, and so climbed the side of a higher eminence beyond. As they angled up the shoulder of it, they gained a wider view of the rolling land behind them, only rarely broken by patches of trees and groups of rocks that glistened in the moonlight. Now, not a mile behind them, they saw three riders come over the brow of a hill, clearly outlined for an instant against the sky, and then lost in the next hollow.

The Graneys had seen the trio. The girl's cry came needle sharp, and she reined suddenly back beside the sheriff. "It's Dirk Van Wey and two of his men!" she exclaimed.

"Take the chestnut for yourself. Give Pringle to Jimmy Bristol. You'll have a fair chance to get into town ahead of them, then. As for Father and me, they won't harm us. We're not afraid."

"It's the one way!" cried Joe Graney. "Dirk Van Wey will have the blood of both of you unless you take the best horses and ride like mad for it."

"And he's likely to have the blood of you two, if we leave you behind," said the sheriff. "Heaven knows what's best to do. We're no faster than the slowest horse in the lot."

"You can do one thing," said Bristol. "Take my word of honor to ride into town freely and give myself up after this brawl is over . . . and let me have my parole and my free hands for tonight."

The sheriff groaned. "Graney," he said, "can you handle a rifle?"

"I've lost the thumb from my right hand," said Graney. "I can shoot a rifle, but I only hit a target now and then."

"Ride on. Ride like hell's after you," said the sheriff. "I'll try to think. The devil's behind this. I never saw worse luck. The devil's in it all!" He groaned again as he said it, and lashed the mule that carried Bristol.

They topped the hill and swung recklessly down into the small swale beyond it. Again they reached a crest, and, looking back, they saw that the three pursuers were near and gaining with a bewildering speed at every moment.

"Make your choice, Sheriff!" shouted Graney. "Make a choice now, or you'll be the death of all of us . . . and free hands for Jimmy Bristol could save us, maybe."

The sheriff was totally bewildered. He looked at Jimmy Bristol and saw in him a prisoner of price, a captive who would give him fame. He looked behind and saw ruin sweeping up on them. Finally, with a shout of despair, he drew a key from his pocket and leaned toward Bristol.

"What your word of honor's worth, heaven knows, not me," said Tom Denton. "But I'll take it."

181

"I give you my word," said Bristol. "Fast, man! They're walking up on us!"

The sheriff had barely turned the key that gave Bristol the freedom of his hands when they had terrible proof of the nearness of the pursuers. It could not have been more than a snap shot, a long chance taken, but a rifle bullet clipped through the head of Tom Denton's horse. The poor brute dropped and pitched down the slope, throwing his rider from the saddle. Far ahead of the mustang the sheriff hit the ground and lay like a stone.

XI

"VAN WEY'S OFFER"

"He's sure dead!" shouted Joe Graney. "Bristol, you take this horse and ride. I'll double up with Margie. D'you hear me, Bristol?"

Jimmy Bristol had leaped to the ground while the mule was still cantering, and he raced forward to the spot where the sheriff lay. If Tom Denton were dead, there was no harm in leaving him there on the ground behind them as they fled. But when he pressed his ear to the breast of the stunned body, he heard the faint beating of the heart. It was like a death warrant to Bristol.

"He's living," he said, without rising from his knees.

"Then we've got to stay by him!" exclaimed Graney, jumping to the ground in turn. "Look yonder, Jimmy. There's a nest of rocks where we can hold 'em off. I'll help you carry him. Margie, slide onto Pringle and burn your way to town as fast as he can gallop."

What girl, thought Bristol, *could have failed to appeal wildly to her father to join her and ride for freedom, leaving the sheriff and the outlawed man to fight it out alone?* But no such thought seemed to enter her mind. Like an athletic boy she was instantly off the chestnut and onto the rangy form of Pringle. There was no time for her even to touch their hands. She could only cry out a farewell to her father. But to Jimmy Bristol she suddenly threw out her hand, calling: "Jimmy . . . if we ever meet again, we. . . ." Then the sweeping gallop of Pringle carried her away, riding for her own life and for theirs.

If they never met again, what was he to understand by that impulsive gesture? He knew what meaning he would put upon it, and a grim joy began to surge in his heart as he helped Graney lift the body of the senseless sheriff. The rocks were not far away, an irregular outcropping of small boulders and large that had been exposed by the wash of water down the hollow during the heavy rains. In hard clay and gravel those big stones were embedded, and, as the two got their burden to the center of this meager screen, they saw the three riders come over the top of the next hill and plunge at them.

Bristol, on his knees behind a rock, found Graney's rifle thrust into his hands. He fired at the central rider, for it had the great shoulders, the unhuman bulk of Dirk Van Wey. The bullet missed. The instinct of the true marksman told Bristol that he had fired a trifle high and to the right—that commonest of all faults. The second shot would not miss, however, he promised himself as he drew another bead for the same target.

Dirk Van Wey and the others, at that first shot, had split their charge and were swerving off to the sides, yet Bristol caught the big outlaw full in his sights, swung the gun with the target until he knew that the life of Dirk was in the crook of his forefinger, and pulled the trigger. There was a muffled explosion. The gun jumped like a wounded thing in his hands, and he knew that good Winchester was hopelessly jammed. From under his eyes the three riders swept off to present security and left him there with the injured man and poor Graney, half helpless with that mutilated hand.

He considered the condition of their shelter. There were enough big rocks scattered about to shield them fairly well from any fire directed at them from the level, but high over them towered the head of the hill, where even a child could take control of them, firing sharply angled shots until they were killed one by one.

"The gun's gone, eh?" asked Graney.

"It's gone," said Bristol curtly. "And you could be off there on the edge of the horizon, riding safe and fast for town."

"Well," said Graney, deliberately taking out a pipe and beginning to load it, "I wouldn't mind living a while longer as a man, but I don't hanker to crawl around the face of the earth as a yellow dog. Taking things the way that they've come, I'd rather be here with you, Jimmy, than sitting on top of a throne with a crown on my head, kicking a couple of prime ministers in the face and ordering up champagne for supper."

Bristol looked at him with that involuntary smile of his that meant well-being of mind and of body. "All right," he said. "All right!" He meant more, far more, than the words said. He saw, in the small speech of Joe Graney, more of the character of the rancher than ten years of other acquaintanceship would have shown to him. That was why he smiled, for he saw that the whole soul of the man was clean, selfless, and sound to the core. He was a proper father of such a girl as Margaret Graney.

If we ever meet again, she had cried as the stallion swept her away to hunt for help in the town. Well, he could extract the best meaning possible from those words, since it was very highly probably that they never *would* meet again. He kneeled by the body of the sheriff. "If he comes to and gets to his feet again," said Bristol, "that will make two and a half of us, Joe Graney. And we can give Dirk Van Wey some sort of a fight."

"He won't be getting on his feet again any too soon," said Joe Graney. "There's not much chance of that. Listen to his breathing. Listen to. . . ."

The hurt man groaned out at this moment: "Put more wood on the fire, you lazy hounds. You want us all to freeze and . . . ? Where am I? Where are we, boys? Where . . . ?"

"You're flat on your back. They snicked a bullet through the head of your horse just after you set my hands free," said Jimmy Bristol to him. "We carried you in here among the rocks. Dirk Van Wey and two of his thugs are somewhere, trying to get a shooting position at us. How are you? Can you sit up?"

The sheriff tried to do so, propping himself with his hands until he was supported halfway from the ground. Then he gasped and fell back. "My back's gone," he said.

"His back's gone," said Bristol calmly to Graney, as though the rancher might not have heard. Then he added: "Sheriff, if you can lie on your face and use a rifle that way, you may help to save yourself and the rest of us. Can you manage it?"

"I can try anything," said the sheriff huskily, "as soon as the fireworks stop in front of my eyes."

He began to edge himself over, but when he was lying on his side, he fainted and dropped back to his first inert position.

"He's no more than a bag of sawdust now," said Jimmy Bristol.

"You and me will be the same before long," answered Joe Graney. "Look!"

He had his pipe going by this time, and, as he puffed at it, he pointed toward the brow of the hill that almost overhung the rocks among which they lay. Utterly black it rose against the brightness of that moonlit sky. Jimmy Bristol saw a figure scurry from one bush to another. A silence followed.

"No," said Bristol. "This is about the finish. Except for the sheriff, we might make a break for it and try to run down the hollow to those trees."

"Yes, *except* for the sheriff, we might do that," said Graney, with an emphasis that Bristol did not miss.

"We're goners, then," remarked Bristol.

He sat down beside the older man and made a cigarette.

He felt a certainty that he was about to die, and he was more than sure that he could not die in better company.

"Margie . . . she's what I wonder about," said Joe Graney.

"She'll be all right," said Bristol.

"You think so?"

"I know so. A girl like that couldn't do the wrong thing. Any man with a brain in his head would want to marry her. She'll have the whole land to pick from."

"The pick of the land'll have to wait a while, then," said Graney. "You made a kind of an impression on her. She knows that you're back here with me because you wouldn't ride on through the Gap about your own business on the back of Pringle, with a thousand dollars in your pocket. And she's not a girl to forget. You saw her wave to you when she rode away?"

Bristol nodded.

"Well, she meant something by that. This is going to be a black night for us, Bristol. But it's a black night for her, too. She's going to lose a father she's fond of. She's going to lose a man that maybe she's fonder of still."

A rifle cracked above them, sounding strangely far away. At the same instant a bullet kicked up the dirt at their feet. Neither of them moved.

"No, there's no getting away," said Graney calmly.

"If I could get a fair crack at just one of 'em . . . if one of 'em would come inside revolver range," muttered Jimmy Bristol.

He reached out and pulled a revolver from the holster at the thigh of the sheriff, and, as at a signal, the sheriff roused himself again, groaning once more.

"They won't come in range," said Graney, "unless they keep in cover of those bushes. Instead of being whittled away, maybe it's better to stand up and let them clip us off quick."

"Maybe that's the best way," said Jimmy Bristol.

Another rifle bullet beat the ground.

"That's in the same place," said Graney. "I should think

they could shoot a whole lot straighter than that."

"Oh, they can," agreed Bristol. "They mean something by it."

The meaning was announced suddenly from a point not far away and in the huge voice of Dirk Van Wey. "Hey, Jimmy Bristol!" that voice called.

"Here," called Bristol instantly.

"I guess we got you bozos, all of you," cried Van Wey.

"You've got us, Van Wey," agreed Bristol.

"Stand up, then."

Bristol rose slowly to his feet. He reached out his hand. Joe Graney mutely gripped it in farewell.

"Where you die don't matter, Bristol," said Van Wey. "But if you come over here, I'll give you a favor before you kick out."

"What sort of a favor?"

"The life of either of those fellows that are with you. *Either* of 'em."

"He lies," said Graney eagerly. "Don't do it, Jimmy. He wants to torture you before he finishes you. There's more devil in him than in any red Indian."

"Don't go, boy," said the sheriff faintly. "Graney's right. They'll devil you to death if you go there."

Bristol hesitated. If torture were in the mind of Dirk Van Wey, there was no doubt that the man would be a consummate artist in his practice of the evil work. Merely to remember the gross, inhuman face of Van Wey was enough to curdle his blood.

"You hear me?" shouted Van Wey.

He was about halfway up the hill, hidden in deep brush.

"I hear you," said Bristol, still hesitant. "How am I to know that you'll let one of these fellows live?"

"Why, son," answered Van Wey, "the fact is that you *don't* know. The fact is that all you can do is just take the word of Dirk Van Wey. If he don't feel like keeping his word, he ain't going to keep it. Understand?"

"I'm going up to you," called Bristol.

"Good boy," said Van Wey. "I've got a kind of a reception committee waiting here all ready for you." He laughed, a brazen peal that thundered through the still air of the night. Somewhere out of the distance a cow began to low mournfully. It was like a ridiculous echo at which Bristol could have laughed at any other time.

"Don't go, Jimmy," said the sheriff. "Stay here, and we'll both take our medicine with you. Besides, what he promises won't keep. I know him."

But Bristol shook his head. "I've made up my mind," he said. "Any kind of a chance is better than no chance at all. Graney . . . Denton . . . so long, and good luck to you."

With that he stepped straight forward among the rocks and began to ascend the hill.

XII

"RIFLE DUEL"

The brush was taller than it appeared from the rocks below. He was soon swallowed up by bushes that rose as high as his head. As he climbed, he was aware of a great form that stalked him from behind. At the top of the hill he came out on a small platform that was so level it looked as though it have been shaved off by human masons. It was solid rock except for a little sifting of soil that appeared here and there, scarcely deep enough to afford rootage for the grass. At one side of this little plateau rose a great tree, a single plume on the head of the hill. From where Bristol stood, the moon appeared exactly behind the tree, turning its leaves into black shadow and a silver luster.

Under that tree sat two forms, and he was able to recognize them presently as Dan Miller and that terrible young fellow with the golden hair and the dark-blue eyes—Harry Weston. And now, behind him, strode Dirk Van Wey up the slope of the hill.

"I told you I'd get him, boys," said Dirk Van Wey.

"I've got him covered," said Dan Miller from behind his

rifle. "None of the rest of you has to worry none. I've got him ready to plant."

"We're going to take some time to do that planting," said Harry Weston. "How does he come to be a big enough fool to come up here when you ask him, though? That's what I don't make out."

"Sit down or make yourself easy, son," said Dirk Van Wey. "Smoke a cigarette, Jimmy Bristol. I'm kind of glad to see you ag'in."

"Thanks," said Bristol.

He was panting from the climb, but he noticed that the slow labor of the great chest of Van Wey had hardly been increased in rhythm. There was no possibility of exhausting the brute, it appeared. His endurance was like his actual strength—extra-human.

"Who's down there behind you?" asked Van Wey. He added: "I mean, besides old Joe Graney."

There was no point in hiding the truth. "The sheriff is down there," said Bristol.

He expected a great outburst of rage. Instead, Dirk Van Wey merely nodded his head. "He's kind of a decent fellow, that Tom Denton is. Got plenty of nerve, too. Three more like him would run me out of the Gap. How come you and him didn't join forces ag'in' me, Bristol?"

"Because," said Jimmy Bristol, "he had handcuffs on me."

There was a deep shout from Dirk Van Wey. It sounded almost like a yell of joy. "Had 'em on you?"

"Yes," said Bristol.

"Wait a minute. Lemme get at something. He had the braces on you and . . . ?"

"I told you he shot too straight to be honest," said Harry Weston, approaching.

"What they want you for?" asked Dirk Van Wey, his face working to an extra hideousness as he asked the question.

"Murder. Shooting a fellow in Tombstone three months ago."

"Good," said Dirk Van Wey. "Damn me, but that's pretty good, all right. I kind of guessed that there was something to you the minute that I laid eyes on you, and that's why I give you a chance to try out the four boys I had along with me. Men . . . they'd always seemed, to listen to their talk and their bragging. Men, and hard-boiled, was what they wanted to seem. But a lot of fresh-water clams was all that they turned out. Fresh-water clams!" He laughed, and his laughter was a snarl. Then he made a brief, ugly gesture toward the two. "I banked on 'em . . . I left four of 'em, counting the cook, to trim you to the quick. And you went through 'em like nothing at all. It took Dirk Van Wey to run you down. It took Dirk to handle you." He laughed again. The snarl was one of triumph now.

"How's Lefty Parr?" asked Bristol.

"Lefty? He thinks that he's going to die, and I wish he would. But he's going to live. Rance is taking care of him, and he's sure to live. You done him in proper."

"I didn't shoot him," protested Bristol.

"No. That's the howling beauty of it," said Dirk Van Wey. "You held him like a light and let one of his own partners put him out. I never seen such a fool as Weston is . . . and I used to think he was a bright kid. I'm a fool, too. That's what I am."

"It was dark," said Harry Weston savagely. "It was dark, and there wasn't any fair chance to get at him. That's the only thing that saved his hide. I'd like to have another whirl at him."

"Would you, now?" asked Dirk, with something almost plaintive in his voice.

"Yeah, I mean it. I'm not afraid of him. I'm not afraid of any man that walks except you, Dirk. And you're not human."

"What about you, Danny?" asked Van Wey.

"It goes for me, too," said Dan Miller.

"You'd fight him ag'in, you would?"

"I'll fight him right now," said Miller.

Dirk Van Wey pulled from his holsters two revolvers

with barrels of an extra length—great guns that would have bent the wrists of most men, though they were mere toys to him.

"Well, boys, you're going to have your chance, and that's why I called Bristol from them rocks, where we could've snagged him dead easy, and no trouble to anybody. You're going to fight him, the pair of you. Understand?"

They blinked at him. There was no answer. Then they stared at one another, but still without comprehending. The first grim flash of understanding came to Jimmy Bristol as he listened.

"Those two down there," said Dirk Van Wey, "which of 'em is to live? Speak up, Bristol. One of 'em has to die, and one of 'em can live. I promised, and my promises go. I promised you the money and the hoss, didn't I? And you got 'em. I didn't say nothing, though, about taking 'em back ag'in." His mirthless grin stretched his mouth once more. He added: "Speak up. Which man is it to be . . . the sheriff or old Joe Graney?"

"Graney," said Bristol slowly. "I suppose it has to be Graney."

"Good," answered Van Wey. "I'd kind of miss him if I didn't have him around to cuff now and ag'in. He's used to it, and I'm used to it. It's fine to have him on the old ranch." Then he turned to his two men. "Danny . . . and you, Harry . . . here's your chance. I got the idea when I come back and found him gone with my hoss and the money. Kind of a funny thing, Jimmy. I waited till I thought you'd never begin to bust loose, or the boys would never go after your hide. Then I took a walk, and, while I was a ways off, damn it, I hear the guns and start back on the run. But I was too late. I only come up in time to hear Lefty Parr yelling and Harry and Dan Miller cussing a little. And so I says to myself right then and there that it's a pity I've missed watching such a good fight. I missed watching you open up them soft-shelled, fresh-water clams. And I says to myself that I'm going to take the first chance and put you together with 'em. Miller!"

Miller started. "Yeah, chief?" he said then very mildly.

"You're pretty good with a rifle, ain't you?"

"I've handled a rifle now and then."

"You've kept us in venison, anyways. And now you're going to have a chance to shoot something better'n deer. Him." He pointed toward Jimmy Bristol. "Bristol," he added, "are you any good with a rifle?"

"I'm fair."

"Was it you that took the flying shot at me from the rocks?"

"Yes."

"You're good, then. It was an inch from my nose. Why didn't you shoot ag'in?"

"The rifle jammed."

"That's a better reason than no reason at all. Harry, give Jimmy your rifle."

Silently Harry extended the rifle.

And then Van Wey went on: "You two can have it out with rifles, first of all. Then we'll see. Stand up there back to back."

So they stood together, Dan Miller and Bristol, in the center of the little moonlit plateau. Each had a Winchester rifle held in both hands, diagonally across the body.

"When I give the word," said Dirk Van Wey, "you're going to start marching. I'm going to count to ten, and each of you is going to take a step every time I count. If one of you tries to take them ten steps faster than I count, or if one of you tries to turn and start shooting before I reach the end of the count, I'm going to put a slug through the head of that fool. Y'understand?"

"I understand," said Jimmy Bristol.

"I understand," said the iron voice of Dan Miller. "Harry, I know this game. Put a bet down on me with the chief."

"I'll bet you a hundred," said Dirk.

"I wouldn't bet on the little runt," said Harry Weston,

"except that he's too damned small to be hit very easy. I'll bet a hundred with you."

"That's a go," answered Dirk. He began to laugh a little as he stood there, enormous, with his great shadow spilled behind him, and the wind furling the brim of his hat so that the moonlight could get at his ugly face.

"Look at the fun I show you, Harry," said Dirk Van Wey. "Look at the game I show you. Maybe better stuff than this is going to come afterward. I've got my hundred on you, Jimmy Bristol. Mind you, Dan Miller is sure a poison rat. You gotta move fast and shoot straight when I count to ten. Start in. *One ... two ... three ... four ... five....* "

It came to Jimmy Bristol, as he paced those grim steps through the moonlight, with his shadow sloping before him, that a rifle is not, after all, so very much heavier than a revolver. If it had been revolver play, he would hardly have feared for the outcome. He knew exactly what he would do. If the rifle were longer and heavier, there was the stock that would fit under the forearm. Suddenly he gripped the weapon in his right hand, alone, with his forefinger on the trigger and the stock extending up under the powerful cushion of his forearm.

"*Ten!*" shouted the thunderous voice of Dirk Van Wey.

Jimmy Bristol whirled, leaping far to the side as he turned, and swinging the rifle up like a revolver in his right hand. Without aim, shooting only by the marksman's sense that he had learned in the handling of a revolver, he took a snap shot at the body of Dan Miller.

The speed of that firing quite eclipsed Miller's return shot. As it was, the sharp-faced little man merely pulled his trigger to fire a blind shot, and then spun half around, and dropped to one knee, groaning and cursing.

"Finish him!" yelled Harry Weston. "The dirty cur ... he's double-crossed me and beat me out of a hundred bucks when I'm broke. Finish him, Bristol. Kill him like the dog he is."

"Go on!" shouted Dirk Van Wey savagely. "Kill him like a pig, Bristol!"

With his two revolvers, he dominated the scene.

"No," said Jimmy Bristol. "He got that through the shoulder joint, I think . . . and that means he's never going to pull another gun in a fight as long as he walks."

Dirk Van Wey shouted with glee. "That's better than killing him. That means that every Chinaman can kick him in the face. I'm done with you, Miller. You can go rot, for all of me. Now I see what my men have been like. They're glass, is what they are. They're all glass! Nothing but glass." He cursed loudly, and then cried: "Now it's your turn, Weston. Stand up and show us what *you* can do!"

XIII

"A GUARD FOR BRISTOL"

Harry Weston was not dismayed. He merely smiled and threw back his head until the moonlight glimmered over his handsome face. He shied his sombrero to the ground.

"I want him!" cried Harry Weston. "Make it knives, chief."

"Knives!" cried Dirk Van Wey. "Why, you got a brain, after all. I ain't seen a knife fight since I was last in Mexico. This is going to be a show. Here, Jimmy. Here's a knife. This Weston is a hot trick with a knife. You wanta watch yourself."

"I'm going to carve him down to my size and then cut him in two," said Weston, drawing a Bowie knife.

A knife of exactly the same pattern was tossed into the air and landed at the feet of Bristol. He picked it up.

"*Down guns!*" shouted Van Wey. "Shell out, boys . . . on the ground with 'em."

They laid their Colts on the ground.

"Now at it, wild cats. *Yow!*"

Harry Weston answered that yell with another. He hopped up a little, as though to test the limber speed of his legs. Then he came racing in, swerving a little from side to side, like a snipe flying down the wind. Bristol stood straight as a ramrod, so straight and still that Dirk Van Wey yelled: "Watch out, Bristol! He'll cut your heart out!"

Only at the last instant Bristol sprang sidewise, bending his body to avoid the thrust and slashing for the throat. He missed in his turn. They swept in a circle around one another, crouching. Weston leaped in, stabbing and slashing, yelling like a fiend. Bristol gave ground again. He stabbed at the body with the knife in his right hand, but in mid-air he tossed the knife into his left hand and slashed for the face. He felt the grit of the keen blade against the bone, and Harry Weston reeled back with a scream. The handsomeness of that face was ruined forever. A dark tide of blood flowed down over it from the forehead.

Dirk Van Wey yelled with laughter. "A two-handed man! *A two-handed man!*" he shouted. "Get out of my sight, the pair of you sick rats. Miller . . . Weston . . . move on! I'm through with you. I've found a man!"

They got on their horses, the two of them, and rode off. The hands of Weston were covering his face as Bristol saw him last. And Miller, bent low in the saddle, gripping his wounded shoulder, was leading the way. So they dropped below the shoulder of the hill and out of sight.

"I've found a *man*," went on the booming voice of Dirk Van Wey. "And a two-handed man. Boy, I want you, and I'm going to have you. You and me can do business together. You and me go halves. That's what I think of you. Halves!"

"Or else, what?" asked Bristol.

"Or else," said the giant, "you drop that knife, and we have it out with bare hands."

His laugh once more was thunder as he said it. For what hands could match his?

It seemed to Bristol that he saw, in that instant, the calm face of Joe Graney as he had sat among the rocks, puffing at his pipe and waiting for death, resigned utterly. And he saw the girl, throwing out her hand as she cried: *If we ever meet again. . . .* If he joined Dirk, they would never meet

again. He would never dare to stand before her. He hurled
the knife from him as far as he could fling it.

"Come on, Van Wey!" he called.

Dirk Van Wey nodded. "Maybe it's better this way," he
said. "Maybe I was a fool to think of anything else. Maybe
it's better to have the feel of you in my hands. I'm going
to break you, kid. I'm going to tear you and twist you in
two . . . slow and easy."

He thrust his two revolvers into their holsters along his
thighs as he strode in. To flee was impossible. Those guns
would be out and spitting death, if Bristol ran. In a frenzy
he leaped straight at Van Wey, all his might going into the
drive of his right arm. Fair and truly he smote the corner
of Dirk Van Wey's chin. It was like striking a rock. There
seemed no give in the head of the giant, but a sharp agony
shot up the arm of Bristol, and he knew that he had broken
the bones across the back of his hand. With the right he
could not strike again in that battle.

He danced back, and Dirk Van Wey followed, shouting,
his face insane with the battle lust. His hat was off. His
long, greasy hair flew back in the wind of his own running.
He did not try to strike, but only to grasp with his hands,
and once they secured their grip, the battle was ended, as
Bristol well knew.

"Stand up to me, damn you, or I'll salt you first and tear
you up afterward!" shouted Dirk Van Wey. One of his
hands dropped for an instant toward a holster gun to em-
phasize the point of the threat.

That instant was used by Bristol to leap straight in and
drive his left to the face. It found, not the jaw, but the
cheekbone, and split the flesh. The shock of the stroke
merely turned the arm numb.

The great hand of the giant found a hold on the arm with
which Bristol had struck. The fingers of Van Wey seemed
to find the bone through the flesh. Only by hurling himself
wildly away could Bristol gain freedom, and the empty
sleeve remained in the hands of Van Wey. He threw the
rag from him and rushed on, bellowing. He was drunk with

the fighting now. Fists were useless against that head of iron and that body of well-ribbed India rubber. Bristol flung his whole body at the knees of the giant. Van Wey went down under the impact, his head hitting the ground with terrific force. For the first time Bristol was on top. At last the balance had tipped in his favor.

Desperately the giant clawed at the revolver whose butt appeared above the edge of the leather holster that was strapped to his thigh. But Bristol knocked aside his hand and grabbed the butt of Van Wey's six-gun. Dirk Van Wey felt the drawing of the revolver and yelled with rage and fear. With a swing of his great shoulders, he flung Bristol from him, and, as Bristol struck heavily and rolled, he saw Van Wey stride after him, his other gun in hand, shooting as he came.

The stolen revolver was in the broken right hand of Bristol, but he could not waste time in shifting it to his left. The moon blazed against his eyes, but he could not even turn on his side to get a better light. He had to fire half blindly at the vast silhouette, and he knew, as he pulled the trigger, that he had fired lower than the body of the outlaw.

Yet Van Wey, striding forward, at his next step crumbled suddenly and lay face downward on the rock. It was as though a miraculous hand from the sky had struck him down. There was no sense of triumph in Bristol as he leaped to his feet and leveled his gun on the mark. There was only a profound sense of gratitude to—he knew not what. Fate, he might call it, or the great god of chance.

The giant propped himself up on both arms. He was quite calm. He seemed almost contented and happy as he boomed out: "Well, kid, you snagged me. I guess you busted the bone of the leg. Poison in both hands, eh? Oh, you're the real two-handed man."

To the bewilderment of Bristol, Dirk Van Wey began to laugh. It was as though the beast of him had been so contented by the battle that he cared not for his own defeat, his pain, or the death at the hands of the law that might now loom before him.

*   *   *

They put the wounded sheriff on a litter when the men from town reached the place, with the girl on Pringle showing them the way in the gray of the morning. They made another horse litter, on which they heaved the bulk of Dirk Van Wey. Then they stood in consultation.

"This here is a wanted man," said the deputy sheriff to Tom Denton, pointing toward Jimmy Bristol. "They want him pretty bad, down there in Tombstone."

"They don't want him so bad, brother. They don't want him so bad," drawled the sheriff. "It was a card game, by what I've last heard. And down there in Tombstone they've likely found out a good deal about the kind of *hombres* that were playing against Bristol in that game. Murder was what Bristol was sitting with in that game."

"Five thousand dollars," groaned the deputy. "Five thousand whole dollars locked up in that hide, and we gotta let it go?"

"We can keep that hide in jail," said the sheriff, "till he's wanted for trial or out on bail. And when the gents in Tombstone hear what Bristol has done in this part of the world, they're going to hand him his freedom on a silver platter."

The other men grinned, and the rising sun gilded their lean, brown faces. The girl, who had brought all this power of the law to the place, drew closer to Bristol, watching him with the grave happiness of possession in her eyes.

"Come here, kid!" roared Dirk Van Wey. "Come here, Jimmy."

Bristol stepped to the litter and looked down at the brutal mirth of that grinning face.

"What tickles me," said Dirk Van Wey, "is that you done it with my own gun. I'm going to be laughing at that when the rope strangles me. Swipes my gun off'n me and drops me with my own gat."

"You went for the Colt first," Bristol reminded him.

"Oh, yeah, yeah," said Dirk Van Wey. "But why bring up the little things? It was a good fight, was what it was.

So long, kid. See you in hell, if not sooner."

The horses that supported the litter of Van Wey started on.

"Who's going to guard Bristol?" asked the efficient deputy sheriff.

The sheriff bellowed at the deputy: "Why, you fool, he doesn't need guarding, does he? D'you think he's going to try to run away from all the glory that newspapers and the whole West can give him? D'you think that he's half-wit enough to run away like that when a week in jail will make him free forever? But hold on . . . wait a minute. I'll give him a guard, at that. I'll give him a guard that looks as though she'll keep him in hand the rest of his days. Miss Graney, will you take hold of Jimmy Bristol and deliver him safe and sound at the jail?"

She laughed at the sheriff joyously and without shame. She and Bristol were already on their mounts when Joe Graney shouted: "Wait a minute! I'll come along with you brats, so's you don't miss the way."

They did not pause, but let their mounts go on at the softest of dog-trots. Now and then, of a mutual impulse, the girl and Bristol would look at one another, but as a rule they stared straight before them, as though they were alone in a great space and had before them the longest journey in the world.

Viva! Viva!

Strictly speaking, "Viva! Viva!" does not belong in this collection. It is most certainly "wild," brimming over with rousing Max Brand action, yet it is obviously not a tale of the West. The story's subject matter is revolution in a fictional Latin American country. So why include it? For the simple reason that I could not resist the story's ferocious energy and bold design. Faust must surely have enjoyed writing it because exactly one week after revising the final draft which was first published in Argosy *on January 2, 1937, he completed a stirring book-length adventure using the same revolutionary background and locale: "A Seabold Fights," serialized in* MacLean's Magazine *(11/15/36–2/15/37). "Viva! Viva!" offers ironic proof that not all revolutions achieve their goals. For big James Easter, who fights his way into Rio Negro, the payoff he expects is not the one he gets.*

General Agosto Hurtado had his revolution all ready to start. He had two three-pounders, ten machine guns, three hundred and fifty rifles. To man the rifles he had eleven hundred soldiers with machetes. To assist in the command he had six generals, who were José Díaz, Manuel Mureno, Sam Israels, Jeff Muldoon, Jesús Maria Valdez, and Honey Parker. He had the ammunition packed, and he was ready to board the train for a swift ascent from the sea coast to San Esteban. Then a hurricane nipped in from the Caribbean, blew the banana farms flat, stamped the jungles into a wet mess, and twisted the rails right off the ties, and finally snapped the cables of the tramp steamer, *Santa Maria*, that had brought Hurtado and his revolution near San Esteban.

The old boat smashed to flinders on the beach, thereby breaking down the bridges of retreat behind the army of the revolution. For twenty-four hours that storm kicked Porto Blanco in the face and poured two feet of water onto the main street. When the wind died down, and the rain let up to a thick drizzle, Hurtado buckled on his wooden leg and went out to inspect, but all that he saw was trouble, so he went back to the *cantina* where his six generals were looking at a map on the wall and drinking rum.

Nobody said anything, because there was nothing to say, and Agosto Hurtado sat down, rested his wooden leg on a second chair, and, with dreaming eyes, began to pull at his black string of a mustache. Colonel Popez brought him a rum, but he failed to see it.

"How long will it take us to clear the railroad?" asked Hurtado at last.

General Honey Parker, who had the brow and the brain of a bull, answered: "After we've cleared it, how long will it take us to rebuild it? Where the devil can we go from here?"

"Could we get to Rio Negro, up the coast?" asked Jesús Maria Valdez.

"Rio Negro? That's where I'm going. Sure we'll go to Rio Negro, all of us," said a voice from the doorway. A big young man was standing there, dressed in a banana leaf and nothing else. He added, as he entered the room: "To

201

Rio Negro, *amigos!* And let's start now. I'm overdue there. Has anybody got a spare cigarette?"

General José Díaz gave him one.

"Who are you?" asked Hurtado.

"I'm an extra part for your army," said the big, bare man. "You can always use another general, can't you? My name is James Princeton Easter."

The roof of the *cantina* was corrugated iron, and the rain came down on it just then with a drum-crash and a rolling that made the generals duck their heads. James Princeton Easter found a chair, sat down, crossed his legs, arranged his banana leaf a little, and took a deep inhalation of smoke that lifted his big chest and flattened his stomach to a corrugation of muscle as hard as the roof above them.

Agosto Hurtado looked at those muscles with interest. "How did you get to Porto Blanco?" he asked. "And why?"

"I was bound up the coast in a schooner for Rio Negro," said James Easter, "till the storm smashed her to bits and blew me and a bit of wreckage right into the middle of your revolution." He shook his fist at the ceiling and yelled: "¡*Viva* Hurtado! *¿Que viva?* Hurtado? Hurtado! ¡*Viva* Hurtado!" After that he leaned back and grinned at the general.

"What did you want in Rio Negro?" asked Hurtado.

"It's none of your damned business," said Easter.

"Shall I throw that bum out on his ear?" asked General Honey Parker.

Hurtado shook his head. He crossed his legs with the wooden one on top and began to stroke the battered shaft of it while he studied Easter. "We're marching on San Esteban," he said. "You can go along with us."

"I don't want any part of San Esteban," answered Easter. "It's Rio Negro or nothing, for me."

"Well?" said Hurtado, turning his eyes of calm question on the others. He was not big, except in spirit. He was young, also, but a deep love of his country gave him a greater dignity than years. "Well?" he repeated. "Before we can rebuild the railroad, Ramírez will have ten thousand men armed and waiting for us in San Esteban. If we stay here, no boat is expected for three months. Where can we go, except through the jungle to Rio Negro?"

"¡Viva! ¡Viva Hurtado!" yelled big James Easter.

"We'll starve in the jungle like wet cats!" declared General Moreno.

"To Rio Negro!" shouted Easter.

And to Rio Negro they went.

The trouble was that the storm had beaten the jungle into a tenfold confusion, and the trip took eight days instead of five. For four days they ate rations. For four more days they chewed green things, and in general lived on their bile, but the army went on hewing a path with machetes through the warm green shower-bath of the forest. It rained all the time, sometimes a miserable drizzle, sometimes a tremendous gushing from the sky. The shoes rotted on their feet. The cartridge belts turned green and greasy with mold. And the weaker spirits began to turn back before the march was two days old. The others went on.

In the evenings they built shelters of palm branches against the rain and rubbed one another with kerosene to get off the ticks that showered down on them during the march. The bare-footed operated on one another with needles, picking out from the thick calluses or from under toenails the little white sacks of eggs that, in time, would rot a man's foot away. All the mosquitoes in the world gathered in a dingy cloud about them, a cubic league of mournful sound. They ate quinine for three days. After that, malaria chattered their teeth with cold or burned their eyes yellow with fever.

"Find out," said Hurtado to General Sam Israels, "why this man, Easter, wants so badly to get to Rio Negro."

Sam Israels went up to the head of the column where Easter, as usual, was swinging a tireless machete, giving edge to the steel with the force of his strokes. His coat and shirt, already rotted by the rain, split open with every sway of his arm to show the muscles that worked like long fingers across his shoulders.

"Leave me spell you, kid," said the general.

Easter straightened and made a pause. As though at a signal from their chief, the peons gave up laboring also, so that for the moment there was only the noise of dripping water through the jungle, the panting of the men, and the multitudinous whine of the mosquitoes.

"I don't need to be spelled," said Easter. "I'm working up a new set of blisters, and I don't want my hands to get cold before they break."

"What's eating you that you want to get to Rio Negro so bad?" asked General Israels.

Easter pointed up the narrow gap they were cutting through the jungle. A big *zopilote* hung in the air high above them, pasted without motion against the gray ceiling. "You see that buzzard?" asked Easter.

"Yeah, what about it?" answered Israels.

"If you knew what I was after in Rio Negro, you'd borrow that pair of wings and try to get there ahead of me," said Easter.

General Israels went back to Hurtado and shook his head. "Just kind of a nut, that's all," he said.

On the fourth day General José Díaz and Manuel Mureno melted away to the rear. One the fifth day General Sam Israels was turned into a shuddering wreck by malaria, and an escort—commanded voluntarily by General Jesús Maria Valdez—took Sam Israels back toward Porto Blanco through a jungle that had already grown up rank over the new trail. On the sixth day General Jeff Muldoon disappeared. On the seventh day James Princeton Easter said, as he chewed the tender inside of a strip of bark: "There's only Honey Parker and you, Agosto . . . you've got to have at least three generals for this man's revolution, don't you?"

"Sure," said Honey Parker, "one general gets stuck in the mud. Another one gets plugged. And the third one takes the city. Go ahead and be a general, Easter."

So Easter tied around his throat the red neckerchief that made him a general.

"D'you know a fellow called de Prida who lives in Rio Negro?" asked Easter.

"Sure," said Honey Parker. "Juan de Prida is the mayor and *commandante* and customs collector and parliament representative of Rio Negro. He has so damn' much money, it's a wonder he doesn't make a strategic retreat to Paris."

"Juan de Prida," said General Hurtado, "is a swine."

"He is not," stated Easter. "He's no swine at all."

Sometimes Hurtado was violent. Sometimes he was polite. On this occasion he reached first for a handy machete, but then he changed his mind and merely said, without smiling: "In the Spanish language the word *no* does not exist, *señor* my general."

Easter looked at the machete and said nothing at all.

So Honey Parker changed the subject by remarking: "We've faded out to three hundred men. What the hell's the use, Hurtado?"

"Three hundred is all we have guns for," said Easter. "Why have a lot of waste tissue for the other fellows to shoot at?"

General Hurtado pulled both sides of his stringy mustache at once. *How long I have been alone in the world, waiting for man like you, general*, he wondered.

On the morning of the eighth day they got to an inland bay and captured an Indian fisherman. He had a small quantity of *pésol* that Honey Parker divided into tiny portions and fed by hand on the end of a knife into the mouths of the soldiers. The fisherman had something more than *pésol*, however. He had news that General de Prida expected the coming of the army of the revolution and had fifteen hundred well-armed men in waiting at the top of the bluff, or at other strategic points. He had posted cannon, also, and plenty of machine guns in the hands of experts who could shoot the buzzards out of the sky. The fisherman had seen them do it.

"Get into your boat and sail," said James Princeton Easter. "When you get to Rio Negro, tell 'em that we've got three thousand wild men with us."

The fisherman sailed away. Three generals watched him with hungry, mournful eyes.

"Yeah, but what's the use?" asked Honey Parker.

"Are you going to start that again?" asked Easter. "¡*Viva* Hurtado! *!Viva! !Viva!*"

The army answered the cheer, but only as briefly as an echo. And some who stood up to shout, staggered before they sat down again. So Hurtado made a speech.

"Friends of the Republic," he said, "at the foot of the bluff of Rio Negro there is a village full of fat chickens and pigs and *pésol*, and *agua dolce*, and we shall fill our bellies and smoke a cigarette before we climb the hill and stretch ourselves out in the good soft beds of the town. Be happy, children. One step more and we shall be home."

"*!Viva! ¡Viva* Hurtado! *!Viva!*" roared James Easter, and his voice seemed louder than the shout of the whole army.

They got on more easily that day, for they found game trails through the jungle, and it was lucky for them that they did. When they had to carve a way through the jungle, the machetes fell from their weakened fingers. Only Honey Parker, the skin of his heavy jowls now hanging loose as a muff, and Easter, as gaunt as an old greyhound, and Hurtado himself, wooden leg and all, made effective play with their big knives, tirelessly slashing and living off the bigness of their hearts. So, in the late afternoon, the army straggled out of the jungle and saw the promised village. It had been swept as clean as a whistle.

There was not the sign of a dog or a cat. There was not a swine to grunt or a mule to bray or a chicken to cackle. The corn bins were empty. There was not so much as a string of chili peppers drying. And from the trees that screened the face of the bluff of Rio Negro, the big hill that sheltered the landward side of the port, long-drawn, derisive yells came floating down to the army of the revolution. Three hundred rifle bullets answered those shouts and silenced them.

Then the three generals stood and looked at one another, and the army looked at its generals.

"Yeah, I knew it was no use," said Honey Parker.

"We can't go back," said Easter, looking up toward the

smoke that blew dimly into the sky above the town, smoke fed by the fires on a thousand hearths where chickens turned on the spit, and fat pork was roasting, and the deep pots of *frijoles* were steaming with fat bubbles bursting and browning at the lips of the jars

"Sure we can't go back," said Honey Parker. "But Rio Negro . . . it's a funny place to rot in. It's a hell of a long ways from Brooklyn. Do we start the climb now or wait for dark, Agosto?"

Before Hurtado could answer, a sound thinner and more piercing than any flute and far sweeter to the ear of that army than any music, broke out on the verge of the empty village. It was the squealing of a pig, and three hundred mouths watered.

The human screaming of the swine came nearer, and now the generals could see a little, lean porker, weaving among the legs of the rabble of the army. The pig ran with his trumpet never silent, but the army of the revolution was silent. Men with faces stretched by grins of quiet earnestness were taking great strokes at the beast with their machetes. The broad blades flashed even in the dingy mist of rain. Dozens of soldiers had rifles at the ready or revolvers poised that they dared not fire because the pig was dodging through such a tangled mass of revolutionists. He was a pig with a calculating mind, and it seemed to him that the best way through a throng was to run between the legs of soldiers, rather than to try to dodge wide around them. Behind him the soldiers crashed against one another, staggered, fell headlong.

There was a certain magnificence about General Hurtado. The long labor through the jungle had taxed him and his wooden leg brutally. The high-heeled boot he had thrown away for a peon's sandal. His trouser leg had been rolled to the knee. His coat hung from his shoulders in tatters, and yet he kept his dignity. From a moldy growth of whiskers, his mustaches thrust out with a fierce jauntiness, and his sunken eyes were still bright as he watched the pig career through his men like a ball through ninepins.

"Do you see, General Easter?" he asked. "One pig is enough to beat our army." He laughed as he watched.

James Princeton Easter was laughing also, and he had began to shout through his mirth—"Hurtado! ¡Viva! ¡Viva Hurtado!"—until the entire throng of ragamuffins was yelling and laughing also and—"¡Viva Hurtado!"—went howling up the bluff as merrily as a drinking song.

The pig was a born gambler, and, having gotten out of the mob for a moment, it bolted straight for the three generals. Hurtado tried a cleaver stroke with his machete, but only sunk the point deep into the ground. However, General Honey Parker, making a tackle in a big way, caught the porker by a hind leg. The whole army yelled with delight, but Easter stepped on the arm of the prone general, and the pig was away in a moment.

"What in hell did you do that for? I gotta mind to break you in two!" cried Parker, getting to his feet.

"Settle that after we've settled Rio Negro," answered Easter. "Don't you see? There's no place for that porker to run except up the hill . . . and a little pig shall lead us. ¡Viva Hurtado! ¡Viva!"

The army, scattered along the foot of the slope, cut off escape for the pig in that direction, and now he carried his fluting squeal of terror up the bluff toward the entrenchments that crowned it. The army followed on, without thought. Laughter, more than rum, had warmed their hearts. The three hundred went on through the fringe of trees and palms at the base of the bluff and so up the face of that impregnable slope, still shouting with laughter, sliding in the mud, pausing to lean on one another, and laugh again until a voice yelled above them: "¿Que viva?"

James Easter roared back: "The army of the revolution! Hurtado! . . . and the pig! ¡Viva! ¡Viva!"

"A pig! A pig!" cried the army of the revolution, still laughing. "¡Viva! ¡Viva! The pig and Hurtado!"

The sentry screeched out something that was drowned by the bellowing laughter. He fired blindly into the air and, leaving his rifle pit, fled up the slope. A moment later a rocket streaked up from the trenches that crowned the rise of ground, burst high above, and fell in streaming banners of flame. The flare lighted the entire hillside, the grass, the slippery mud, the dim palms, and, near at hand, that reeling, hysterical mob that brandished rifles and climbed and fell and climbed again. The squeal of a pig still fluted before them, and the mob followed it, blind with laughter.

From the trenches came a long, muttering groan of fear and then a screeching voice that yelled: "Hell is open and the devils are loosed at us!"

"Roast pork and red wine!" shouted James Easter. "*¡Viva! ¡Viva* Hurtado!"

"Hurtado . . . and the pig!" laughed the army of the revolution and burst in a noisy wave upon the trenches.

Off there on the left a staunch platoon was firing blindly into the dimness. On the right a pair of machine guns began to saw the night open. But all the central portion of the trenches was empty, and a frightened crowd of defenders fled from maniacs who laughed as they charged that Gibraltar. So in a moment the fighting was ended from one side of the bluff to the other.

Half of the army found rations in the trenches and paused to eat them, which was the reason why Hurtado had men sufficient to man the height and turn the guns so that they commanded Rio Negro. The rest of the revolution flowed on down the slope into the town, and General James Easter was among them.

A tardy fugitive slipped into a muddy ditch, and Easter picked him out by the nape of the neck. "Where is the house of de Prida?" asked Easter.

"*¡Viva* Hurtado!" yelled the poor man, sputtering out mud and water.

"You lie," said Easter, "you haven't been with Hurtado. There's an inch of fat on your ribs. But show me the house of de Prida, and you'll be as safe as any general of the revolution."

So he went down into Rio Negro with the mob about him. They still wanted a leader, the place looked so strong to them, so bulwarked with many big houses. When they got down to the streets of the town, every householder was writing in chalk on his front door: "¡*Viva* Hurtado!"

The rain stopped, but still the water was slopping and squeaking in their shoes when they reached the central plaza.

In the lighted interior of a clothing shop Easter saw General Honey Parker with a large sausage in one hand and flask of wine in the other. Three or four of the shopkeepers were displaying uniforms glorious with golden lace, but they had only succeeded in fitting his taste, so far, with a magnificently cockaded hat that had a large flow of feathers down one side. "Who *vivas* Honey?" called Easter.

"Hai, James Easter!" shouted Honey Parker. "The pig *vivas*, by God, and so does the revolution. Come in here and start *viva*ing yourself, will you?"

But Easter went on. He had no need of a guide because an entire throng was yelling—"Down with de Prida! Down with the traitor!"—and pouring around a house that lifted big shoulders above its neighbors. They were working over the locked house like ants over some great, helpless beetle, a certain prize for the nest but safe for a moment because of its bulk. Some of them were already on the roof, hammering at the trap door. Some had climbed up to batter the shutters. The voice of their general, bellowing from the street, stopped all that activity. In the pause they could hear him beat with the butt of an automatic on the door of the house, shouting: "Open to the revolution and General Easter!"

Here the door swung open. A burst of light struck James Princeton Easter, and before him stood a fat little general, complete with epaulettes and mustaches. The mud of the trenches was still on his khaki trousers. Despair rather than fear had swept him away in the rout, but, now that his time had probably come, he wanted to die in half full-dress, at least, so he had huddled into his coat, pinned on the biggest of his medals, and belted on his largest sword.

"I am de Prida! Do your worst to me, but spare my unhappy family," said the general.

His heart enlarged and his chest with it. He could see those words carved in stone, and tears glittered suddenly upon his eyelashes. But the huge, dripping, half-naked man who had come out of the night merely laughed. His laughter seemed louder than the roar of the crowd as it yelled: "Down with de Prida!"

"Don't you know me?" asked Easter. "I met you that night in New York. James Easter. You'd better start remembering, you need a friend in this mob."

General de Prida stared at the extended hand that was covered with exactly those blisters that long swinging of a heavy machete will give. He looked up, and saw around the throat of the monster the red neckerchief that was the badge of a general. Life, which had been ebbing from the hope of de Prida, returned in a great, sobbing breath. Plainly it was not a moment for halfway measures. De Prida threw his arms as far as they would go around the big man, hugged him tight, and kissed both of his hairy cheeks.

"My friend, my general!" said de Prida.

A yell of disappointed astonishment roared at them from the street. Easter disengaged himself. He turned to the crowd, his wet arm around the shoulders of the little man.

"*¡Amigos!*" thundered Easter. "He is my friend . . . he is your friend . . . he is a friend of the revolution . . . he has given us Rio Negro. *¡Viva* de Prida!"

The rabble, their mouths watering for the loot of that fat mansion, gaped and was still.

"Talk to 'em, de Prida," said Easter. "Tell 'em you're opening some casks of wine in honor of the revolution. Tell 'em anything you please. Hail de Prida! *¡Viva* de Prida!"

The crowd echoed his cheer feebly, and de Prida, stepping into that small breach, seized his opportunity with a magnificent gesture. He began his speech in a ringing voice, as Easter, turning from him, saw at the end of the lofty hall a girl with a cloak thrown about her, the hood over her head as through she were prepared that moment to run out

211

into the night. He could not see her face clearly, but he cried out—"Alicia!"—and strode toward her.

She shrank away from him through a doorway, and he, following, found himself in a big room, all paneled in the glow of maroon-colored Spanish cedar. A chandelier hung like the reflection of a frozen fountain from the ceiling, and the girl stood beneath it with the cloak slipping away from her. She was tall and slim. Her dress was a soft flow of green chiffon.

The children of de Prida were well and delicately nurtured, but, when she saw Easter clearly, it is sure that she swore not entirely beneath her breath. She said: "God is of value to me." In Spanish this is an oath. She added: "Jeemmy, it ees you?"

A double "e" was in the "Jimmy" and the "ees" made a music that lifted the chest of Easter in a long, long breath. It seemed to him that her eyes were almost too wide, almost too perfectly deep and brown.

"When I asked where I could call on you," said Easter, "when you told me Rio Negro . . . that was a laugh, wasn't it?"

The crowd in the street began to cheer, and she pointed with exultation. "My father, he ees so wonderful," said Alicia. "But you are the one who wheestled them to your heels. Oh, Jeemmy, so big, so strong."

She made, with both hands, small gestures toward that bigness and that strength, and had to tilt her head back a little in order to read his face, where she found such a strange story that she was lost in wonder reading it. He could have caught her in his arms that moment except that he was aware of the pool that spread around his feet, dripping down from his drenched rags. The green chiffon was as perfect, as light as a cloud in heaven. Stampeding footfalls had begun to stream around the side of the mansion as Easter picked up from the couch a folded, knitted throw of tan-colored silk and flung it around his nakedness.

"No, no, no!" said Alicia. "Let me see you, Jeemmy . . . my general! Did you make the revolution for me? I want to see how the jungle has beaten and torn you. And your poor hands! Poor, poor hands all bleeding."

"Oh, damn all that," said Easter. "Sit down here, Alicia. Let me look at you for a long time." He signed. "It's not what I remembered, but better."

Here, through a window at the end of the room, he saw lights flood a big, arcaded patio into which the mob of the revolution was pouring. Active little house *mozos* in white were rolling onto the patio whole kegs of wine. Other servants carried out an endless procession of baked bread, of heaped tortillas, of soggy, white *pésol*, of corn husks packed full of salt, and burning little chili peppers or dried meat and fish, of cans with bright-colored American wrappers. The procession hardly entered the patio before the burdens it carried were snatched away by the grimy hands of the Hurtadistas, and the eyes of James Princeton Easter swam with desire, his stomach closing its walls together like the palms of two sore hands.

"Tell me everything, Jeemmy," she said. "Every*theeng!*"

"Say that again."

"Why Jeemmy?"

"I like the way you say it. I like everything you say. Where do I start?"

"Where eet began."

"When I saw you dancing."

"Was eet nice?"

"They just step, usually, but you flowed around."

"Then?"

"Well, when I went home, there wasn't any taste even in a Scotch and soda. I kept thinking, Rio Negro! Rio Negro. I kept seeking a white beach and palm trees . . . and Alicia."

"Ah, Jeemmy!"

"Then there was a boat. It didn't come straight. But it came near to Rio Negro. I grabbed it. I shifted to a coast schooner that would touch here . . . hurricane . . . old tub went down."

"Jeemmy!"

"I got ashore."

"Darleeng!"

"I couldn't cut my way through by myself . . . so I picked up a tidy little revolution and brought it along with me. It's costing your father something to feed that revolution, just now."

Alicia de Prida slipped from her chair to watch the festival on the patio. Naïve, delighted as a child, she drew herself close to Easter and from the broad shadow of his protection, as it were, peered out upon this strange picture.

"Are those the men, Jeemmy?" she asked. "Are those poor theengs the ones? Ah, but with you to lead them they *would* be men."

She lifted her head slowly and looked up to him with parted lips, avoiding his face and centering her attention on his eyes only. He would have given a nameless price for a clean shave, but he felt himself strong, controlled, like a rich man who may take what he pleases and when he will.

"I should have shaved and cleaned up, Alicia," he said, "before I came here. But the mob might have smashed into the house if I'd waited. . . ."

There was a new delight in her eyes that forgot his words as she looked past him, as though her own conception had carried her into a waking dream. *The beauty of women is of the spirit, really,* he thought. *When we look at them with true eyes, the gates open, and it is heaven that we see. Shakespeare's girls . . . Desdemona . . . Juliet . . . !*

That joy that was in her made her body tremble against his arm. "Who ees he, Jeemmy?" she asked.

She was, in fact, staring out onto the patio of the house, and there was no doubt on whom she was looking. Her father was stirring about busily through the crowd, giving his smile like a benediction to those hungry men, but de Prida was as nothing among those tatterdemalions compared with a new figure that had come among them, striding splendidly. The rain could not dim the luster of those boots. The spoon-handled spurs rang out with little golden voices as he walked, a tumbler of wine in one hand, the other resting on the hilt of a great sword that had a golden swishing of tassels at the butt. From shoulder to shoulder his breast was covered with medals, or what seemed to be medals, and his plumed, cockaded hat cast no shadows upon the face of Honey Parker.

"Ah . . . Jeemmy . . . *who* ees he? Ees he your friend? Ees he one of the heroes?"

"Hero? Sure, he's a hero," said James. His mouth pulled awry, but that made no difference, because she was not watching him.

"How beeg! How beeg!" said the girl.

"In a fight, he's a knockout," said Easter. "Like his looks?" He stared at the face of Honey Parker. Famine had not been able to starve all the swine out of those jowls.

"So beeg!" breathed the girl. "And . . . and *like* a general!"

She did not stop trembling. This quivering of soft flesh created in Easter a cold current that reached his heart and chilled it. He looked down at the dark silk of her hair. He looked forth onto the patio at the full glory of Honey Parker. The voice that came out of his throat was as flat as the croaking of a frog.

"Yeah, he's as brave as they come," said Easter. "Shall I call him in?"

"But weel he come eef you call?" breathed the girl.

"I dunno," said Easter. He leaned at the open window. "Hai, Honey?" he called.

"Hai, kid," said Honey Parker. "What are you doing up there, bozo?"

"Come on in," said Easter. He stepped back. "I'll bring him in."

"Weel you, Jeemmy?" asked the girl. "Weel you *really* bring heem?"

"Yeah, I'll bring him, all right," said Easter, and looked once at her brown, slender hands that were clasped against her breast. Her eyes were almost too wide. He thought he could see a slight stain, a smoke of yellow in the whites of them.

In the hall he met Honey Parker.

"Go on in, Honey," he said. "De Prida's gal is in there, waiting for *the* general."

"Yeah?" said Honey. "It's a funny thing how quick they fall, ain't it?"

"Yeah, it's funny."

"Come on in and introduce me, James."

"I couldn't do you justice," said Easter, and left the house.

He found Hurtado in the rear room of a *cantina*, seated all by himself, while a mob of his revolutionists howled and laughed and dribbled wine over themselves in the front room. Hurtado had his wooden leg at rest on a second chair while he leaned back with half-closed eyes and played old airs on a guitar, close to his canted ear.

When he saw Easter, he removed his leg from the chair and waved him into it.

"Ah, my general," said Hurtado. "You could not find her?"

"Oh, I found her, all right," said Easter. "How did you know there was a *her*?"

Agosto Hurtado put out a dirty hand and clasped that of Easter. "I am sorry from my heart, brother," he said.

"Are you?" answered Easter. "Pass me that wine bottle, Agosto, and then I could listen to a song."

The Taming of Red Thunder

Appearing in Esquire *in September, 1942, this was Faust's last published Western story, ending twenty-five years in the genre that had made Max Brand a household name. Working on the Dr. Kildare films and novels in Hollywood since 1938, he was into a new phase of his career. Heroic Western fiction no longer excited him. He had explored every possible variation in the field by then, and, although he did involve himself in scripting a few Westerns for Hollywood, his main interests lay elsewhere. "The Taming of Red Thunder" was his last hurrah in the genre, a lightly written lark of a story, reflecting the author's rejection of Western stereotypes. No quick-draw gunmen. No great wonder horses. No larger-than-life villains. Faust was saying good-bye to the thunderous melodramas of his pulp years in a casual, at-ease-with-the-world story that pointed away from his past toward the reality of his future.*

There was a man named Harter who was more self-made than anybody you could imagine. He was born with an impediment in his speech, and the first time he tried anything, he always failed. He had to be either very patient or go crazy, so he turned into the most patient man in the world. He was nearly thirty before he worked his way through college, and he was all of thirty-five before he finished his law course. The reason he won so many cases was that the judge and jury sympathized with his stammering. He sweated so hard and was so honest that twelve men and women always sat on the edges of their chairs and hoped he would win. He was forty when he married and at sixty-odd he had a comfortable fortune plus a beautiful twenty-year-old daughter who knew three modern languages and had friends all over Europe. He would not have been surprised if she married a title, but instead of that she decided on a return to the soil.

What she admired in her father was not his victory over the world, but his conquest of himself which began on a Middle Western farm. She went farther west and bought a large acreage of California hills in the Coast Range. It was in the books for her to fail, but she had the sense to find a good foreman and use his brains. The result was that she did fairly well, and, though Harter was not pleased, he could not complain, until at the end of the fourth year she decided to marry her foreman.

This was a shock to Harter. On his last trip to California he had met Joe Langley and liked him, but a thirty-seven-year-old cattleman was not his idea of a son-in-law. He thought of Cecilia in cowhide boots, leaving the raising of his grandchildren to some Mexican wench who would fill them with bad Spanish and worse manners, and he decided that the time had come for him to act. He knew, from experience, that he could do nothing with Cecilia, so he looked about for help. He wanted a young man of breeding and education to throw into the breach, but the only one he knew with these qualities was the son of his dead partner, and the lad was not promising. Young Quigley had managed to pass the bar examination, but he was no more use than a rubber stamp in the office. Frank was a long, lean, casual fellow who never had learned how to make an effort. Tutors had helped him through school, and he knew European beaches from Biarritz to the Riviera. These limited talents Harter knew about, but he was not acquainted with any other eligible male. Besides, he always believed that a good workman never complained about his tools. He could not help remembering that Frank Quigley, Senior, had seemed just such another as his son, a man of vast silences and unending inertia, but he had been capable of such strokes of insight as mean the difference between success and failure in the law courts.

"No," said Frank, when Harter called him in and told him that he needed a change, "I hate changes. Now that I've learned the way of the office, I'd rather stay put."

"The fact is," said Harter, "that Cecilia is in trouble."

"Who is Cecilia?" asked Frank.

To be sure for some years the pair had not been together, but half the summers of their childhood had been spent side by side. Harter took off his glasses and polished them for a long time. "Cecilia," he said at last gently, "is my daughter."

"Oh, Cissy," said Frank.

"She's in trouble," said Harter.

"What sort of trouble?" asked Frank.

"I don't know," said Harter. "That's what I want you to go to California and find out."

"Why me?" asked Frank.

"Because you're an observer. You're the only man I know who can spend a whole day without moving. It's a great thing to be an observer. It leads to contemplation, religion, and a lot of things. Ambition."

"I've thought of a schooner," Frank answered, sighing, "not too big . . . and sailing somewhere in the Trades with a good, steady crew . . . a hammock slung somewhere and a clean sky to look at . . . and knowing there is a bit of white beach wrapped up in the blue of the horizon, somewhere."

Harter was polishing his glasses furiously, as though he were trying to rub out a flaw. "You like the sea," he said, perspiring a little.

Max Brand

"It's all right to look at," said Frank.

Harter jammed on the glasses, but he used them to look out the window at the ugly city distances. "Well," he said, "you go to California and look around. If you can find out what's wrong with Cecilia, maybe we'll see about that schooner and a good, steady crew."

That was why Frank arrived at the Circle C Ranch. A letter from her father had reached Cecilia before her guest. He wrote:

Dear Cissy,

I'm sending Frank out for a rest. I wish you would treat him with something less than your usual levity and try to find out what is troubling him. There is something on his mind, and I can't find out what it is. You like hard problems, and perhaps you'll be able to fathom even a contemplative brain like that of Frank's.

He had an answer from her a few days later which ran:

Dear Pops:

Frank is here, and I'll try to find out what's on his mind. I never knew he had a mind, but, if you've discovered one, I'll take your word for it. He spends most of his time in a handy nook which he's rigged between a live oak and a pine tree. Maybe he's contemplating, but it looks to me like sleep. It's a bit tough, having a lug like Frank on one's hands, but I'll put up with him as well as I can.

I've had some rotten luck. Nearly ten thousand dollars that I sank in the hide of a pedigree bull has gone native on me and lost himself in the back country. Getting him out is like pulling tar out of your hair. He's gored two horses and put one of my best men in the hospital, but I'll beat the rascal if it's my last act.

Cissy

P.S. Joe sends his best.

The temper of Cecilia had been short when she wrote that letter, and it grew shorter as the days went by. To Frank Quigley they were flawless and beautiful, but Cecilia neither could sleep nor eat while the great red bull wandered through the hills. He was Grand Champion Horlock's Red Thunder, and she had put in him a part of the profits of four years. Joe Langley had opposed the purchase, but to Cecilia the bull was a symbol of what she had accomplished on the soil and also of the greater future that was beginning to live in her imagination.

She showed her unhappiness this morning by saying: "There's Alec again, out there smashing things. I wish you'd take him to the butcher, Joe."

From the direction of the barn came a steady groaning and screeching of timbers. Langley finished off his coffee and wiped his mouth on the back of his hand. He went to the door and stood with arms akimbo. A life in the saddle had bowed his legs, and the blue jeans fitted them all too accurately.

"Yeah, it's that damned Alec," he said. "He's pretty near got the fence down again. Give him a call. He won't pay no attention to me."

She lifted her head and whistled the frown from her forehead. In that instant the Cecilia of the Circle C was replaced by someone far more familiar to Frank Quigley.

"Mosshaven," he murmured.

"Well, Alec heard you, all right," said Langley at the door. "I'd take him to the butcher right now, except that we've got to put the day in on Red."

"What did you say about Mosshaven?" asked the girl.

"You looked like the old days, just then," said Frank. "When you whistled and smiled . . . Mosshaven, and the rocks, and the sea."

"That looney steer is trying to come to you," complained Langley. "The fool's trying to break down the fence."

"Shall I go let him out?" asked Frank.

Langley turned and pushed back his hat. "You ain't afraid of them horns?" he asked.

"No, we get on together," said Frank.

He rose and walked out toward the corral, where a mountainous brindle steer with a foolish white face had pushed his head between the second and third bars of the fence and was leaning his weight towards the house and Cecilia. Alec, four years ago, had been a knock-kneed orphan that Cecilia had raised by hand until he followed her like a dog and came to her call from as far as her voice could carry. Under such cherishing as she gave him, Alec waxed into a prodigy of bone and flesh. He was as tall as a moose; his horns had the spread of a hammock. There was no malice in Alec, but he was continually inspired by an appetite as huge as his body. He never used his horns to demolish the fences, separating him from the grass beyond, but before the leaning tower of his bulk they sank to the earth, groaning.

The fence was beginning to sag when Frank opened the corral gate and called. Alec came towards him with a splay-footed amble. During several of the preceding days Frank had shared the shade of the same tree with Alec, and they were friends. Now the great steer permitted himself to be held by the ear until the gate was closed, after which Frank hoisted himself up and sat at ease between the horns. It did not occur to him that this was spectacular. It was merely a device for saving a number of steps back to the ranch house. Both Langley and Cecilia stood in the doorway as he slipped to the ground and dusted his trousers, while Alec tried to lick the hat from the head of his mistress.

"You're worthless," she scolded, putting her gloved hand on the beaded wet of his nose. "I've got nothing for you."

"He would eat the rest of that loaf of bread, I believe," Frank suggested.

"Eat *what?*" cried Cecilia.

"A steer eat bread?" scoffed Langley. "Are you looney?"

Frank brought out the loaf and offered it. Alec blew out

the humid sweetness of his breath upon it, then engulfed it. The stale crust crackled for an instant, then the bolus slid down the throat into the vast interior caverns.

"Now, how would *you* know the fool would eat bread?" swallowed Langley.

"He has shared my lunch on several occasions," explained Frank.

"Maybe you've got a way with beef," said Langley, with a half smile on a face so stained and weather-toughened that it could give way only slightly to the emotions. "You ought to come along today and watch us work out on Red. We've got Pedro Mendoza to head up the show."

"Have you a gentle horse?" asked Frank lamely.

A shadow passed across the eyes of Cecilia. She turned away with a shrug, and he knew that he had dropped through dark leagues and leagues of contempt. But he was rather afraid of horses, and he rarely chose to lie. It was too much trouble afterwards. But to be despised by Cecilia made him surprisingly unhappy.

"You find me rather a ratty fellow," he said to her.

"Don't be silly, Frank," she answered. "It's only that you're a city mouse."

So the city mouse was given a safe mount and rode out with the others to find Red Thunder. The country from a distance had seemed very large, but to ride among the hills magnified everything. It was like seeing the waves from the deck of a liner as against rowing among them in a skiff. There were hollows of withering heat and stillness and heights that held him up like the shoulders of Atlas. He had imagined men, galloping down the steeps and along the dizzy edges of nothingness. Instead, this group went at a walk or a dog-trot all the way.

Mendoza was the focal point, the *pièce de résistance*, of this expedition which Langley swore would succeed where so many others had failed. They had tried to snag Red Thunder with ordinary light forty-foot ropes before, but Mendoza brought along twenty yards of rawhide lariat that was as supple as quicksilver. This Mendoza was powerful and chunky, with a big-nosed, Indian face. He had spurs, and, when his horse stumbled, he used them to draw blood. Frank drew away from him with a feeling that he had fallen a little too deeply into the dark ages and needed to return to the light.

When they got into the back country where live oaks and brush clawed at their legs, Frank understood why it was so hard to get at Red Thunder.

"Hai!" suddenly called Cissy at his side. "They've found the sign of Red."

The track was not hard even for Frank to follow. In a moist hollow the footprints of Red had been driven into the ground as though by a piledriver, and they loomed as big as the flat of his two hands. They strung out, Mendoza in the lead, then Langley, then the girl, then the three cowhands, with Frank at the rear. Now and then Mendoza lost the trail, but he always found it again in a moment and led them on.

Red Thunder did not wait to be routed from some thicket. As they went up a gully, a patch of sunshine among the trees—a somewhat redder patch than usual—turned suddenly into a charging future. It seemed to Frank more in the air than on the ground, like a rampant figure on a coat of arms. There was about a ton of him placed as close to the ground as possible and driven by high-octave hatred of all things human. The apparition was aiming directly at Frank, and his cow pony at once went to another place. By the time Frank got him headed around, there was no sight of the bull or the hunters, but a thin cloud of dust was traveling above the brute and beyond the nearer trees. The roar of Red Thunder filled the hills.

Just then the whole cortège plunged from the woods into the open. Two of the horses were carrying double. The great Mendoza himself sat behind the saddle of Cecilia, embracing her with much determination. Joe Langley was up behind one of his men. Behind them the bellow of Red Thunder repossessed the wilderness.

They retreated slowly down the gorge, because Mendoza

had to be persuaded against taking a rifle and going back to say the last word to Red. It appeared that his rawhide lariat had been left, gripping the horns of the bull. Parted from his rope, the Mexican was a man whose soul is lost.

At dinner that night Langley said calmly: "Turn that bull into dog meat, Cissy. We'll never get him out of that jungle ... and what's the use of throwing good horses after bad bulls?" This sally touched his funny bone, and he chuckled.

Cecilia stood up from the table, whole inches taller than her height. "I'll have him out or *die*," she declared, and flung into her room.

Frank was tired enough to fall asleep without undressing, but woke up before midnight with the white of the moon in his eyes and a strange, cold sense of fear in his soul. There had been an event this day, he realized, that had gone through him like an arrow fresh from the string. It was not the terrible charge of the bull, he decided. It was rather the passion of Cecilia. The red bull, he began to see, was more than mere flesh and blood to her. It spelled four years of victory or defeat, and she had the soul of a conqueror.

After a while he got up. The muscles on the inside of his thighs were sore. He was very glad that he was not Joe Langley with the need of facing Cissy in the morning. Perhaps it was the need of friendliness that drove him out to the pasture. Alec was lying down, but it was not hard to identify him. Flat on his belly he was almost as tall as the heifers that still grazed in the moonlight. A thought came to Frank.

He went into the barn, found Joe Langley's saddle, and took the neatly coiled rope that was tied by the cantle. Then he returned to the field and took Alec by the ear. When the rope was noosed securely around his horns, he allowed himself to be led placidly up among the hills. Each heave and swaying of the live oaks startled Frank with the thought of Red Thunder, rushing on him from behind.

He had come to the edge of a clearing, and at the top of the rise appeared the unmistakable silhouette of Red Thunder himself, offering the authentic challenge that sounded right before him and seemed to engulf the world. In the near distance some of the cows, gathered under his protection, lay close to a thicket, but the bull stood on the hilltop, pawing the ground and booming insults at the moon. From his horns, sleeked with moonshine, ran the thin streak of one rawhide lariat.

To the end of the trailing rawhide was only ten steps for Frank, and he made them, though they were like ten strides along the edge of a cliff. He carried with him the rope that was fastened to the head of Alec, and, kneeling on the dead grass, he started tying the knot that would join the two lengths. The rawhide, like a living snake, slipped and avoided the knot. Then something began to bawl loudly, pitifully. It was one of the wild heifers that had started to her feet at the sight of man, the universal danger. The bellowing of the red bull suddenly grew louder. Frank, looking up, saw the big fellow, facing toward him from the crest and lowering his horns for the charge. He took one last pull at the ropes, then fled. He bounded into the first wide forking of an oak and was still climbing when he heard the sock of a great impact.

He had not been the target in the eyes of the bull. Instead, Red had locked horns with Alec. The shock slewed them around so that there was no advantage in the slope for Red. That low-flowing strength of his kept urging and pouring against the steer. A rage for destruction was in him. The moonlight trembled on his silken hide. But Alec, leaning steadfast against his attack, seemed hardly more interested than when he put his weight against the corral fence and yearned toward the sweeter grasses of a neighboring field.

Now Red Thunder bellowed mightily. The greatness of that sound seemed to shake the branch on which Frank was sitting. For half an hour, without moving a hoof, the two strained until the delicate hide of the bull was drenched with water. The foolish cows drifted nearer and stared. Sometimes one of them would lower her head and make threatening gestures with her horns, right and left, showing a mild desire for combat.

Frank lighted a cigarette and relaxed. Even the wind seemed to be pausing to watch. The hush spread until he could hear the breathing of the great beasts. The bull made the first move. He slipped his horns out of lock, swerved aside, and reached for the flank of Alec with an upward thrust. He might as well have tried to pass a phalanx of leveled spears at the enormous armament of Alec. No malice on the part of the steer but Red's own furious lunge caused the point of one of those spears to gash open his neck and shoulders. Once more they were head to head. The minutes passed. The cows came closer. Frank was on his fourth cigarette when Red Thunder bellowed, a new, lamentable note, and slipped to his knees. The weight of Alec still crushed down upon him from a strategic height. He regained his feet with a mighty effort and stood a yard or two away, roaring his rage, tearing up grass and earth.

Alec took this opportunity to withdraw in the direction of the Circle C corrals, far away. He came to the hundred foot end of the rope. Against the restraint of it, he leaned patiently, persistently, without malice. The double rope grew taut. It made a dull sound like a loosened violin string, vibrating out of all key. Frank climbed down the tree.

The dew was once more on the corral dust when Cecilia hustled the breakfast onto the table, bringing with her the smell of fried steak and potatoes from the kitchen. Joe Langley, tilted back in his chair, was waiting at the table, but there was no sign of Frank Quigley.

Cecilia went to the closed door, rattled the knob, and called. She announced—"He's gone."—and pushed the door open.

"Gone?" said Langley. "Now where would that fool take himself to?"

"What makes you so sure he is a fool?" asked Cecilia, still with her back turned.

Langley lifted his head. There was something in the tone of Cecilia that he had never heard, but, before he could make an analysis, another sound came wavering and booming from the direction of the corral.

Cecilia got to the door first. The rising sun threw a dazzle into her eyes, but then she saw Red Thunder, standing at the open cow gate. His head down, he was braced against a taut line, the other end of which connected with the horns of Alec and on the back of Alec, sitting sidewise and smoking a cigarette, was Frank Quigley. Red Thunder presently gave up. Staggering drunkenly, he reeled through the gate and stood with his head hanging down, down, until his breath raised the dust into a little cloud.

Later on this day Frank read aloud to Cecilia the letter he had been writing to Harter.

> Cecilia feels that four years of the soil and a net of over ten thousand dollars prove that she is not effete, and now she thinks of coming home, if you agree. Besides, she can sell this place to advantage. Her chief regret is in leaving Alec, but perhaps a place can be found for him near New York.

He looked up from the letter.

"Do you think that says it?" he asked.

"I suppose so," she answered. "Though he may wonder who Alec is. . . ."

"Well, I suppose I better be going," said Joe, pushing back his chair noisily.

He made further noise and closed the door, but the two seemed quite unaware of him.

"You're daydreaming," said Cecilia. "What are you thinking of? Mosshaven?"

"No, not at all," said Frank, startled from his thoughts.

"What is it, then?" she insisted.

"You'll think I'm frightfully silly," he told her.

"I'll *never* think you're silly," said Cecilia.

THE END

About the Author

Max Brand is the best-known pen name of Frederick Faust, creator of Dr. Kildare, Destry, and many other fictional characters popular with readers and viewers worldwide. Faust wrote for a variety of audiences in many genres. His enormous output, totaling approximately thirty million words or the equivalent of 530 ordinary books, covered nearly every field: crime, fantasy, historical romance, espionage, Westerns, science fiction, adventure, animal stories, love, war, and fashionable society, big business and big medicine. Eighty motion pictures have been based on his work along with many radio and television programs. For good measure he also published four volumes of poetry. Perhaps no other author has reached more people in more different ways.

Born in Seattle in 1892, orphaned early, Faust grew up in the rural San Joaquin Valley of California. At Berkeley he became a student rebel and one-man literary movement, contributing prodigiously to all campus publications. Denied a degree because of unconventional conduct, he embarked on a series of adventures culminating in New York

City where, after a period of near starvation, he received simultaneous recognition as a serious poet and successful storyteller. Later, he traveled widely, having made his home in New York, then in Florence, and finally in Los Angeles.

Once the United States entered the Second World War, Faust abandoned his lucrative writing career and his work as a screenwriter to serve as a war correspondent with the infantry in Italy, despite his fifty-one years and a bad heart. He was killed during a night attack on a hilltop village held by the German army. New books based on magazine serials or unpublished manuscripts or restored versions continue to appear so that, alive or dead, he has averaged a new book every four months for seventy-five years. In the United States alone nine publishers now issue his work. Beyond this, some work by him is newly reprinted every week of every year in one or another format somewhere in the world.

Acknowledgments

MAX BRAND

THE ABANDONED OUTLAW

No writer captures the American West better than Max Brand. And nowhere is Brand's talent more evident than in these three classic short novels, all restored to their original length, and collected in paperback for the first time. In "The Gold King Turns His Back," young Miriam Standard is more than capable of running her father's ranch, but finds she has much to learn about the Westerners' meaning of honor. In "The Three Crosses," an ominous prediction leads a cowpuncher to a showdown with a notorious gunfighter. And the title novel finds a young woman caught in the middle of a lifelong rivalry between two men, one of whom is an outlaw. Experience the West as only Max Brand could write it!

___4465-X $4.50 US/$5.50 CAN

Dorchester Publishing Co., Inc.
P.O. Box 6640
Wayne, PA 19087-8640

Please add $1.75 for shipping and handling for the first book and $.50 for each book thereafter. NY, NYC, and PA residents, please add appropriate sales tax. No cash, stamps, or C.O.D.s. All orders shipped within 6 weeks via postal service book rate. Canadian orders require $2.00 extra postage and must be paid in U.S. dollars through a U.S. banking facility.

Name_____
Address_____
City_____State_____Zip_____
I have enclosed $_____ in payment for the checked book(s).
Payment <u>must</u> accompany all orders. ☐ Please send a free catalog.

MAX BRAND

SAFETY McTEE

Here, in paperback for the first time, restored from his own typescripts, are three prime examples of Max Brand at his rousing best. In "Little Sammy Green," a son has a difficult time living up to the reputation of his gunfighter father, until fate forces him to prove himself. "Black Sheep" is the extraordinary story of a nine-year-old tomboy who comes up with a scheme to win an outlaw his freedom, even though it puts her own life in jeopardy. And "Safety McTee" tells of a gunfighter who earned his nickname by merely wounding, not killing, his opponents. But when he's forced to shoot an old man in self-defense, he finds himself hunted by a lynch mob that doesn't appreciate his past mercies.

____4528-1 $4.50 US/$5.50 CAN